MEET ME IN WONDERLAND

IN THE CAROLINAS
BOOK 3

ANGEL ANDERS

To the readers who want a little ho ho ho in their lives. Sometimes, you just want to read about someone getting a happily ever after with their ex-boyfriend's dad.

ONE

Ellie

"I LOVE YOU. You know I do..." Harper pauses.

I shut my eyes and internally groan for what's to come. This conversation is getting serious if Harper's already using my name and this exasperated tone. At least I'm still lying in bed for this conversation.

"But?" I finally ask.

Harper sighs loudly through the phone. It's almost as if she's actually in my bedroom with how jarring it was.

Opening my eyes, I begin to play with the ends of my hair as I wait for her to say what she needs to get off her chest. I notice her hesitation lingers as she weighs whether or not to address this further.

Since she is one of my best friends, I already have an idea of what she's about to say regarding my current work situation. In Harper's mind, I have a crush on my boss, Fisher Underwood. She thinks the reason I don't want to take a new job opportunity is because of him and not because of the experience I'm gaining at Rain Peak Corporation.

The idea that I have romantic feelings for Fisher is so preposterous that I can't even entertain the concept. It would never work between us.

For one, Fisher is my boss. I'm not exactly allowed to date someone I report to. Then there is the fact that he's about twenty years older than me. Dating someone so much older isn't the norm. And the most important factor that would hinder any chance of Fisher and me ever being together is that I've already dated his son.

That's right. I have already been in a relationship with Knox Underwood.

Even if I did happen to have feelings for Fisher, it's not like I could do anything about them. These three reasons alone are enough, and there are so many more that I could add to the list.

"This is the job opportunity you've been waiting for. I know you love Daddy Fisher's attention," she starts.

"Hold it right there."

I sit upright, startled.

"How many times do I have to tell you to stop calling him Daddy Fisher?" I ask.

She starts to laugh.

"Fine. My point is that Troy Medical Company is the chance for you to finally transition into a management role. You know you're more than qualified to take it on. It's time to spread those wings and fly," Harper finishes.

I know Harper's intentions are coming from a good place. I have stayed on as Fisher's assistant far longer than I ever intended to.

When I graduated college, he offered me the role of his executive assistant because of my situation with Knox. His son suddenly broke up with me to pursue his dream of becoming a professional musician. This coincided with my search for a job in Seattle so that we could stay together. Fisher needed an assistant, and I believe he thought he was softening Knox's blow to my heart.

As the years passed by, I became addicted to studying the way Fisher operated. He has a brilliant mind, and I've learned so much by being his assistant.

Early on, I noticed that Fisher appreciated my enthusiasm in the workplace. He started to involve me more in his day-to-day, and I took every opportunity he offered. The more time we spent together resulted in most of our boundaries disappearing altogether. The truth is, he knows me almost better than my best friends do because of how much time we spend working together.

"I know you want what's best for me, and it is a good career opportunity, but I'm just unsure. That doesn't make me any less grateful for the offer."

Harper lets out a frustrated moan. Evidently, my friend is very annoyed with me.

"Yes, this is a great opportunity, but think about what it all means. You could finally get out of Seattle and move to Charleston. You'd be closer to friends and your dad."

All valid points.

I've never wanted to move back to my hometown in Florida, but I always imagined I would live on the East Coast. It was because of my job with Fisher that I kept putting off searching for a new role somewhere else. That is until Harper emailed me the application for this job opportunity in Charleston. I know she sent it to me because she would love for me to live in the same city she's in.

"Will Grayson be upset if I don't take it?"

"Definitely not. This isn't about Grayson; it's about you.

Just because he knows the owner and made a call, you taking or not taking this role doesn't impact him at all."

"Well, having his connection did help me get noticed out of the sea of applications."

"Don't talk down about yourself like that. Connections always help, but you're the one who secured that job offer, not Grayson."

"True. I just wouldn't want your fiancé to be upset with me."

"Now you're trying to distract me with wedding talk? I'm onto you, young lady."

We both erupt into a fit of laughter.

Harper is the first to recompose herself.

"What is important is that this is a manager role. This is what you've been wanting for some time now, and the salary is much higher than what you currently make! Plus, you're such a good fit, and this company has so much growth potential for someone as talented as you are."

"Stop making such good points and paying me compliments," I tease.

When I got the job offer, I considered turning it down immediately. I never thought I would actually get the role since I live on the other side of the country. After speaking with the recruiter again, she told me to get back to her with my decision by the new year. The company shuts down around the holidays for two weeks, so I had time to decide.

I didn't need to make an immediate decision, even though I should have still told her no during that conversation.

The issue now is that I've been considering taking the role more than I'd like to admit. If I left Fisher, I would potentially be causing a host of issues for him, and that means Rain Peak too. I don't want to let the team down by leaving.

It's just not a simple decision to make. Some days, I'm adamant that I can't leave, and then other days, the allure of living in Charleston starts to draw me in.

I take a deep breath in and out to settle my nerves. Harper will understand when I finally admit this truth.

"I don't think I'm ready to fly," I confess.

I continue to play with the ends of my hair as I cross my legs over one another. Once settled, I pull the white comforter over my lap.

She gives me a knowing sigh.

"This is a fantastic opportunity for you. It's time that you take the next step in your career... and life."

"I know it is."

"I think you need to take the time they've given you to really evaluate what you want out of life. Don't take it because I want you here, and do not stick around in hopes that Fisher smiles at you."

"Hey! That's not fair. I happen to get a smile every day now."

Harper tries to stifle her laughter.

"See! You're only proving my point."

I wince and fall back onto my pillows.

"Why don't you use this time to muster up the courage to finally tell him how you feel. Admit it to yourself first and then to him. Maybe that'll help you make the right decision."

I rub my forehead as I process everything she's saying.

"You want me to tell Fisher I have feelings for him?"

"Yes, because you do," she draws out.

I nervously twist in my bed as I'm suddenly feeling restless.

"Hypothetically, let's say I do. I should what? Just announce it out of nowhere at the client retreat in the middle of the mountains? That sounds like a terrible idea."

"It's not a terrible idea. Tell him or come to Charleston. I won't let you continue to torture yourself like this."

I let out a long sigh as I sit upright once again.

"This is a lot to take in... but I will think about it all."

"Good! I really hope you come to Charleston though," she says cheerfully.

"I know you do," I say with a laugh.

My alarm clock rings loudly on my nightstand.

"Alright, well, it's finally a decent hour here on the West Coast, so I have to go and get ready for work."

"You get ready for work at five in the morning?" Harper asks, surprised.

"Yes, some of us work out before we get ready to start our day."

"Wow. Meanwhile, I'm just at home avoiding writing this magazine article."

"Stop procrastinating and go get it done, *young lady*."

Harper laughs freely, and I hear shuffling in the background. I'm assuming it's Grayson with how distant she suddenly seems.

"Call me later. Love you," I shout.

"Love you too," she shouts back and then hangs up.

Quickly, I hop out of bed and change into workout clothes. My spin class starts in thirty minutes, and I can't be late for it. Working out is where I get some of my best thinking done, and I definitely need it now that Harper has told me I need to assess my feelings for Fisher.

I can't believe I have to deal with *my feelings* now on top of everything else I have to do today. My schedule is jam-packed already because of the upcoming retreat.

I have to wrap up a few retreat tasks, and I have a slew of personal errands I need to run as well. When we decided to host a family-friendly holiday retreat, I didn't realize how excited our clients would be for it.

We invited some of our top customers and, to our surprise, they all accepted. I can admit that it's an amazing trip we've put together, but it was risky for us to do so, given the time of year. Who knew that so many people would be willing to travel so close to the holidays?

"HI, ELLIE," my spin instructor, Josie, greets.

"Hey, Josie."

"Pick any bike you'd like when you go into room A. You're the first one here."

"Got it, thanks," I reply as I start to head into the studio.

Having a fitness studio on the ground level of my apartment building is a godsend. There is no way I would have the time to work out as frequently as I do if it wasn't this accessible. I have such little free time because of my job that it would be hard to fit it in otherwise. I like to get into the office early to have time to review Fisher's daily schedule. That way, I'm prepared for any issues that may arise throughout the day.

I pick the spin bike I'm going to ride this morning and realize that my thoughts always involve Fisher in some capacity.

Harper is right. I do have complicated feelings for the man. I just can't say it out loud.

I'm twenty-six years old and have a secret schoolgirl crush on my much older boss. It's almost pathetic. I know that we can't be together, which is why I like to pretend as if my feelings for him are nonexistent.

There. I did it. At least I finally said that to myself.

Fisher has no idea how I feel. We may be close, but we're always professional. Any boundaries that have disappeared have made us more like friends than anything.

If only it were different.

"Did you say something?" Josie asks as she walks past me and heads to the main spin bike at the front of the studio.

Did I say that out loud?

"Oh, no. Sorry, I'm just thinking about the day ahead."

"In here, you only need to think about clearing your mind! Get pumped. I have the best playlist planned."

Looking around the studio, other people have arrived. I've been so wrapped up in my thoughts that I didn't notice anyone else was here. All because I can't stop thinking about my boss. Maybe I'll stop thinking about him during this workout... I hope so, at least.

"Good morning! Let's get started!" Josie shouts.

Now it's time to pretend like I enjoy spinning for the next forty-five minutes. I've perfected the art of lying to myself, so it should be no sweat.

I SETTLE into my desk quickly.

It's a little later than I usually like to arrive at the office, but I had to run one of my errands before coming in this morning.

As I unpack my tote bag, I notice that Fisher already has someone in his office. Whoever it is isn't on his calendar. Hopefully this doesn't drastically impact his schedule the rest of the day. This is exactly why I like arriving early to the office. If I had come in when I normally do, I would know who is in there.

I start preparing the paperwork needed for the upcoming leadership meeting.

"Good morning."

I look up to find Doug, the vice president of operations, standing in front of my desk.

"Good morning. What can I do for you?"

I stop going through the documents to give Doug my full attention. His department is the one I would want to transition into if I were to stop being Fisher's assistant.

Lately, Doug has been coming by my desk and asking me all sorts of questions. I really don't understand why, but I go along with it.

"It's a beautiful day, isn't it?"

"What is it today? Need me to solve more problems in your department?" I tease.

"Wouldn't that be wonderful," he retorts playfully.

"If you don't have anything, I do have to prepare for Mr. Underwood's meeting at nine."

"I'll be in that one."

"I know. You are a leader, after all." I let out a small laugh.

"See you then."

"See you soon," I reply with a wave.

Looking down at the clock on my computer screen, I see I do have to quickly finish prepping for this meeting. I didn't have time last night to print all of the documents I need for it.

For certain meetings, Fisher prefers to have hard copies to write notes on instead of using a tablet or laptop. I take digital notes for him to reference later if needed too.

Once this meeting is over, a ritual Fisher and I have is to do an immediate data dump. We review our notes, and he shares more thoughts on what was discussed. From there, I'll handle any follow-up needed.

I have a strong feeling this leadership meeting is going to create a stir. Doug has been working on streamlining a lot of initiatives that span multiple departments. It's the first topic on the agenda. If we get to another one, I'll be pleasantly surprised.

Finding the remaining documents, I print them out and organize the packets.

IN THE CONFERENCE ROOM, I finish preparing for the meeting and feel satisfied. Everything is laid out correctly, and I secured my spot next to where Fisher will be seated.

I head back to my desk to finish my last task before this meeting—preparing our morning coffees. The coffee machine is in his office because it's for his use only. Well, technically, our use. An insignificant wall we broke down early on in our professional relationship.

Back at my desk, I notice Fisher's door is still closed. I'll wait until his meeting is finished to go in and make the coffees. Fisher is always punctual, so I know it will finish soon.

Right on cue, his office door swings open, and Doug walks out.

Wait a second... He wasn't the person who was in there earlier. A short time ago, he was talking to me. This is odd.

"Doug? How did you get in there?" I ask, perplexed.

"I saw Sara coming out, and Fisher knows I've been needing just a few minutes of his time."

"Oh, okay," I respond, still confused.

The conference room isn't far from my desk, so I don't know how I didn't see all of this happening. Very strange, but so be it.

"If you'll excuse me," I start.

I can't finish because suddenly, my skin starts to prickle with goose bumps.

A strong, broad frame pauses in the doorframe I have to go through—the reason my body is reacting this way. Sometimes, it's hard to control my natural reaction to being around my boss.

"Good morning, Ellie," Fisher rasps.

His voice sends shock waves throughout my nervous system. The way his tone has me electrified should be terrifying, but it's not.

I smooth out my dress as a distraction and smile.

"Perfect timing. I was about to prepare coffee for the nine a.m. meeting," I say while trying to still pull it together.

Fisher gestures for me to go into his office as he takes a step forward to make room for me to pass.

"Thank you," I murmur.

As I approach the doorway, I pause. Looking back, I meet Doug's gaze.

"Glad you were able to get in without being on the calendar," I tease.

Suddenly, I hear a low rumble vibrating nearby. Turning my attention away from Doug and to Fisher, I find two eyes peering at me. Fisher's jaw is twitching as if he's holding back from saying something for some reason.

"See you in there," Doug calls out as he walks away.

Doug is completely unaware of Fisher's change in

demeanor, unlike me. I'm not sure why Fisher's acting like this.

His chest rises and falls repeatedly, and I watch his Adam's apple bob as he swallows thickly.

"I'll make the coffees and be in the conference room soon," I murmur.

I head to where his coffee station is set up and avoid looking at him as I put together the coffees, needing this time to recompose myself again after that interaction. Sometimes, it feels as if I'm making more out of some of our interactions.

I stretch slightly from side to side as the coffee finishes brewing and can feel his stare on me.

I try to avoid thinking more about it as I methodically prepare our drinks. I know I have to face him momentarily, but I'm embarrassed by how much my imagination has been running wild. It would really help me if he would just leave the room and put distance between us. I'm not sure why he's lingering instead of going to the meeting without me.

With both coffees in hand, I turn around to finally face him again.

I yelp and nearly toss the coffees into the air because of his proximity. He's so much closer than I assumed he would be.

"Sorry, I didn't realize you were right here," I breathe out.

His arms are folded across his chest, making his muscles more apparent. The way his suit clings to his body makes me wonder what's underneath. I know he has some tattoos, but I'm dying to know where they all are.

I bite my bottom lip to stifle an embarrassing moan from slipping out.

"I thought we would walk together," he coolly replies.

"Oh, that's... nice," I whisper.

I smile to ease the tension as he takes a step back. It gives me the opportunity to hand him his coffee.

"Here's your coffee, sir," I say with my smile still in place.

"Ellie," he scolds.

He hates when I call him sir.

"Force of habit," I weakly admit.

I try to keep it as professional as possible when we aren't behind closed doors, especially in the office. Most employees naturally address Fisher in this manner. I don't want to appear like I get any kind of special treatment.

Fisher takes the coffee, and I leave his office first. The office door closes behind us as we walk to the nearby conference room.

"Doug is going to cause a stir," he mutters.

"He is." I sigh knowingly.

"It's key to remember that disruption can be positive for an organization. It keeps us effective," Fisher says.

Fisher opens the conference room door and gestures for me to go in first.

"Fair point, sir," I say as I walk through it.

"Ellie," he draws out as he follows behind.

"Force of habit," I say to remind him.

We take our seats next to one another. As I continue to get settled in mine, I watch as Fisher pulls out his thick, black-framed glasses from his jacket pocket and puts them on to begin reviewing the meeting documentation I prepared.

"Remind me after we do our debrief that we need to talk about our travel plans to North Carolina too."

"Of course."

The conference room begins to fill with his leadership team. It's time to get started.

TWO

Fisher

"WHAT TIME DOES our flight leave for Asheville?"

"Wheels up at six a.m.," Ellie states.

I grumble as I adjust in my seat, eliciting a small laugh from across my desk.

The sound of Ellie's laugh is sometimes the only positive point of my day. I'll consider it a win even though she's laughing because of how much I dislike early morning flights. Ellie knows this, and yet, here we are, leaving tomorrow at six in the morning.

Most of my employees aren't as comfortable around me as Ellie is. I foster a dynamic environment where we're open to change and new ideas, but typically, I'm all business. If I had any free time, I would enjoy hearing about so-and-so's child or pet. I simply don't have it because of the growth that Rain Peak has been experiencing over the past few years.

It's one of the reasons I'm grateful to have Ellie by my

side. I can let my guard down, and there is never any awkwardness between the two of us. I don't have to sugar-coat or mince my words.

"I know it isn't ideal; however, there is a snowstorm that may impact our travel."

I rear my head back at this news.

"It may not, but I had to move up our plane departure time to ensure we're there ahead of any clients," she finishes.

Removing my glasses, I set them on my desk and rub in between my eyes.

"Did you say snowstorm?"

"Yes. It's really unusual timing for North Carolina to get a snowstorm, from what I'm told, but here we are," she gripes.

I settle back into my chair as I consider our options.

Ellie moves the sleeves of her fitted black blazer back down from her elbows. It's so easy for me to follow all of her movements. I have to stop myself whenever I notice I'm paying closer attention to her than I should be. It doesn't matter how comfortable I feel; she's my assistant. I can't be studying her movements as if she were just any attractive woman. If I did, it would cross one of the remaining boundaries we have in place after all these years.

Ellie straightens her posture and waits.

"What about the clients? Shouldn't we be rescheduling this retreat if a snowstorm is heading that way?"

"I already called each and every one of them and offered an alternative. I let them know they could participate in a different retreat we'll host soon. They all said they were going to still come. It's out of our hands," she concludes.

I tent my fingers against my mouth and hum as I weigh

what this means. We really can't cancel if all of the clients are willing to chance it. If they aren't concerned about a potential snowstorm, then the show must go on. We just need to make sure all of our bases are covered in case something unplanned occurs.

"Fine," I bark out.

"The plane will be fully stocked with your favorite espresso and blueberry muffins, so I think you'll be just fine."

Ellie gives me a knowing smile.

"Are all of the cabins secured on the property in case of emergency?"

"Yes, Mr. Underwood," she sing-songs.

"Easy, Ellie."

She rolls her eyes playfully.

"I'll email the full retreat agenda and supporting materials over to you shortly. I'll also have a printed copy ready for you to review on the plane."

"Thank you."

"If that's all, I'll be wrapping up and heading out soon."

I look down at the clock and see it's close to the end of the day. Ordinarily, Ellie stays until I do or vice versa. It's another sign of how in sync we are with one another. I've come to value her input in the business, and her role has naturally expanded past what a typical executive assistant would do.

"You can't stay late?" I ask.

It's out before I even consider the meaning behind those words.

A warm smile spreads on her expression. She bites the bottom of her plump lip, one that I shamefully can admit I've thought about too often.

She gives me a sincere look back and shakes her head no.

"Not today. Since we are leaving so early tomorrow, there are a few errands I need to take care of before we head out."

"Like what?" I can't help but ask.

She gives me an amused look but refrains from laughing.

"If you must know, women don't naturally look like this," she says while motioning down the length of her body.

"You always look nice."

The amused expression morphs into a more thoughtful one. If I thought it was possible she'd be interested in a man my age, I'd almost say it's one of desire.

"Well, I have upkeep to do tonight to keep being so nice to look at," she teases.

We pause at the same time, and Ellie's eyes widen as her mouth slightly parts. It's almost as if we were just flirting with one another.

"I'll check in before I leave," she chirps.

She gets up and smooths out her dress. The heels she's wearing elongate her legs, ones that I've imagined being wrapped around my waist a time or two.

I need to stop thinking about Ellie in this manner.

Ellie is only twenty-six years old, seventeen years younger than me. She's not jaded by the outside world like I've come to be over the years. Her upbeat, take-charge personality has smoothed out my roughness.

Over the past few years, I've come to realize I need her to center me as we tackle the chaos of Rain Peak expanding so quickly. I initially hired Ellie because my son had just broken up with her to become a musician. Given the tough job market, she was having difficulty finding the right entry-level position, and I wanted to help. My last assistant wasn't up for the demanding hours and had just quit. It was mutually beneficial for her to take the role.

My son and I have a complicated relationship, so I thought it would be a positive for him as well. He didn't care at all what happened.

Eight years ago, Knox had showed up at the front desk of the high-rise apartment I call home demanding to see his "deadbeat father." A son from a one-night stand I had twenty-six years ago and was never told even existed. His mother had my real number and never had the decency to call me.

After that night together, I tried to give her a call so that we could see each other again, but she had given me a fake number. Imagine my surprise when a Greek restaurant asked if I was calling to order takeout.

Knox didn't care to hear the truth and, to this day, still hasn't accepted my side. He wants to continue to believe that his mother would "never do something like that." I'm not about to ruin his perception. Too much time has passed.

After he finally gave me a chance, I found out that his mother needed to enter a rehabilitation facility but couldn't afford it. I offered to pay for it since that's clearly why he tracked me down. Then, I presented another offer—move from California to Washington for college. If he did, I would take care of his expenses.

He accepted my offer.

During his junior year Christmas break, he visited with the brunette bombshell I now call my executive assistant. The one who has honey-brown eyes and naturally tanned skin and whom I'd be lost without. Ellie keeps me organized and in line. There is no replacing her as my assistant; no one will be able to meet the same level of standards.

Which is why I've been repeatedly telling my vice president of operations no to making her *his* operations manager. He's having a hard time accepting that response.

I know it's a good career opportunity for Ellie. Eventually, I'll have to agree to it, but I just can't bring myself to say yes quite yet. If I do, I'll see less of her every day.

I have to accept reality and finally give her this promotion; otherwise, she may go somewhere else, and I'll lose her for good. Ellie will leave if she doesn't get career advancement soon.

I know what I have to do. At the end of this retreat, I'll have to face the truth and tell her about this new role.

"Knock, knock," a sweet voice murmurs.

It's none other than woman consuming my mind.

"Everything okay?" I ask.

She's lingering in the doorway instead of coming into my office.

"Everything is good. It's five, so just checking in before I head out for the day," she replies.

I roll up one of my dress shirt sleeves to find my watch.

How did the afternoon get away from me already? Running this company has taken over my very existence; there is no stopping at the end of a traditional workday.

I roll up my other sleeve, revealing more of my black-lined decorated forearms, ones I got done in my youth. The black ink swirls up toward my shoulders, but no one has seen that far in ages.

"Right. Well, have a good evening," I answer.

Glancing back up to Ellie, I see her eyes simmering with the same look I thought I saw earlier today. I know it can't be. If it were, then maybe these intrusive thoughts I have would make sense.

"Ellie?"

She doesn't realize that I'm watching her drink in my movements. Over time, I've gathered she's a fan of my tattoos. These days, she's one of the only people to see any part of them. It's a sick pleasure of mine to watch her study my ink.

She meets my gaze and nervously chews on her bottom lip before smacking them together.

"Yes? Sorry," she stammers.

A light flush stains her cheeks. I can't help but smirk because of her reaction.

Ellie likes a man with tattoos. I'll pretend that includes me.

"I'll just be heading out. See you on the plane tomorrow bright and early," she finishes.

"Have a good night."

Ellie stands tall as if she's redrawing the professional boundary between us. It's almost laughable that I'm pining over this woman in secret.

We both examine each other for a beat before Ellie nods her head and gives me a tight smile. She taps her knuckles quickly on the open door and disappears.

As much as I wish she were staying at the office longer, I do enjoy watching the way her body sways as she walks away. I'm out of my goddamn mind.

My cell phone vibrates on my desk, pulling me out of my trance. I slide my chair back slightly and look at my phone, my eyebrows pinching inward.

Knox. He never calls me. Well, that's not entirely true. He does if he's low on funds or needs to deliver some type of news. I hit accept.

"Hi, son, how are you?"

He clears his throat.

"Hey, Fisher, good, good. I'm in New York this week."

I sigh and brace for what's to come.

Today, he's calling me Fisher and not Dad. This isn't a good sign. Knox does this when he's trying to create even more emotional distance. No matter how hard I try, he's never truly let me in.

"Are you enjoying it?"

"It's been a blast."

"Good, that's good."

"Yeah, it's good here. You have to visit the city sometime soon again."

"I do."

Silence stretches on.

"I have some news. I'm not coming back to Seattle or going to California for Christmas. I have an opportunity in Nashville."

I grumble louder than intended.

"Don't do that," Knox says defensively.

"I'm worried about you. I'm allowed to be worried. What kind of opportunity is it?"

"To audition for a new band who got a record deal. A friend of a friend connected me with the lead singer who is holding auditions for the lead guitarist spot. Their longtime guitarist just dropped out because his wife is having a baby, and he doesn't want this lifestyle anymore."

I fiddle with paperwork as I continue to listen.

"This is a real chance for me. They have a pretty decent following in Nashville and are in the running to open up for a major artist going on tour soon. I haven't gotten all of the details just yet."

If this is really his chance to pursue his dreams, I want him to take it.

"If you think this is the right step, I'm here for you."

"Thanks, Dad."

Back to Dad, it is. I'll take it as a victory. My shoulders begin to relax now that we're back to this dynamic.

"Keep in touch better than you have been," I say.

Knox chuckles.

"Can do, but hey, I have to run. Call you from Nashville."

As we get off, I consider what's happened between us over the years. He's never made it easy on me. Regardless of our rocky relationship, I just can't be the one to tell him to give up on his dreams. I need to be supportive if he's this confident about it.

I'm glad he's finally getting a real opportunity. The music industry is hard to break into, and he's had a tough path attempting to find success. There have been some months where I've sent him more money than a parent should send to a struggling musician. On the other hand, there have been months where the odd gigs he takes have kept him afloat.

Hopefully, this opportunity in Nashville will finally be his ticket.

A ding chimes from my computer. My last notification of the day alerting me to a meeting I have with our team based in Sydney, Australia.

These long days are getting exhausting, but it's all been in pursuit of making Rain Peak a global brand. I've accomplished what I set out to do, and I've put my blood, sweat, and tears into making it successful. It is now a global market leader.

I can't help but think about what's next. At my age, I don't want to be in this rat race much longer. I've given up so many years to my career and left everything else by the wayside.

I never take a vacation. In fact, the last time I did was

for my pseudo-daughter's wedding. Avery's wedding was in Charleston, South Carolina, where she now lives.

Avery's father, Todd, was my best friend and mentor. He founded Rain Peak and offered me a job almost right out of college. Tragically, he passed away several years ago.

Avery and the board of directors decided that I was the right person to take over as CEO of the company when he died. I was the senior vice president of operations and had been the closest executive to Todd.

Avery knew it. I knew it. Everyone at Rain Peak knew it too. I made the most sense to be his successor, so that's what I became.

Making Todd proud is part of the reason I've worked so hard to grow Rain Peak.

Ding.

I heave a heavy sigh as I pull up the notes for the call. It's time to keep going.

"EVENING, SIR." My doorman pulls open the door for me to go through.

"Hi, Joe," I say with a curt nod.

Walking into my building, I head past the reception desk and right for the bank of elevators, taking one to the best view in the city—my penthouse.

As I walk into my home, I take it all in.

It's the entire top floor of the building. With floor-to-ceiling windows that look out across the water, it's the reason I picked this building to live in. I have no place as a single man in the suburbs. Somewhere like this feels right.

"Good evening, Mr. Underwood."

My house manager, Letty, reaches for my coat as I slip it off.

"Evening. Everything in good order?"

"Yes, Mr. Underwood. Chef Theo has prepared a delicious meal for you this evening. I will bring it into the dining area for you now that you're home."

"I'll be out there soon."

Placing my hands inside my pockets, I walk toward my bedroom.

I change into a pair of black joggers and a matching T-shirt. I have a long night ahead of me still.

Heading back out to my dining room, I find Letty waiting nearby.

"Mr. Underwood, after your meal, I'll meet you in your office to review what will be happening at the house while you're away."

"Not necessary, you can go home," I encourage.

Letty has my personal affairs running smoothly. She's someone I can trust to handle whatever situation arises.

"I insist, Mr. Underwood."

"After dinner," I relent.

I see that she has already set the table with my meal. It looks delicious, like always.

I'm going to miss Theo as my private chef. He's off to New York to open his first restaurant. I'm sure his departure is just one of the items on Letty's list to review. This is an opportunity to see someone I rely on leave. Maybe it's a small glimpse into my future with Ellie.

Sitting down, I take in the aroma of the bruschetta grilled chicken he's prepared. Theo gets it right every time.

I turn my phone on silent so I can enjoy dinner without any distractions. It's one of the only times I'm granted silence.

I'm lucky this evening because as I stare out the window, it begins to rain—one of my favorite sights to behold. This view is everything and one that is meant to be shared with loved ones.

I POUR a sizeable whiskey as I settle into my home office. After firing up my computer, I start to review new emails that have come in over the past few hours. There's one particular email I didn't review in the office and need to this evening—the one from Ellie.

The retreat agenda is packed. We have a combination of activities planned for clients and their families. It's one of the opportunities I created to showcase how we don't just look at customers as if they are revenue and that we actually care about what's going on with their companies.

"Mr. Underwood?" Letty calls out.

"Please, take a seat," I answer and motion to the open chairs.

"Thank you."

Letty sits down and instantly pulls out her tablet, tapping away using the electronic pencil.

"If I may?" she starts.

"Please do."

I take a sip of my whiskey.

"As you know, Chef Theo is leaving this week. I am finalizing his replacement and have found a few excellent local candidates."

"We will be fine."

She raises one of her eyebrows and purses her lips together.

"I'll have his replacement ready for your return."

I signal for her to continue.

"Next, I have a list of services that will be done to the house this week. I'll forward it to your email for reference."

I nod my head and take another sip of my whiskey.

Letty continues with her list until we reach the last point.

"And lastly, Mrs. O'Connell and I spoke earlier today. She asked if you had made any decisions regarding Christmas." Then she pauses.

"I'll give her a call myself regarding the matter."

"As you wish," she answers.

She looks over her list once more.

"That's all I have for you this evening, sir. I packed your suitcases earlier today, and they are now at the front door. Your car will arrive at four-thirty in the morning to take you to the airport."

"Thank you."

"Safe travels, sir."

"Good night."

Once she leaves, I focus back on the retreat agenda.

Stretching my neck from side to side, I lean back in my seat and close my eyes. Some nights, I wish I wasn't this busy. At least the documentation is prepared exactly like I need it.

There is no slowing down for me—not anytime soon, at least.

THE DRIVE to the airport at this time in the morning is somber, with only the city lights illuminating the early morning sky. One would look at it as almost peaceful, but I know what it really means. A new day is dawning, with more madness in store for the bustling downtown.

The inside of my jacket vibrates.

I reach into it and wonder who's calling me this early in the morning.

Oh, of course. It's Avery.

The person I did not call last night to address my plans for Christmas. Even if Knox wasn't going to be in Nashville, there was little chance he would have planned to spend it with me over his mother. I was bound to be alone for the holiday.

I've been actively avoiding the Christmas conversation. Normally, I'd try to stay in Seattle, have a meal by myself, and then get back to work. I know that's not healthy, but it's what I'm used to and something that Avery constantly tells me is problematic.

"Avery," I finally answer.

"Hello."

An uncomfortable silence continues from the other line. I can feel her debating how to phrase what she's going to say.

"How are you?" I finally ask to break the tension.

I probably should have just gotten the Christmas discussion out of the way. It's around the corner, and I know Avery likes to plan.

"Pleasantries, is it? Okay then. Well, my non-profit, Save The Day, is doing well. The gala I just hosted for it was a success."

"That's wonderful. I knew you'd be able to get it off the ground quickly. When is the one-year anniversary?"

"In March. Now, do you want to share why you've been ignoring my calls regarding Christmas?"

"Avery..."

I exhale loudly.

Looking out the window, I see we're pulling up to the airport.

"You can't work yourself into the ground," she says.

"I know." I sigh.

"Then it's settled. I expect you on my doorstep no later than Christmas Eve."

"See you then."

"Good," she answers excitedly.

It has been a while since I've seen Avery.

"I'm off to North Carolina; I'll send you my details when I can."

"Perfect," she replies.

The car parks in front of the airplane. The steps are already rolled down, and I know I'll find Ellie waiting for me inside.

Avery's words ring true. Work is all I know. It's all I've ever wanted—to get to the top. I've been here for so long that I now question what my next step should be in life. At this rate, I just don't know if it's even possible for me to stop working.

I'll have enough time to think about Christmas and my future after this retreat. Right now, I get to see the one person who makes me feel alive.

THREE

Fisher

AS I WALK onto the plane, I immediately notice two long legs crossed over one another in a pair of high-heeled boots.

Ellie's already seated and focused on her laptop screen. I take in her attire—a crisp white button-down and a gray pencil skirt. It's like she's taunting me on purpose. This is one of the exact looks that makes me have inexcusable thoughts about my assistant.

Walking closer to where she's seated, I notice the exact moment that she registers I'm on the plane now too.

"Hi," Ellie chirps.

"Good morning," I respond gruffly.

"Someone needs their first espresso," she sing-songs as I take a seat across from where she's seated.

Ellie looks to the front of the plane, where a timid flight attendant stands by. She catches the woman's attention, and she quickly scurries over.

"He'll have an espresso and blueberry muffin."

"Yes, right away."

The flight attendant rushes to the galley to start preparing my espresso and muffin.

"Happy?" Ellie asks.

"I will be," I grunt.

"I never know which it'll be," she murmurs.

"What's that?"

Ellie looks up from her laptop with a cutting stare.

If looks could kill. Maybe she needs another coffee too.

"I never know if women are going to throw themselves at you or be scared of you."

Well, this certainly has my attention. I lean forward with my hands folded together.

"Those are the only two possible options?"

She laughs and then returns her attention back to her laptop. Interesting. I'll save this tidbit for the future.

"I just need a few minutes to wrap up an email," she shares.

"Anything of interest?"

"Just Rod Lohan asking more questions about the retreat," she grumbles.

"Ah, Rod. He's a detailed one."

"Yes, but so am I."

The flight attendant brings me out my espresso. I look up at her as she waits rigid as a stone for me to take it.

"Is there sugar in here?"

"Yes, sir. Ms. Robertson already told me how you like it prepared. I'll be right out with your muffin."

I signal for her to move forward.

Turning my attention to my own email, I lean back and begin scrolling through it on my cell phone. Nothing that needs to be responded to before takeoff.

After taking a sip of my espresso, I set it down on a

nearby tray the moment Ellie snaps her laptop closed. I glance up to find two big honey-brown eyes waiting.

"Are you finally ready?"

I do enjoy pressing her buttons from time to time.

Ellie gives me a pointed stare.

I love it when her professional mask falls when we're alone. It's just another moment where I can pretend like we could be more.

"Here is your file detailing every day of this retreat. I'd like to go over the last-minute updates. Does that work for you?"

"That's fine," I answer as I take the file.

The flight attendant brings me my muffin and Ellie a new coffee.

"What's this?" I ask, bewildered.

From here, I can see it's just a black coffee. This isn't what Ellie drinks daily.

"It's fine, sir," Ellie replies.

Ellie fascinates me.

She has no problem speaking her mind to a room of board members, yet she's too nervous to ask for the correct coffee on the private plane we've chartered.

Ellie and I are having a staredown.

"It certainly is not."

I shoot her a wink.

"Ms.?"

I get the flight attendant's attention.

"Yes," she replies.

"What's your name?"

"Samantha."

"Samantha."

"Yes, sir," she replies.

"Ms. Robertson here takes a latte with oat milk and no sugar. Please see to it before we take off."

"Sir..." Ellie interrupts.

"Of course," Samantha squeaks.

"Let's go over the updates once we are in the air," I say.

Ellie gives me a placating smile as she settles back into the seat.

"Whatever you want, Mr. Underwood."

I give Ellie a coy smile.

She can be such a brat. Some days, I dream about what I'd like to do to her when she gives me this attitude.

The flight attendant rushes over with Ellie's correct coffee.

"Better?" I ask as the captain announces it's time for us to take off.

"Yes, thank you."

"Good."

I watch as Ellie places her new latte carefully into the cupholder right before we start to take off down the runway, the speed climbing faster.

Ellie closes her eyes and grips the edge of her armrests.

"Ellie," I huff.

"I'm fine," she snaps.

I unbuckle my seat belt and move to the seat next to Ellie. After buckling myself in, I take one of her hands in mine.

"You don't have to do this," she groans.

"Again."

"Yes, again."

"I know."

Her hand grips mine tightly as a bright white color floods her knuckles, surrounded by a deep red. Instinctually, I rub my thumb against the back of her hand to try and get her to relax.

Ellie's fear of flying only recently came to light.

Typically, she's stayed behind in the office to keep a handle on the day-to-day affairs. It wasn't until we started these client retreats this year that I found out.

The first time I saw her white-knuckling the seat, I knew I had to immediately try and help ease her discomfort. I didn't care what boundary I was breaking, and she didn't seem to mind either. After that incident, this song and dance has become almost routine-like.

"Better?" I ask as the plane steadies in the air.

"Much, thank you," she mumbles.

Ellie lets go of my hand like it's on fire. I take that as my cue to go back to the way we were seated beforehand.

"Next time, you can just sit next to me," I remark.

She looks up at me through her long black eyelashes, and a faint blush appears on her cheeks.

"Yes, I know how much you love people in your personal space. I'll just plan to hold your hand because of my fear of takeoffs." She groans.

"Ellie," I scold.

"Yes, Mr. Underwood?"

So goddamn sassy.

She smirks as she picks up her laptop.

"Ready to go over the final changes?" She's grinning at me knowingly.

"Proceed."

I tent my fingers over my mouth as I wait for her to speak. Ellie straightens as she looks over the materials on the screen while I open up the file and pull out the documentation she's about to run through.

"You and I are the first to arrive today. The clients will

be arriving throughout the day tomorrow, and I have a detailed list attached that says who is coming in and when. There have been revisions to the order due to flight changes."

I nod thoughtfully.

"When will Grant arrive?"

"Mr. Sinclair arrives tomorrow at four thirty in the evening. His assistant shared he would be in on time for evening drinks with you."

"Very good."

Ellie raises an eyebrow, waiting.

"Continue," I say.

"Then, throughout the next three days, everything is still on track leading up to the formal reception with the new product launch. There are minor changes to the reception, but I think it'll all still be to your satisfaction."

"And you're sure James is coming in tomorrow to present?"

"Yes, Mr. Vice President of Product wouldn't dream of having anyone else present at these retreats," she mocks.

I chuckle before taking a sip of my espresso.

"You know how James is."

"Oh, yes, I do. I'm the one who has to make a thousand edits to his presentation each quarter."

"You shouldn't be doing that. Get his assistant to take over."

"You trust someone else with the final presentation?" Ellie asks skeptically.

"No, I don't."

A victorious smile stretches across her face.

"Do you want me to go into each day now to see if there are any final changes you'd like to make?"

"Yes, now's the time before we get off this plane."

"Alright. I'll make edits on the digital copy as you review."

It's difficult trying to review this as I watch her bite into her lower lip.

My eyes travel down to where her skirt has started to rise, giving me a better look at her golden thighs. I clear my throat before reverting back to trying to focus on this documentation.

I know Ellie has perfected the agenda to account for everything we've previously discussed. She's been a whiz at planning these and knows how I like every single detail to be handled.

It just adds to the reason why I'm struggling to let her go as my assistant. The sooner I break away mentally, the better. But how can I? Not when she's taking care of so much for me.

"Before we continue, Letty reached out to me to remind you to contact Avery if you haven't already," Ellie shares.

Letty knows how much I adore Avery, but she's beginning to be the mother I didn't ask for. She is another woman whom I am grateful to have in my life, no matter how much she interferes outside of her responsibilities.

"I already spoke to Avery," I admit smugly.

"Really? Did you decide to travel to Charleston for Christmas?"

"I'm expected on Avery's doorstep by Christmas Eve."

"That'll be nice for you," she says warmly.

I know I shouldn't, but I can't help but ask.

"What are your plans?"

Ellie's eyebrows furrow together momentarily.

I almost regret asking her something this personal. If it were anyone but Ellie, I probably wouldn't have even bothered. It's the pull to know where she'll be when she's not by my side that's addicting.

"It's still up in the air," she answers.

"Not going back to visit family?"

I take another sip of my espresso.

"Maybe. It's a long way to go back and forth after this trip."

"Nonsense. You can come with me on the plane. I can drop you off in Florida first."

She tilts her head to the side.

"I couldn't possibly take advantage of you like that. You know you've been too kind to me with using the company plane."

I give her a pointed look.

"Ellie, being stuck in Charleston because of a hurricane does not count as me being generous. I couldn't have you stranded on the other side of the country."

Her cheeks flush as her mouth turns down slightly.

"Right. Of course. I know that," she stammers.

"Well, when you decide, just add it to the itinerary."

"Of course, sir."

"Ellie," I grumble.

She won't look back up at me. It's almost as if she wants to avoid continual eye contact after that discussion.

The truth of the matter is I want Ellie to be safe and taken care of, regardless of the circumstances. It doesn't matter if she's just my assistant—if she needs help, I'll be there.

"Will Knox be joining you in Charleston?"

I remain stoic as I focus on Ellie. She still won't look in my direction.

Is she interested in Knox still after all these years?

Christ. I should have known that she could still have feelings for my kid.

"No, he actually just got an opportunity with a band in Nashville. You know how Knox is."

"I do," she replies.

I have to stifle my jealousy.

Considering that she may have lingering feelings for Knox is still a punch in the gut. It makes me want to throw this laptop across the plane and bend her over backward to redden her perfectly shaped ass for even bringing up her ex-boyfriend. I don't care that he happens to be my son.

I try to breathe in and out to prevent myself from behaving in a way I'll regret.

I should be trying to get these two back together instead of getting jealous. I have no reason to be territorial over her like this.

"If you'd like, I can tell him you say hello," I grumble.

Ellie's eyes finally snap up to meet mine.

"That's not necessary."

She returns to what she was previously focused on.

I can't tell how she meant that. Normally, I can pull back the curtain of Ellie's professional mask. Now I'm not so sure.

I finish my espresso.

"It's not an issue for me to ever pass along a message. I hope you know that."

Why am I digging myself a deeper hole? I don't want to pass along any messages between my assistant and my son.

Ellie's eyes shoot back to find mine, this time, searching for more. I can tell she's trying to assess what my motive is. Hell, I'm not even sure what my motive is.

I must be a glutton for punishment at this rate. Hoping that she doesn't want to speak to him, yet begging for her to give me the kind of response I need to hear so I can get these sick thoughts out of my head.

Give me a reason to stop wanting you.

"No, Fisher. Honestly, I hope this is okay to say..."

"You can say anything to me."

Her shoulders naturally relax as her mouth forms a pout.

"I really am not sure how Knox and I were ever even together. I wish him the best in what he's trying to accomplish. It's admirable even that he has this type of perseverance."

She pauses as I watch her mouth twitch while trying to find the right words.

"But if it wasn't for you, I would have forgotten he even existed," Ellie finishes.

I'm not stunned exactly, but this is a new development. We don't typically speak about him, and now it makes sense why.

If it wasn't for me, she and Knox would be completely in the past.

"I understand. I hope I didn't make you feel uncomfortable."

"No, of course not."

She gives me one of the few breathtaking smiles I get to witness behind the façade.

"Good. Now, let's go over the daily itineraries?"

She shakes her head slightly in amusement before returning to focus on the laptop screen.

"ANYTHING ELSE?" Ellie asks.

I lean back in the chair and assess all of the plans for the last time.

"It's good. Well done."

She closes her laptop as her eyebrows shoot up skeptically.

"Well done? What has you in such a good mood?" she taunts as she leans back into her chair now too.

"Easy, Ellie."

"It's always 'Easy, Ellie' when you're being teased," she muses.

Right then, the flight attendant interrupts our verbal sparring.

"Is there anything I can get either of you?" she asks.

It would be polite of me to focus on Samantha, but I can't look away from Ellie's gaze. I don't care if the flight attendant thinks I'm rude or cold or whatever else. Not when I have Ellie's attention.

A small smirk forms on her lips, and she finally breaks eye contact first.

"No, thank you, Samantha. Mr. Underwood and I are fine," she answers.

"Of course. Please just let me know."

"Actually, Samantha. I'll take another double espresso," I say.

Ellie's eyes shoot back to me.

"Oh, of course, one moment."

Samantha scurries away to the back of the plane.

"Really? Since when do you have more than one before ten in the morning?"

"Since today."

"I see."

Ellie clacks her long nails against the armrest as she crosses one leg over the other. To distract myself, I pull my tablet out of my briefcase and settle in to review the latest proposals I have from Doug.

Through the peripheral of my eyes, I see Ellie flipping through her cell phone.

"You have done a good job on these retreats. You should be proud."

"I am," she answers, and I can hear the hint of pride coming through.

"One of these days, you'll be off leading your own teams on a regular basis."

I notice Ellie stops scrolling on her phone.

"Why is that?" she asks hesitantly.

Now's not the time to mention the potential job change.

"You know you're more than capable. You won't be my assistant forever."

"Would that be such a bad thing?"

Turning my attention fully to her, I see she's waiting with bated breath for my answer. I don't want Ellie to think I don't want her to stay on as my assistant, but I can't trap her into staying in the role.

"One day, someone is going to snatch you up from under me, and I'll be damn proud to see you succeed."

Ellie gives me a hard smile and returns to browsing her phone. The look on her face almost appears upset.

I furrow my eyebrows together for a moment. Could it be that Ellie hates the thought of leaving me too?

FOUR

Ellie

THE NERVE.

The nerve of this man.

This beautiful, cold, unnerving man.

One day, someone is going to snatch me up. And he'll, what, be okay with it? As if I've barely meant anything to him over all these years. It's as if he's almost ready to find a new assistant. Like my time is almost up with him after everything I've done.

Frustration bubbles up. I don't know what I've been thinking lately. I know I should be using this as a sign to take the new position in Charleston and to put thousands of miles between Fisher and me.

There is just one problem.

One gorgeous, annoying problem.

The problem, which is sitting in front of me and answering emails as we are driven up a windy mountain to the resort.

All arrangements have been made to exceed Fisher's standards. I know what he likes and how to deliver. The only problem is that I've wanted him to see how valuable I am to him for far too long.

"Ellie." Fisher's smooth voice fills the silent car.

"Mr. Underwood?"

Fisher hates when I call him Mr. Underwood as much as when I refer to him as sir. His eyes always darken, and I feel like his arms tighten no matter the position or place we're in. It's almost as if I'm getting under his skin.

He groans and removes his glasses. Placing them firmly in his lap, he turns to face me more directly in the SUV. I wait patiently for what's to come.

"Don't be childish. If something is the matter, you should know by now you can just say it. I don't have time for these games."

I roll my eyes and look out the window.

I'm not going to talk about it. If he doesn't know how offensive he was, then he'll just have to figure it out on his own eventually.

As I focus on the scenery, I notice that the snow is starting to fall earlier than the weather forecast said it would. It's coming down almost magically. The pine trees are beginning to have a light dusting of powder, and the ground is sprinkled with it. A few deer are in the distance. Truly the start of something magical.

As I sit here, infuriated by what Fisher just said, I can't help but love where we are.

Wait. Did he call me childish?

"Excuse me?"

My head snaps over to him, where he has a smug smile plastered on.

"Had to say something to get you to talk to me."

"Ugh."

"What is it? You know this isn't us," he almost pleads.

If Fisher ever did plead, this would be the closest I've seen him come to it in all these years.

It makes me flinch in confusion.

"It's nothing."

"Don't do that."

"Do what?"

"Shut me out."

I look back out through my window and watch as the snow falls down harder.

The driver suddenly slams on his brakes, and the tires screech along the icy roads. Fisher's arm stretches out in front of me, and my body flushes against it. Even with my seatbelt on, I couldn't avoid it. The SUV skids before coming to a final halt.

"What the..." I manage to breathe out.

My hands are holding onto Fisher's arm.

I glance over and see his chest expanding in and out so vividly as his face remains calm.

"Are you okay?" he finally asks.

"Yes."

"Are you?" I get out.

"Yes."

Fisher's gaze finally meets mine, and I see a blaze there that I'm not familiar with.

Slowly, I peel my hands away from his arm and drop them to my sides.

The sound of the driver door opening and shutting breaks me of my Fisher-induced trance.

"I wonder why that happened," I ask.

"I'll go take a look," Fisher says.

He hops out of the SUV to join the driver.

I see them both examining the front of the car, talking frantically to one another.

The driver suddenly darts past where I'm seated to the trunk. I hear it pop open right as I focus back on Fisher. He's taken his suit jacket off and is rolling up his sleeves.

I watch as his swirling ink starts to appear with each roll on the left side, followed by the right. The way his veins protrude makes me forget all about the situation we're in.

Focus, Ellie. Now's not the time to be staring at Fisher's body art.

The driver runs past the doors back toward Fisher with something in his hands. He gives it to Fisher and goes back for something else in the trunk. Fisher leans down below the car.

"What's happening here?" I murmur.

Looking around where I am, I see my jacket and Fisher's glasses are on the ground. I pick his glasses up first to inspect them. Not broken.

The driver rushes past the side again.

I slip my jacket on to bring Fisher his glasses.

It's cold. Much too cold to be outside wearing a skirt and heels. I can admit that I dressed for Fisher and not for the snow—a choice I'm now regretting. The chilly weather and wind gusts are not helping.

Both sides of the road are desolate. If we weren't out here, it'd feel like the middle of nowhere. It practically already is.

The retreat is in a mountain town that you have to take a thirty-minute drive from the closest airport and go up the mountain. It'll be worth it in the long run if we can make it there.

I pull my jacket tighter around me before slipping my hands inside of my pockets.

"What's going on out here?"

I round my side of the car to see Fisher and the driver hunched in front of a tire. The old man is shining a flashlight where Fisher is working.

I lick my lips as I watch Fisher's arms pumping the device around and around.

I can't be thinking this way right now. We're practically stranded, and I'm lusting over his arms.

"We ran over a nail. Since we're on the mountain, putting the spare on is the easiest and quickest solution," Fisher answers while staying focused on the task at hand.

"Sorry, miss. I did offer your husband here for me to call the company's tow truck."

"My boss," I correct.

Fisher pauses, and his gaze shoots up to mine. His swirling hazel eyes take my breath away, except they are looking at me with something new in them.

"What? You are."

He grunts and returns his focus back to changing the tire.

"And we didn't want to wait for help?" I ask.

"No time if the snow keeps falling like this. Who knows how long it'll take someone to get up here to help," Fisher answers.

"That's fair."

"And why would we wait when I can do it?"

"I didn't realize you knew how to do manual labor," I tease while trying to lighten the mood.

The snow has started to fall harder in the short time since we've been outside.

"There's a lot you don't know about me," he shoots back, and it takes me off guard.

"Is that so?"

Well, now I'm intrigued. Fisher doesn't pause or give any indication of what that means.

"That's right, *assistant*."

My body shivers from the demanding tone. I wish I could say it's because of the cold air swirling around.

Huh.

He didn't like that I said he wasn't my husband. It just doesn't make sense why that would bother him.

Several minutes go by as the driver and I both wait for Fisher to finish fixing the tire.

"That'll do it."

Fisher stands and places his hands on his hips as he inspects his handy work. There's something attractive about watching my normally buttoned-up boss know how to do something so rugged. It's entirely unexpected. I would have laughed if someone told me this story, and I wasn't here to see it with my own two eyes.

"Thank you, sir. Once again, I deeply apologize, and you'll be receiving a full refund for this trip," the driver says.

Fisher wipes his hands against his pants.

"Get in, Ellie."

"Yes, sir," I automatically reply.

My body wants to follow any command he gives me in that tone.

Fisher's eyes flash up to mine.

"Now, Ellie."

My eyes shoot up from his arms and chest to his face. His jaw is tight, and I notice a small tick.

"Now."

Hurrying around to the other side, I slip in and sit in

disbelief as I wait for Fisher and the driver to get in too. What on earth has gotten into my boss?

***

"THANK YOU," I say to the driver as I step out of the car.

We've finally made it to the resort after our action-packed drive here.

I'm glad Fisher took charge of the tire fiasco and found an immediate answer to solve it. Fisher is meant to solve problems. He's good like that every single time I've witnessed him in a tough scenario.

"Of course, miss," he answers nervously.

"Will you be okay waiting here?"

"Don't worry about me, miss. Have a wonderful stay."

I give him a curt nod and head into the resort. I see the valet already has the bags and is putting them onto the luggage carts.

Fisher is standing next to the closed car door, waiting. Walking past the bellhop, I come face-to-face with the man of many talents. You can't even tell he was changing a tire in the snow twenty minutes ago. Meanwhile, I was just standing around, and I'm sure I look like a mess.

"Ready?" he asks.

"Yes," I answer excitedly, trying to come across as upbeat.

Fisher studies me for a moment.

"Everything is fine. That was a hiccup."

"I know."

We walk up the beautiful stone steps to the main lobby to check in. Normally, I would do this myself, but Fisher insisted on coming with me this time.

I walk ahead of him to try and give myself some space to

regroup. It's been an interesting day with him, and this retreat is only just beginning.

———

"GOOD AFTERNOON. Welcome to Valley Bridge Resort. Do you have a reservation with us?" the front desk woman asks as we approach.

"Yes, I'm Ellie Robertson with Rain Peak Corporation. We have the retreat taking place."

"Yes, of course. Welcome, Ms. Robertson. Thank you once again for choosing us as your destination. Mr. Peters will be out momentarily to show you around the meeting space first, as requested. We'll have your luggage sent to your cabin immediately."

"Thank you."

The front desk woman calls my resort contact, Russ Peters, to let him know I've arrived.

"Mr. Peters will be right out," she shares.

"Perfect. And can you please have Mr. Underwood's luggage sent to his cabin as well?"

"Yes, of course. We have Mr. Underwood staying in the Luxury Deluxe Mountain Cabin."

The door behind the woman swings open, and a tall, blond man who looks like he stepped off a fashion runway appears. He's in a fitted navy-blue suit, and his hair is neatly styled.

"Ms. Robertson?" he asks with a blinding smile.

"Yes, that's me," I almost stutter.

"It's a pleasure to meet you finally," he says, with an outreach of his hand.

"You as well," I answer as I shake Russ's hand.

My body begins to prickle automatically. I feel his presence behind me without even hearing his movement.

The way Russ's eyes widen as they travel to behind where I stand gives me the final confirmation.

Fisher's body is mere inches away from me, and I feel the heat radiating off his frame and onto mine. It's still somehow professional despite the way my body starts to feel achy all over. I really need to pull it together when I'm around this man.

"Mr. Underwood, it's a true honor to make your acquaintance," Russ exclaims.

Russ lets go of my hand immediately and steps to the side to greet Fisher properly.

"Yours as well," Fisher replies coldly.

Fisher looks down at Russ's hand and gives it a firm shake. I notice the way Russ flinches and lets go of it as quickly as possible.

"Well," Russ says.

He takes a substantial step back and clears his throat.

"Right this way to see the meeting space."

He turns, and the clack of his designer shoes sounds against the stone as he leads the way.

I glance up at Fisher to see a small smirk. Another smug one. Only this time, I get the odd feeling it's because of what just transpired.

I let out a loud exhale.

Maybe Harper is right, and I do need a break from Fisher. I'm imagining one too many scenarios, and it's only getting worse.

"Fisher," I start.

"Don't."

I open my mouth and snap it shut. We're distracted by a server walking into the same main ballroom as we just did.

"Champagne?"

"Thank you," Fisher answers.

He collects two champagne glasses from the server and hands one to me.

"Thank you."

My fingers graze the back of his hand, and I feel a current sweeping between us from the slight touch. Fisher's expression is overwhelming as I watch his eyes lift from our connection and up to my mouth.

"This is our main ballroom. We'll be hosting each meal inside of this room, and this is also where the evening receptions will be held. As you know, we have ways to quickly maximize the space to make the evening as enjoyable as possible for your guests," Russ shouts.

Fisher and I both immediately straighten and focus on Russ. It's a needed reprieve from what's happening.

He starts to pace around the room as Russ continues sharing more details, and I follow along a few steps behind. It's a familiar routine we have.

I confirm the details, and Fisher examines the space from the viewpoint of the clients. They are giving up valuable time to come here for this retreat.

"Good?" Fisher asks me.

"Good," I confirm.

"Next room, please, Russ," I say, interrupting his speech.

"Oh yes, of course, right this way," he stammers.

Fisher and I both trail Russ as he leads us to the world-famous Après ski lounge area.

"Is it meeting your expectations?" I ask.

"Exceedingly," Fisher answers.

"Good, I'm glad."

"Were you worried?"

"No. I mean, yes. I want to please you."

Fisher comes to a sudden halt, and I nearly bump into one of the double doors we're about to open.

His eyes darken, and I see a battle within them.

"You always please me."

I suck in a deep breath and feel like the wind has been knocked out of me. Fisher grins and strolls into the lounge, leaving me breathless.

FIVE

Ellie

"THIS IS YOUR CABIN, MS. ROBERTSON," Russ says as he holds the door open.

"Thank you."

I walk into the cabin, and my breath is taken away again. Only this time, it's because of the beautiful place I'll be calling home while we're here and not because of Fisher.

The cabin is all wood with modern details. It looks like the perfect high-end destination for someone who wants to escape to the mountains but get all of the amenities of a five-star hotel.

"You did good," Fisher whispers into my ear.

"Thank you," I murmur.

I soak in more of his praise.

"Is this to your liking?" Russ asks as we're all lingering in the front foyer.

"Yes, it's perfect," I respond warmly, and I hear Fisher growl under his breath.

What is wrong with him lately? He's been acting so strange.

"Wonderful," Russ says.

Suddenly, a loud sound cuts through the cabin. I shriek right as Fisher grips my shoulders to steady me.

"What happened?" I ask, panicked.

"Nothing to worry about, I assure you. Let me take a look around," Russ answers.

"Yes, that's probably a good idea," I stammer.

I watch as anxiety takes over Russ's demeanor, and he suddenly dashes into a nearby room.

"This isn't promising," I whisper.

"No, it's not, but there is no reason to worry until we know what happened."

"How can you stay so calm?" I ask.

"Worrying won't help us. We need to assess the problem at hand. It could be nothing."

I start to pace as we continue to wait for an update.

"We know it was something," I interject.

Nothing? We know it's something, but I get his point.

I find Fisher is watching me with an amused expression. There is a crinkling around his eyes and mouth.

"Am I entertaining you?"

"Very much so."

I ignore his rebuttal and continue to pace.

We wait for several more minutes in the foyer, then a resort staff engineer comes through the cabin door.

"Good afternoon," he says.

"Hello," I answer, while trying to force a smile.

He gives us a curt nod before hustling into the same room that Russ is in.

"He called for backup," I groan out.

"Still could be nothing," Fisher adds.

"Right," I say sarcastically.

I start pacing around the foyer again as we wait.

A chill falls through the air, creating the need to pull my jacket tighter to keep warm. It's gotten exceptionally colder in this cabin.

The cabin door opens again, and it's another engineer.

"Hi there, folks. Shouldn't be too much longer," the man says.

"Great," I force out.

He scurries back into the same room. At this rate, we're starting to collect hotel staff in this cabin.

I come to a halt as realization dawns on me.

"Has it gotten a lot colder inside of here to you?"

Fisher looks around the room momentarily.

"It has."

"You realize what's happening?"

"I do."

"The cabins are sold out. The main lodge is sold out. Everyone is arriving tomorrow," I say frantically.

Fisher's expression remains stoic. We're in a battle of emotions as I start to panic, and he remains calm.

"Ms. Robertson, Mr. Underwood," Russ calls out. We both break our trance to see him coming back out of the room.

"Yes?" I ask.

"Unfortunately, we have a situation on our hands. Let's head up to the lobby and see what other sleeping arrangements we have."

"Other sleeping arrangements?" I croak.

"Yes, unfortunately, the heat has stopped working. It's very unusual. The team is diligently working on it, but I'm afraid it won't be fixed today."

"Oh," I reply, stunned.

"Yes, let's head to the front desk, and we can see what I can do."

Russ is trying to remain calm, but this isn't a huge resort. We don't pick those kinds of places for the retreats on purpose. The main lodge has to have less than twenty rooms. It's a destination people choose to come to far in advance.

Everything is sold out. He knows it, and I know it. Only we are both hoping for a miracle.

Russ leads the way to the main lodge as Fisher and I trail behind him once again.

"Regretting this outfit?"

"You cannot be serious right now." I huff.

I fling my hair back and continue walking to the lodge. Fisher chuckles.

The man chuckles.

I don't know what's going on with him, but first, I get a show with Fisher sexily changing a tire, then he becomes possessive in front of Russ, and now a chuckle. I must have hit my head at some point because this feels like an alternate reality.

I come to another stop inside the lobby. It's filled with guests—almost as if the resort is sold out like I assumed it would be.

"This doesn't look good."

"Don't worry yet. There is a solution to every problem."

We linger near the guest relations stand and watch Russ behind the counter, trying to magically find a room. Fisher is remaining collected as we wait. Easy for him—he's not the one out a place to stay.

"What's the situation? Give it to us straight," I finally ask.

Russ looks up from his screen with a panicked expression.

"Well, Ms. Robertson, you see," he begins.

"The situation."

Russ gives me a tight smile.

"We're completely booked out. I don't have another room for you tonight. You could always stay in one of the cabins you reserved for other guests, and we can take it on a night-by-night basis. I assure you, my team is working hard to solve the heating issue in your cabin," he spits out.

I watch Fisher listening intently next to me.

"Well," I start.

"Send Ms. Robertson's belongings to my cabin. She'll stay with me this week until the heating issue is resolved in the original cabin. I expect some type of apology will be given to Rain Peak for the inconvenience?" Fisher cuts in.

"Of course. Of course," Russ stammers.

Russ snaps his fingers and begins giving orders for his team to take my bags to Fisher's cabin. I feel dazed as I process what Fisher just said.

Me? Stay in his cabin? I couldn't possibly. Fisher likes his space and privacy. There is no way he wants his assistant to stay with him for a week.

"Fisher," I whisper.

"Don't."

"I don't mind staying in different cabins as needed."

"You will do no such thing. There are two bedrooms in my cabin, correct?"

"Well, yes."

"Problem solved. You can take the spare room. We'll be working nonstop all week; it makes sense for this to be the solution until your own accommodations are guaranteed to be fixed. Do you really want to be switching around every day?"

"Well, no."

Okay, I understand where he is coming from, but it just feels awkward. I don't want Fisher to feel forced to do this.

"Let's go then."

Fisher turns on his heels back to Russ.

"Can someone take us there now?"

"Yes, of course," Russ answers.

Fisher pulls out his cell phone and answers it as I stay in this fog-like state.

Russ and two bellmen start leading the way to Fisher's cabin, the same one I am now temporarily staying in.

As Fisher continues his call, reality hits.

I'm about to be sleeping in Fisher's cabin. We'll be sharing a space together.

Oh no. I'm going to be sick.

How am I going to get through the night? Being around Fisher is already a difficult enough experience. I don't know why, but his presence makes me feel uneasy. I mean, am I supposed to make my morning coffee in my pajamas and ask my boss if he wants any? So weird.

Nope. No way. I mean...

I need to get a grip on what's happening. It's going to be fine. I've got this.

I slam into the back of someone who feels like a wall of hard muscle. As I stumble, this person swoops around and pulls me into his arms.

"Are you okay?" he rasps.

Of course it's Fisher. Of course he's now swooping in to save me.

I KNOW I have to come out of my bedroom sooner rather than later.

None of the guests are arriving until tomorrow, so tonight was going to be my time to review the client list one more time and eat a bowl of pasta and maybe have a glass of wine or two. Riveting, I know.

It was the calm before the storm, but now I'm debating how to act in Fisher's cabin as we share this space.

I start to pace behind my closed door, looking down at what I'm wearing. It's still appropriate—a cozy sweater and a pair of jeans. Easy and relaxed.

"Ellie," Fisher calls out.

I freeze as if he can see me nervously walking back and forth behind the door.

"You can do this," I mutter.

Slowly, I crack the door open to peek out. I see Fisher sitting in a pair of fitted lounge pants and a basic T-shirt, which is stretched across his chest, with his phone in hand.

Seeing him like this is something else. I love when I get glimpses of his tattoos, but right now, they are fully out on display.

It's like seeing a different side of Fisher that no one else gets to see—a version reserved for those in his comfort zone. I'm not sure why the idea of me being part of that circle makes my insides feel jumbled up.

"Ellie," he says, breaking me from my daze.

This isn't good. I'm not someone who daydreams like this. I step completely out of my room.

Alright, Ellie. Be natural.

"Don't feel obligated to say yes, but I'm going to order room service for dinner. Care to join me?"

Fisher is finally looking at me instead of his cell phone. He's always checking in with work.

"That sounds great."

"The menu is on the counter if you'd like to take a look."

"Great."

I shut my eyes tightly for a moment.

Oh god, I need to pull it together better than this.

I head to where the menu is and start glancing at my options. Hopefully, they have a bowl of any kind of pasta on it.

Suddenly, I feel Fisher's presence nearby.

"Anything look appealing?"

It comes out huskier than I think he intended, and it makes my body squirm.

I nod my head slowly as I avoid looking over to him.

"What will it be?"

"The chicken alfredo pasta."

"I'll call it in."

"Wait, no, I can do that. It's my job."

He sighs as he rounds the kitchen island to one of the landline phones.

"Don't start that."

"I'm your assistant."

"And tonight, you're my guest."

Fisher doesn't give me a chance to challenge the situation and begins calling the room service line.

"Why don't you change into something more comfortable? You can be yourself with me here. This is your cabin too."

"Okay..."

I really thought I was dressed comfortably, but I suppose he's right.

I head back to my bedroom and close the door, leaning against it as I process what's happening.

What *is* happening?

He's just my boss being nice. That's all. And for that matter, we are friends. I would never say that out loud, but I know we are.

I'm overreacting because of my...

I'm not going to say it. If I string these words together, it'll make it real.

I hang my head back and breathe in and out.

"Everything okay?" he asks.

In a panicked state, I collapse onto my bed and rub my temples.

"It's all great," I shout.

I'm grateful he can't see me because I feel like I want to die with how many times I've been using the word great in the past ten minutes. I need to figure out how to use a different word when responding to him tonight.

Straightening up, I need to get back to my usual self.

I need a new plan to get through the night. I'll simply get changed and go out there like it's nothing, eat the pasta, check the paperwork, and then head back in here to go to bed. It's all simple enough.

That all sounds good and well, but I do have one major hiccup to the plan: I don't think I packed appropriate pajamas. Clothes are something I take great pride in as I like looking my best at all times. Even when I'm alone, I don't sit around in an old T-shirt and mismatched shorts.

Assessing my options, I pull out a pair of black silky shorts and their matching camisole top. It's not overtly sexual. If I don't change, Fisher may think I feel uncomfortable around him for entirely different reasons.

I am overthinking all of this way too much.

After quickly changing, I take a final look at myself in the full-length mirror. This is totally fine to wear in front of him. Maybe I can lie to myself a few more times about it, and it'll be true. There's nothing else I can do.

I open the door to see Fisher has a fire roaring and candles lit around the space. *Nothing romantic about this setup at all.*

I clear my throat to get his attention, and his eyes snap up to mine.

For a moment, I watch as they travel up and down the length of my body. He fixes his glasses and tries to focus back on his phone, but I see them darting back and forth from the screen to me repeatedly.

"Glad to see you got more comfortable."

"I wasn't expecting to be with anyone at night when I packed my bag."

Fisher mumbles under his breath as he stares at his phone.

"What was that?" I ask.

"It's nothing. And your outfit is perfectly you."

I walk toward him.

"Perfectly me?"

"Yes, I wouldn't expect you to wear an old college T-shirt to bed."

I cock my head to the side and fold my arms against my chest. I'm making him have to look up at me.

"Why is that?"

He finally does.

"It's nothing negative. I know you like to dress well and take good care of yourself."

I settle down on the couch. That is true.

"I was planning on reviewing the client list tonight."

"We can do that together after dinner if you'd like."

"That would be great." I wince.

New word, Ellie. Find a new word.

I see his mouth turn upward.

Does Fisher find me... amusing? I need to find out what's going on in these mountains because I am witnessing a side of Fisher that's so different.

"Dinner should be arriving soon. Interested in watching anything on the television?"

I fold my legs under my lap and grab a nearby blanket.

"Does Fisher Underwood watch television?" I mock.

He gives me a pointed stare.

"It is a valid question," I continue.

"Periodically."

I perk up, excited that I'm getting tiny bits of information about his personal life.

"What is one of your guilty pleasures? I know you have to have one."

Fisher places his cell phone on the coffee table and grabs the remote control.

"Buying time, I see," I taunt.

"I'm not embarrassed to say I watch a few reality dating shows," he says with a grin.

"Fisher Underwood and reality dating. Interesting."

He looks over at me as I try to contain a smile, and he simply shrugs. The man is a shrugger now too.

"I have to ask something," I start.

"What's that?" He gives me his full attention, a quality I love.

"You seem different. Is everything okay?"

I see a newfound weight on his shoulders as his playful expression turns contemplative.

"Maybe different can be good," he suggests.

"Maybe," I agree.

The ringing of the doorbell gives us both a needed distraction.

"I'll get it," he says right before standing up.

I can practically feel the drool coming out of my mouth as I watch him do so. His feet pad against the wooden floors over to the door.

As he greets the delivery server, all I can do is fixate on the way his butt looks in these pants. His whole body is hard, but I've never had a chance to just take him in like this. I've never seen him this dressed down before either.

"Good evening," the server greets Fisher.

"Good evening. On this table, please," he answers.

"Can do, sir."

Fisher plucks a wine bottle off of the dining cart and begins uncorking it. Now I'm getting a front-row seat to my new favorite show: watching his arms flex as he opens the wine.

"Have a good evening," the server calls out before exiting.

Fisher brings the two wine glasses over to the now candle-lit table.

"Ready?" he asks.

"Ready."

I certainly hope I am.

SIX

Fisher

"I THINK that's all we need to do tonight," I say.

I don't know what I was thinking, putting myself in this direct line of torture. Having Ellie in my space outside of work is different. Even when she was dating Knox, they rarely came over. He would seldom take me up on my invitations.

This is entirely different. I have to smell her floral scent all night and watch her hair spill over her chest.

"Are you sure?"

Ellie looks up at me through her long black eyelashes.

"You've got it all covered."

She smiles at me like I've given her the world with this small compliment. I'm not sure why, but I like that she wants my praise.

Ellie closes her laptop and sets it on the coffee table, then picks up her almost-empty wine glass.

"Up for a refill?" I can't help but ask.

I want more time with her without it revolving around working.

"Sure," she answers hesitantly.

We both head to the kitchen with our empty wine glasses.

Ellie stops suddenly.

"Is everything okay?"

"Oh, yes, sorry," she whispers.

She points out the kitchen window into the dark abyss.

"The snow is just coming down really hard. Even with what the forecast said, I'm just shocked, is all."

I come up behind her to get a better look.

"We'll work it out in the morning if it becomes an issue."

Ellie glances in my direction.

I know I should take a step back, but this feeling is all I've been craving as of late. The chance just to be near her when I know I have to let her move on. She doesn't need to be stifled by me.

"How can you always be so calm?"

"I don't think many people would describe me as calm," I say with a grin.

Ellie's mouth parts for a moment before she closes it.

"What were you going to say?" My voice comes out deeper than I meant for it to, and her lips part once more.

"I would."

My chest rises and falls.

"I suppose you did."

We're staring at each other like there is more to say. It should be uncomfortable, but it isn't. I watch as her breath hitches. She is debating saying something. I know she is.

"It's because I know you, Fisher. I know you."

"You do."

Ellie's eyes focus on my mouth. It stirs up feelings inside that I need to push down. I want to kiss her, but I can't. Instead of acting on it, I take a step back and brace myself on the kitchen island.

Ellie shakes her head to clear herself from the moment and bring herself back from whatever that was.

"I'll get the wine. Why don't you turn on the news? Maybe we can see what's going on with this snowfall," I suggest.

"Sounds great."

I see her eyes shut for a moment before she spins on her heels toward the living room area.

Focusing on the task at hand, I pour two generous glasses of wine and head back out there. On the television screen, I see what looks like a terrible snowstorm right over North Carolina.

"Can you turn this up?"

Ellie nods as she stares at the same screen and slowly turns the volume higher.

"This isn't good," she whispers.

The meteorologist is sharing that this is shaping up to be one of the worst snowstorms to hit North Carolina in years.

"What do we do?" she asks.

"Don't worry. We'll go to the lodge in the morning and see what's happening. For now, here," I answer as I hand her the glass of wine.

"It's hard not to worry." She sighs.

We both walk over to the couch and take a seat.

"We can't change the course of the storm. On the upside, we have heat and wine. Looks like a good combination to me."

Ellie laughs and runs a hand through her hair.

"True. And delicious wine at that."

"We have another bottle."

"That's probably not a great idea," she counters.

"I have a strong suspicion this retreat isn't happening tomorrow. Or this week."

Ellie leans back and takes a gulp of her wine.

"I have a bad feeling about it too."

We both sit in that confession. This whole day, we've both been coming to terms with the fact that this retreat is not happening. We just haven't wanted to be the one to voice it.

If the storm is as bad as they claim it will be, I doubt any clients will be able to arrive tomorrow as planned.

"Movie?"

A smile stretches over her face.

"A movie sounds great. You can pick," she says.

"I don't think so."

"You're right. Of course I should pick. Otherwise, we'd be getting some type of cheesy movie that could compete with reality TV dating," she says with a laugh.

"Don't knock it until you try it."

"Whatever you say."

"WHAT DO YOU MEAN? How is that acceptable for a resort of this caliber?" Ellie shrieks.

Russ's demeanor is exactly how he should be acting. He's almost afraid of Ellie. This side of her is one of the reasons I've loved seeing her grow in her role over the years. She knows what she needs to do to get a job done. I may be calm and collected to Ellie, but to me, she's someone who can hold her stance.

"I understand, Ms. Robertson. I do. However, there is

nothing I can do about the snowstorm blocking the roads to the resort."

"It's barely even snowing anymore," Ellie says.

Russ and I make eye contact. It's coming down hard. Much harder than last night.

"Let's figure out what we can do," I interject.

"Right, sir."

"How long is the storm estimated to go on?"

"Another forty-eight hours."

"And then there are going to be days added on for the roads to clear."

"That's correct."

"What you are going to do for us is personally call every assistant on this list immediately regarding the situation. If anyone is, for some reason, able to arrive this week, you will give them accommodations."

Russ looks flabbergasted.

"Mr. Underwood, sir," he starts.

"Also, we'll be expecting our same arrangements to be rebooked for February. Presidents' Day weekend."

Russ's jaw opens before he snaps it closed.

He adjusts his tie to buy time. It's a lot I'm asking for, but I don't care. Russ knows my connections in the community he serves, and it can't get out that he's not being accommodating, even if it is because of a snowstorm.

"Sir, I will do my best to determine what we can do for you. I will call your cabin within the hour."

"Thank you."

Russ scurries behind the counter back to his office.

Ellie sighs loudly. "I had that handled."

"I know you did, but Russ was going to keep pushing back."

"I still could have handled it."

"I know. Next time, I won't intervene. Happy?"

"Yes," she admits.

"Now, let's get back to the cabin and call these clients."

Ellie hangs her head back momentarily before nodding in agreement.

"Let's get to it. I can't even imagine how everyone is going to take it," she complains.

"It's a snowstorm. I bet most people are trapped locally and didn't even get to take off."

"I hope you're right."

ELLIE SLUMPS back into the dining room chair. Her laptop is on the table, surrounded by a second screen and dozens of papers.

As she crosses her legs, I can't help but notice how the black leather pants mold to her body. Her sky-high black boots elongate her already long legs, and I want to bury my face in between her tits in that fluffy sweater.

Fuck. What is wrong with me?

This is Ellie, not some woman I'm taking to a hotel for the night. I need to keep reminding myself of this.

"I'm so glad that's done." Ellie groans.

"Everyone understood."

"That they did. You were right," she admits.

"Of course I was."

Ellie opens her eyes and shoots daggers at me with them, and I can't help but smirk.

"What should we get to work on next? I can sort through our project management system to see what we had after the retreat. Or else we could answer emails. There are endless emails I'm sure we can sift through."

Ellie sits up and begins tapping away on her laptop again.

I thought I was nonstop work. Ellie matches me in almost every way—the determination, the need for success.

"I have a different idea," I say.

I lean against the nearby wall and fold my arms across my chest, waiting for her to answer.

She perks up.

"What's that?"

"How about lunch?"

She arches one of her eyebrows.

"Uh, Fisher. We're stuck on this mountain."

"We'll order room service and have them deliver it to us whenever possible."

Her shoulders visibly relax, and a relieved expression takes over.

"That sounds nice."

"I know this isn't what we planned, but we're here and should make the most of it."

She smiles. "You're right."

"I know."

Ellie gives me a pointed stare, and I can't help but feel smug.

The cabin phone rings.

"I'll get that. Take a look at the menu, and we can put an order in after this."

Ellie gets up and starts heading to the kitchen with me.

"I bet that's Russ."

"With fantastic news, I bet," I say sarcastically, and she grins.

"Mr. Underwood, did you just make a joke?"

"I can make those periodically."

"Something is definitely in this North Carolina air," she mumbles.

I pick up the phone to answer it. Hopefully, Russ will have some positive news.

"Hello," I say.

"Mr. Underwood, Russ here. I have good and bad news to share."

"Continue."

"The good news is that everything has been taken care of. I personally followed up with the assistants as requested."

"Thank you. That's good news, indeed."

Russ clears his throat.

"What's the bad news, Russ?"

He clears his throat again.

"Well, you see, this is something out of my hands," he begins.

"Go on."

He clears his throat again.

"Ms. Robertson will need to continue to stay with you in your cabin indefinitely this week. We can offer additional credits for you to use in the future for the inconvenience."

"Why?"

Ellie looks at me curiously.

"The snowstorm is having a greater impact than ever before, sir. Most of the cabins are now without heat or electricity, and the remaining cabins need to be used to house staff members who can no longer go home."

"I see."

"Once again, I deeply apologize."

"No need to apologize given the situation at hand. Thank you for letting me know. I appreciate the care you are taking of your team. We'll be placing a food order momentarily. I expect food can still be given out to your guests?"

"Of course, sir," he answers.

I hang up and turn my attention back to Ellie.

"What's happening now?" she asks hesitantly.

"Well, the good news is that everything we wanted regarding the retreat is being taken care of."

"That's good..."

"It is."

"What was the bad news?"

"It's all about how you look at it."

Her eyebrows furrow together as she places the menu down on the kitchen island.

"What does that mean?"

"It means you're bunking in here with me this week."

Ellie's eyes widen.

"What?" she shrieks.

"Cabins are out of power and heat. Any remaining working ones are being used for staff."

"An entire week of just me and you?" She practically stutters.

"I'm sorry."

I don't want to make her uncomfortable, but there aren't exactly a ton of options right now for us.

"No, no," she quickly interjects.

"Will this be okay with you?"

"Of course. It makes sense. I just hope the staff will be okay."

"Me too."

I look out the window as an easy distraction from this awkwardness.

"Did you find something you'd like to eat?"

"I have. Let's order."

Ellie rounds the island and comes up to where I still wait near the landline. Her big doe eyes look almost eager—for what, I can't imagine.

"I promise it will be okay this week."

"I know it will be. I have you," she whispers.

My heart comes alive from her trust.

Ellie's mouth parts as she stares at mine.

She's so goddamn tempting all the time. It's hard to remember that she's not mine when she looks at me like this.

"I'm going to make a few personal calls before we order lunch," Ellie declares abruptly.

I'm confused by the sudden change.

"Okay."

She walks to her bedroom quickly and closes the door.

I fiddle with my cell phone and debate making a few calls myself, namely to Avery and Letty. If I call Avery, it'll only come with more questions. Ones that I don't exactly have the answer to.

Will keep you updated on Christmas. The storm is coming through where the retreat is scheduled.

I saw! I've been trying to call you. What are you going to do?

We're sticking it out, nothing else we can do.

Wait, you're trapped?

Yes.

One word answer?

Yes.

Very funny.

I'll keep you updated.

Stay safe!

I SHOULD HAVE KNOWN that Avery would have questions regardless of how I reached out to her from here. Now, onto Letty, who will surely have dozens of updates for me.

She was more concerned about Chef Theo leaving me than I have been. The kid has talent, and I always knew he would move on to bigger and better jobs as he should be doing. He can't be a private chef in Seattle forever.

It's almost the same way I feel about Ellie. I know she has to move on from being my assistant, only it's harder for me to let her go after all this time. My feelings for her are complicated, to say the least.

Back to Letty.

"Underwood residence," Letty says.

"Letty, it's me."

"Hello, Mr. Underwood. I've been expecting your call, given the news of the snowstorm. Are there any arrangements you need me to make on behalf of you or Ms. Robertson?"

"Nothing can be done just yet. I'll give you a call when something can be."

"Of course. Is now a good time to give you updates on outstanding items in the household?"

"You may."

I settle onto the sofa, and Letty begins to give me countless updates. I appreciate her work; she's one of the only people I can rely on. Letty and the woman on the other side of the wooden door, whom I can't wait to see again.

SEVEN

Ellie

SNOWED IN.

I'm snowed in with my boss. With my ex-boyfriend's dad. With the person whom I am actively trying to come to terms with my feelings for as I navigate this next life choice I have to make.

I need to call Harper immediately. She's one of the only people who knows what I'm going through.

"Hello? Ellie?"

"Hi."

"Oh my god, I've been so worried! Are you still in North Carolina?"

"Yes, but we're fine."

"We're?"

"Yes, Fisher and me."

"Oh," she yelps.

"Exactly."

A silent beat between us.

"I'm freaking out, Harper," I shriek.

"Don't freak out, this is actually…"

"Actually, what? A disaster?"

Harper laughs lightly.

"Are you actually laughing right now? I can't believe I'm now trapped on a mountain in the same cabin as Fisher with everything I have to consider. It's the worst." I groan.

I plop down onto the bed and lie back fully while keeping the phone to my ear. Closing my eyes, I rub my eyebrows as they pinch inward.

"Ellie, I love you, I do. I realize that this isn't technically how you thought it would be."

"Technically?"

Harper laughs again.

"But this is actually perfect. Now you can address your feelings for Fisher in the cabin."

I freeze as I take in what she's saying.

"I can't do that."

"Yes, you can and, more importantly, should," she says.

I let out a loud groan.

"I don't know…"

I get up from the bed and start to pace around it instead.

"What do you want to say, but you aren't?" I can't help but finally ask.

"Look…"

"Don't beat around the bush. It's not like you."

She laughs again, only this time louder.

"I know you think that Fisher will never have feelings for you, but what happens if you never try? I mean, I can be the first one to tell you that there is something about being trapped with the guy you like during a weather-related disaster."

"Okay, well, that's fair," I agree.

Harper was in Charleston for a bachelorette party, and she had a one-night stand with Grayson. A hurricane forced her to stay with him for a few days. It's how they eventually became a couple.

"You have this other job offer. I think you need to use tonight to lay your cards out there. It's only you two in the middle of nowhere while it's snowing. Like, come on, how romantic is that?"

"Well, I suppose that's one way to look at the situation."

"Go for it."

"We'll see..."

Harper sighs.

"Alright, well, at the very least, consider what's at stake. I would love to have you in Charleston with me next year, but if you don't say anything to Fisher, you'll always wonder."

"I'll think about it."

After getting off the phone with Harper, I plug my phone into the charger before changing into a new outfit—a pair of black leggings and a black V-neck T-shirt.

Looking at myself in the mirror, I start fixing my hair to avoid going back out to Fisher.

"You can do this. It's just Fisher," I murmur.

Bouncing on my feet, I try to get pepped for going back out there. Maybe Harper is right to some degree; I don't think Fisher even realizes his effect on me. I have seen him notice me staring at his tattoos, but that could be chalked up to anything.

I can't stall any longer; it's go time.

I walk out of my bedroom and immediately stop in my tracks. Fisher has also changed, and he's far too relaxed-looking for me to have any type of barrier up. We're practi-cally matching. He's in a pair of black joggers and a black T-shirt that looks like it's been painted on his chest, with his tattoos that I love clearly on display.

I instinctively lick my lips as I watch him run a hand through his deep-brown styled hair.

Fisher turns his attention away from the television to me.

Then he does it again.

And again.

Finally, he clears his throat.

"Ellie."

His voice comes out thickly, making heat start to pool between my thighs. I squeeze them together slightly. As I do, I see Fisher's eyes snap to the movement before returning to my gaze.

His eyes darken as we now pretend like everything is perfectly normal.

"Fisher," I calmly respond.

Needing a distraction, I walk into the kitchen and pick up the room service menu, pretending to read it, even though my mind wanders back to Fisher and his black-inked tattoos swirling around his thick, muscular arms. Ones that I want to lick like a sex-crazed maniac.

My eyes keep wandering from one item to the next on the menu, but I can't read a word of it.

I hear Fisher get up from where he was seated and start walking over to me.

Dear god, this man is going to torture me more than usual.

I continue to keep pretending like I'm reading the menu when I feel his presence behind me.

"Find something you like?" he whispers near my ear.

I straighten and try not to feel his heat on my back. I

want to lean into it instead of trying to break free of the feeling of his warmth.

"Yes," I manage to get out.

Fisher puts his hand on the same menu I'm holding up.

"Let me know when you're ready. I found what I'm looking to eat."

A tiny moan slips out.

Both Fisher and I pause exactly as we are.

Suddenly, he lets go and walks away. I hear him clear his throat before he heads to the landline.

"I'll take the Caesar salad and a side of fries."

"Interesting combination," he says with a light laugh.

"It's a girl thing," I try to tease.

Finally, I look over to where he is. The tension is still here, but it's lighter. I don't feel like a thin line is about to snap any longer.

I give him a small smile.

Fisher's expression breaks out into a wide smile, one that I've never seen before. It's unnerving. Maybe I should try to see if he could ever look at me as anything other than his assistant and Knox's ex-girlfriend.

"Got it. I'll order. We can always call again instead of ordering a lot now. Why don't you pour us a couple of drinks."

"Sounds like a plan."

Anything to allow some time to collect my thoughts.

I pull out a wine bottle and pour it into a decanter, carrying it over to the coffee table. Looking up, I see the television is still on, thankfully. Nothing new to report other than the snowstorm is here.

Walking back into the kitchen, I quickly pull out two wine glasses from the cabinet and bring them to the living room.

After pouring two glasses, I nestle into the couch and watch the fire glow.

"Alright, surprisingly, it'll be here in less than an hour," he says as he sits down.

"Maybe we should have ordered more to be safe."

"We'll figure it out as we go," he answers.

"I wish I could remain as calm as you with everything happening," I complain.

Fisher smiles as he grabs his wine glass.

"You're perfect the way you are. No one wants to be me."

He takes a sip of his wine, and I follow suit. Then I frown as I take in what he just said.

"That's not true."

Fisher lets out a sigh and then turns to me.

"My life has been all about work. It's why I'm able to remain calm in any situation. This is my life. Don't let work be all yours."

I nod in understanding.

This is a good chance to ask him something I've always been curious about.

"What about girlfriends? I never see you bring anyone to the functions we have to attend."

Fisher eyes me carefully. I really hope I didn't just cross a line.

"Sorry. You don't have to tell me. I'm not sure why I asked," I stammer.

"No, it's fine. I simply don't have time to date. And let's be honest here, where are all the men you're bringing to these functions?"

I can't help but smile—he got me there. I take another sip of my wine.

"Fair enough, sir," I taunt.

"Ellie."

"I know; I just enjoy seeing you groan whenever I call you that."

"I had a feeling it was something like that." He smirks.

"Have to keep you on your toes, you know."

"You always do."

I rest my head on my hand that's leaning against the back of the couch, looking out the windows behind him. The snow really is picturesque. If this were any other scenario, it would be a perfect night in with a lover.

Just two people making the most of being trapped in a gorgeous cabin while it snows the week before Christmas. If only that were the case.

Fisher mimics my positioning with a stoic expression.

"Why don't you have time to date? You're a catch—any woman with eyes would think so. I'm sure you could find someone who also works hard and would be understanding," I offer.

What am I doing? I'm practically shipping him off to someone else. This is not what I intended.

Fisher's jaw twitches.

"Have anyone in mind?"

My eyes widen momentarily.

"I'm just saying, I'm sure there are women out there like that."

"There are."

"See? You could find one."

"The problem is, I'm not interested in just anyone."

Now, my interest is piqued. What is Fisher's type? Is it the type of woman that I just described? It coincidentally sounded an awful lot like me.

"Who are you interested in?"

Fisher's eyes darken as he just stares, making it feel like his eyes are penetrating into my entire being.

"Another time," he finally says.

The doorbell rings loudly, and Fisher gets up to let the hotel employee in with the room service.

Something is happening between us. I know I'm not going crazy. These feelings and longing stares have to be real.

"Right over there, thank you," Fisher says to the employee.

"Of course," a man answers.

I look over to see Fisher watching the man put out the meals as requested. I can't help but think about Fisher and other women. The thought makes my stomach churn.

"Is there anything else?" the man asks.

"That's all, thank you."

Fisher hands him a one-hundred-dollar bill.

"Thank you very much, sir."

The man leaves the cabin as I walk over to the dining room, and Fisher pulls out my chair.

"Thank you," I whisper as I take my seat while he rounds the table on the other side.

"What did you get?" I ask as I look over to his meal.

"Grilled chicken and steamed broccoli."

I roll my eyes playfully.

"That's why you need to follow my lead. The fries are the treat."

"Next time," he says with a grin.

We eat in a comfortable silence.

"I HOPE the lights don't go out," I say.

Fisher and I are sprawled out on the ground in front of the fire. The heat in the cabin is still on, but the storm has picked up as the hours have passed by.

"The resort will have generators; they're prepared for these situations."

"I hope so."

"Don't worry. We'll be okay."

"I know."

The lights continue to flicker as the winds howl in the distance. Naturally, I pull the buffalo plaid blanket tighter around my shoulders.

"Cold?"

"I'll be fine."

I reach around to the coffee table I'm leaning against and take a sip of my wine. Fisher reaches for his glass at the same time.

As we both gulp down what remains, I don't want this night to end. Not even with how odd it's been between us since coming here. There's been something comforting with having him next to me as the snowstorm continues.

I look up at the weather channel on the television and see it's after eleven at night now. I can't delay this any longer; I have to finally head into my room and get some sleep.

"Well..." I start as I put my now-empty glass back on the table.

"Since we can't exactly do much work tomorrow, interested in opening another bottle?" he interjects.

I smile as his gaze is upon me.

"Isn't it a bit late?"

"Not here. I think we're about done with the rules here, aren't we?"

My throat tightens as I try to gulp.

"What do you say? Have another drink with me?"

"Yes." I beam.

Fisher's legs are sprawled next to me, crossed over one another.

"Come on," he says as he begins to stand, stretching out his hand for me to take. This man has no idea what he's doing to me.

I love the way his glasses match his entire look, something he had to have done unintentionally and not to tease me.

I take his outstretched hand and instantly feel a pulse of electricity coursing through my body as our connection lingers together. Fisher's eyes travel down to where we still are holding onto one another; neither one of us wants to break the connection first.

Reluctantly, I pull my hand away from his and bend down to pick up the wine glasses.

"After you," I say.

He clears his throat.

"Right."

I follow his lead into the kitchen.

"Here," I offer as I slide our wine glasses over to him.

"I hope another red works?" he asks with a cock of his eyebrow.

"Of course." I try to feign that everything is perfectly normal.

That my heart isn't beating wildly out of my chest. That my eyes aren't glued to his frame and the ropes of muscles spilling out from every pore of his being.

"It is what the lodge gave us, after all."

Russ had more wine sent over as an apology gift, and we weren't about to say no.

Fisher slides a glass over. With the kitchen island as the barrier, I reach for it as if I'm not dying in his presence.

"Thank you," I say.

"We haven't had the chance to really touch base in a while. It's all Rain Peak day and night," he says with a light laugh.

"That is our lives." I smile.

He comes around the corner of the island to where I stand.

"Is that what you want to *be* your life?"

His expression is serious as he asks it, and I'm torn between saying yes and no. I do want success but also a life outside of work. I don't want children—I know that—but I do want love, adventure, and companionship.

"No, I mean... yes?"

I take another heavy drink of my wine as I walk back toward the living room.

"It's okay if a young woman like yourself does. It's perfectly natural," Fisher says as he follows behind.

I sit back down next to the fire with my legs curled up.

"Is it perfectly natural if I don't?"

Fisher sits down in front of me while resting his back on one side of the sofa. He stretches his legs out over one another, and the length of them goes along my side. I watch as he settles in with his wine still in his hand.

"Of course it is. Whatever path you want to take is yours. Don't let anyone tell you differently."

I breathe a sigh of relief.

I don't know how I would have felt if Fisher believed a woman couldn't have the same career path and life he's taken. Any path a woman takes should be her choice, and none of them are wrong—whether it's a career woman who stays single, a stay-at-home mom, or a working mom—as long as it's what she wants.

And me? I want a partner and a career, just no children.

Fisher studies me carefully. Being held under his gaze and talking about my future is jarring. It's almost as if he knows about my job offer.

"I want a career, yes. But I also want a partner. Someone who I can go through life with."

"What about children?"

He holds his palm out before I can speak.

"That was inappropriate of me to ask."

"It's fine. I don't want any of my own. I hope to be an aunt one day, the best aunt out there."

"The one who sneaks candy and cookies to the kids?" he says with a smile.

"Exactly." I grin.

"Whatever path you take, you're going to knock it out of the park."

"Well, thank you for the vote of confidence," I say through a laugh.

I hadn't realized it, but our bodies must have been inching closer to one another. Fisher's face is mere inches away from mine, and his formerly relaxed demeanor has changed. I watch as his tense jaw twitches. All I feel is a deep yearning.

Harper is right.

I'm in love with the man in front of me, and it's a major problem.

EIGHT

Fisher

LISTENING to Ellie talk about her future was an interesting experience. I'd always assumed that she would want to have children.

Maybe this is an archaic way of thinking, but I assumed twenty-something-year-olds wish for the cliché American dream that they are told about early on in life—the whole white picket fence, two kids mentality. To be an everyday family, even if they also have career aspirations.

I never once thought that Ellie and I could be on the same page regarding this aspect of life.

From my perspective, I'm too old to start over and have more kids. It's not something I want at this stage—my time has passed. I know people do it all the time, but it's just not what I see for myself when I look ahead ten years.

I never dreamed that the one person I have a true connection with would be happy with a life without children of her own. The more layers I peel back of Ellie, the more I want her for my own. She's intelligent, capable, witty, and determined, and she would rather be child-free.

Now I have to sit here and stare at this beauty, knowing that the life she wants is one I could provide. If only our situation were different, I could be who she wanted. The truth of it is that we have too many obstacles in our way, the first being Ellie has no idea how I feel.

That's the way life goes. Something I truly want for my own is just out of reach. I'll never be able to expect more, and I know this. This is why I'm going to soak in all of the time I can with Ellie this week while we're stuck together.

"What are you thinking about over there?" Ellie's sweet voice fills the air.

"Just time."

Ellie cocks one of her eyebrows up.

"Time?"

"It's so fleeting."

She takes a sip of her wine.

"I suppose it is."

The words are so low I feel like they weren't meant for me to hear.

"That's one life lesson I've been grappling with as of late."

Ellie perks up.

"In what way?"

The blanket covering Ellie's body slips down, and I can't help but watch it pool to her lower legs. I glance over to the fire to try and calm the intrusive thoughts that are starting to arise.

"I've been at this game for some time. I climbed the ladder, as they say. I accomplished my goals. Now I'm sitting here thinking about all of the time I've spent dedicated to Rain Peak and growing the business instead of building a life."

That was too much to share.

"It's nothing," I add as I take a sip of my wine.

I can feel Ellie's thoughtful gaze. I need to change the topic—I'm not usually this vulnerable.

"How about we," I begin.

"Fisher..."

"Think nothing of what I said."

"Don't do that."

"Do what?"

"Shut me out. I think we're getting beyond that, aren't we?"

Ellie is looking at me with hope swirling in her eyes as she tosses my words from the beginning of the trip back at me.

"I suppose we are."

A hint of a smile appears at the corners of her mouth just as a loud crash outside distracts us both.

"What was that?" Ellie asks, panicked.

I walk over to the window to try and figure out what it was. Unfortunately, it's dark, and I can't see much outside of the heavy layers of snow. It's eerie. The wind is howling as if the end of this storm is just starting to brew.

"How did it get this bad?" she murmurs.

I turn slightly to face a bundled-up Ellie standing at my side.

"It'll pass soon. It has to."

She hums in response, and I turn back around to look out into the blackness.

"I think I'm going to attempt to get some sleep," Ellie says through a yawn.

"I'll walk you to your room."

She gives me a shy smile and starts walking toward the bedroom, and I trail not far behind.

Ellie looks up at me through her long black eyelashes—her brown eyes have specks of honey peering through. My favorite time to stare into them.

"Well," she starts.

She rocks on her heels, waiting for me to say something. To be honest, I really didn't have much of a plan when I said I would walk her here. I just wanted more time. I'll never get enough time with this woman.

"If anything happens in the middle of the night, please come get me," I say.

She rolls her eyes playfully.

"I'll be fine."

"Any case, you know I'm here for you. You're special to me, and I wouldn't want you to be frightened in the storm."

That gets her attention, and her face whips back up to mine.

"I'm your friend. I always am, but here, it's different circumstances."

She lets out a deep breath.

"Don't worry, I'll come get you if anything goes bump in the night."

"Good."

I watch as her breath hitches and her lips part. Ellie's eyes focus on my mouth. It's almost as if we are both desperate for the other. Like with that admission, we can test being more than boss and assistant.

My head starts to dip low as Ellie's head tilts upward.

The heat between us is palpable. All of the tension that has been playing out for years is about to snap.

I jerk back.

I can't do this. This isn't the way I want to go about it with Ellie.

I pull away completely and take a few purposeful steps backward. As I do, it's almost as if she is coming out of the same spell I had just fallen under.

"Good night," she squeaks.

Ellie rushes to open her door and shuts it.

"Fuck," I mutter.

I CAN HEAR the snow coming down harshly outside.

All night, I've been tossing and turning in bed. I'm not sure if it's because of the storm or what transpired earlier tonight.

I push the bedroom sheets off, revealing my boxer briefs. I usually sleep naked but decided against that once I found out Ellie would be staying in the same cabin.

It feels more appropriate than being completely nude.

I glance over at the hotel room alarm clock to see it's 2:22 a.m., and I blow out a heavy sigh. This is going to be a long night. Between the winds and thinking about Ellie, there's no way I'll be able to get any sleep.

I pull the sheet back up over my lower body and fluff my pillow, forcing myself to try and get some sleep. I just need to get through the next couple of hours until I can scrounge up some espresso, or hell, I'll take a normal coffee at this rate.

A booming sound echoes in the distance, making me jolt up instantly. Across the cabin, I hear a loud shriek.

"Ellie?"

I jump out of bed and dart to the other side of the cabin

where she's sleeping. Opening her bedroom door, I frantically search the space to ensure she's okay.

"Fisher?" Ellie yelps.

I spot her sitting upright in her bed with the covers around her neck.

"Are you okay? I heard you scream."

I get closer to her and sit on the edge of the bed.

"Yes, I'm good, I..."

"What's wrong?"

I search her eyes to make sure she's okay.

Ellie drops the blanket, and that's when I see her mouth open, and her eyes light up. I look down to see I'm still in only my boxer briefs.

"I'm sorry. I wasn't thinking."

Ellie's eyes roam my body, from my arms to my torso and down to my thighs. I'm covered in more tattoos than anyone would realize.

"No, no, it's okay. Thank you for coming in here. I'm sorry I worried you."

I slowly peel myself away from her bed. I don't want to make this situation any more uncomfortable than it already is.

Walking backward slowly, I'm at a loss for words.

"Wait," she whispers.

I stop right as I'm about to dart out of the room.

"I'm sorry."

"I'm not."

My chest puffs in and out repeatedly as my breath becomes ragged.

Ellie licks her bottom lip slowly.

I need to get a handle on this situation. Ellie is only starting to feel lustful toward me because we're trapped in this cabin. I can't take advantage of the situation, no matter how much I want to.

Whatever feelings are stirring up in Ellie can't possibly be real.

"Good night."

"Fisher…"

"I'm glad you're okay. Get some sleep."

I head out the door before she can get another chance to say anything.

I'm walking faster than I have—outside of the gym—in ages to get back to my side of the cabin.

PACING AROUND MY ROOM, I try to get a handle on what happened.

It was instinctual to check on Ellie after hearing her scream. I had an undeniable need to make sure she was okay. Normally, at work, it's easier to control. But here? Everything has changed.

"Fuck."

I head to my dresser and pull out a T-shirt and a pair of pajama pants. Quickly changing, I settle back onto my bed to catch my breath.

My alarm clock is flashing that it's a little after two thirty in the morning. What better time to start my day? I'll regret it tomorrow, but I've gotten less sleep before and have managed. Hopefully, Ellie has fallen back asleep and won't hear me.

I head to the kitchen to make some coffee. Thankfully, it's not too close to Ellie's room since I'm not sure if I can face her again so soon.

I hang my head back and place my hands on my hips as

I take a steading pause on my walk. There isn't an *us*. Any tension or looks or fucking hell, whatever it may be, is because of the circumstances.

This woman is going to torture me slowly with each day we are trapped together—a form of torture I'll take willingly. There are only so many days left with us here. By the end of this trip, I have to tell her about the promotion, and shortly after that, she'll be working for Doug.

Coffee. Focus on the goddamn coffee and not the brunette beauty in the other room.

Finally, in the kitchen, I get to work making a basic pot of coffee. Finding anything related to an espresso is going to make too much noise.

"Fisher?" I hear being whispered.

Looking across the kitchen, I see Ellie inflicting a new form of torture on me. She's in a deep-red silky nightgown. I wouldn't expect anything less than this, but it's too much to take in.

I clear my throat and focus back on the coffee brewing.

"Did I wake you?" I ask.

"No, no. I couldn't get back to sleep."

I nod as I keep focusing on the coffee.

She's making me feel like I'm having an out-of-body experience. I'm not a nervous kid, and fuck, the only thing that's stopping me from swooping her into my arms is the fact that I know I must be delusional about what's happening.

I clear my throat.

Small steps get closer as I brace my hands on the counter.

"Fisher," she whispers.

"Do you want a cup?"

"Sure..."

I get to work pouring two cups of coffee.

"Can you look at me?"

I pause, letting the sugar spoon fall to the counter. Slowly, I turn my head over to face Ellie finally. Pink-flushed cheeks, a warm smile, and understanding eyes greet me.

"Can we pretend?" she whispers.

"Pretend?"

I swallow thickly.

"Yes, pretend... just for today. I'm exhausted from trying this hard. I'm tired of pretending like you and I... that there isn't something happening. We don't have to talk about it. I'd like to just pretend."

I want to deny what she's admitting to, only I can't because Ellie just said what we both needed to hear. Something is going on between us here. I want it to be real, but maybe what she's offering will be enough.

"I can pretend for today."

A beaming smile stretches across her face.

"Can we watch a movie on the couch?"

"I'll meet you over there with the coffees."

"I THINK the sun is about to come up," Ellie whispers.

Truthfully, I assumed she had fallen asleep with her head resting on my shoulder ages ago. I've been sipping my third cup of coffee, debating moving her back to her bed.

Both of us felt more relaxed with this wall torn down. We haven't talked about what was said or what pretending really means.

"It is."

"Watch the sunrise with me? I think the snow has

stopped falling," she murmurs while nuzzling into my shoulder.

I move her head onto my chest and wrap an arm around her side. Ellie pulls the blanket further over her body.

"Are you sure?" I whisper into her hair.

"Yes, then maybe..." She starts to trail off and lightly laughs.

"Hmm?" I murmur.

"Maybe we then decide if we should nap or see if Russ is around."

"Don't remind me of the real world."

"Never thought I would see the day."

"What's that?"

Ellie perks up from resting on my chest and places one of her hands on me to push herself upright. She smiles brightly.

"There is something in this North Carolina air."

I'm confused by what she means.

"Let's go, Mr. Underwood."

She gets up and extends her hand out for me to get up too.

"I'm not that old." I sigh.

"Believe me, I know that," she murmurs.

I take her hand, and she leads me to the front door.

"Ready?" she asks.

"Let me check outside first."

I open the front door and confirm it's no longer snowing. This scenery is beautiful to behold.

"Wow," she whispers.

Ellie's hands grip my shoulders from behind. It feels more intimate than her even sleeping on me on the couch. This time, I lead her to the swinging front porch bench. Surprisingly, it's not covered in snow.

I sit down first and guide her next.

"Still have that blanket, I see," I tease.

"This blanket has been a lifesaver in this cold."

I hold back a groan. I can't get jealous of a fucking blanket.

I pull Ellie into my side, and she settles in naturally as if we do this every morning.

"Look, over there," she says.

I follow where she's pointing across the snow-covered ground and toward the trees.

"Well, look at that," I say in almost disbelief.

A family of deer is in the distance. It's peaceful to watch them graze from afar as the sun begins to rise over them.

"We're in a movie scene," she comments.

"A movie scene?"

"Definitely a movie scene."

"If only."

"Why do you say that?"

"Then this could be more than pretend."

She sucks in a deep breath.

I don't know why I let that omission slip, but I'm relieved I did. The past few hours have been transformative —pretending that whatever is happening could be something other than our reality.

This snowstorm has been an unexpected opportunity for me to get to know more about who she really is. With that, I finally know we're on the same page. Only I'm not sure what to do about it.

"I HAVE SOME NEWS," Russ begins.

It's early in the morning, but Ellie insisted she needed to get a handle on the situation after the sun rose.

"The snow has subsided," Ellie interrupts.

"That's correct, but unfortunately, snow is still expected to continue throughout the next two days. And as you know, we're on a mountain."

"I don't see what you're getting at here."

She taps her red-painted nails on his desk. Right now, I'm grateful that poor Russ has a barrier between the two of them.

Watching Ellie in her element is how my attraction started. Seeing her being all business and no games is a turn-on. She wants to solve the problem at hand as soon as possible. She's the definition of type A.

Being trapped with her here has given me an opportunity to learn more about this woman, and I like every facet of her I'm getting to see.

Russ straightens his tie, no doubt to give himself time to restructure his plan.

"We're trapped, Ms. Robertson. Simply trapped. Supplies are what they are. There is no way up or down this mountain for days to come. The snow will continue to make things worse for the next two days even though it will be nowhere near as hard as it was last night."

Ellie stiffens.

"Trapped?" she asks.

"Trapped."

"And what do you suggest we do?"

"Make the most of it," Russ offers nonchalantly.

Ellie looks over at me, and I cock an eyebrow. This is her game, not mine. I'm enjoying watching her like this far too much to intervene.

She focuses back on Russ.

"This isn't over," she declares.

"Of course, Ms. Robertson. I'll send room service to you with additional supplies."

"Thank you," she answers curtly.

Ellie confidently turns on her heels and starts back down the lodge walkway. I follow behind, something that's becoming all too common.

NINE

Ellie

WHEN RUSS TOLD us we'd be trapped for the next few days, I was stunned, to say the least. I knew the storm had been bad, but I thought the roads could be getting cleared sometime today.

It's not that it's so terrible of a concept, but what really worries me is being with Fisher for days on end. I already asked him if we could just stop pretending like there isn't something between us. All this time, I thought I was delusional, but I know I'm not now.

Did I think that there was a possibility of Fisher being attracted to me? No, I really didn't believe that these feelings could be a two-way street until yesterday.

When I realized he was looking at me in a new way, it made my heart flutter. It's taken everything in me to not just try to admit my feelings once and for all.

I'm conflicted with officially confessing how I feel and

throwing the rule book out the window versus hiding in my room the rest of the trip.

I know Harper told me to finally talk to him about how I feel, but I just can't come to terms with doing that yet. I was brave when I asked him to pretend with me.

A small test and win, which is not typically something I do.

I'm not the type of person to break the rules or put myself out there in that way. And what if I've been wrong? What if Fisher really doesn't feel the same way about me as I do about him? Then, my job would be completely awkward, and I'd definitely have to take the job in Charleston.

On the other hand, then I'd have my answer.

That's it, isn't it? If I get the nerve to make a move and simply tell Fisher how I feel, then I'll know what I should do.

I groan.

Harper is right. If he denies me, then going across the country is the only reasonable option for how to handle the situation.

I don't care how confident I am in my day-to-day work. If Fisher tells me we can't try to be together, there is no way I could handle seeing him every day.

"Looks like we've lost the Wi-Fi signal," Fisher says.

We've been using the kitchen island as a type of divider since we got back to the cabin.

"Now? The storm has mostly passed," I ask, perplexed.

Fisher shrugs as he continues to work on getting us connected.

I can't help but bite my lower lip as I drink him in— glasses on, sleeves rolled up, and tattoos on display. I won't survive being trapped with this man for days and not telling him how I feel. If there's a chance something could happen, then I need to try.

I watch as he swallows thickly, causing his Adam's apple to bob in his throat.

"What should we do?" I croak.

I look up to find his gaze examining me.

My mouth naturally parts as I fall deeper into this spell I've been under. I can't help but watch as he runs his thumb across his lower lip.

He clears his throat, and my eyes snap to his.

"I'm sure Russ and the team are aware and working on a solution. Why don't we forget about work for the day?"

"You're suggesting we forget about work?" I ask in disbelief.

"Yes. It can't be all about work and no play."

"This is strange," I say with a smirk.

He grins back.

"Indeed. What do you say?"

"Let me go change. I'll be out in five minutes."

"I'll do the same."

I walk around the kitchen island and beeline it for my room. I can't help feeling giddy at this opportunity as I shut the door.

What should I wear in the snow while having... free time? Casual time? Whatever this is with Fisher. The more I get of his personal time, the more I know how right my feelings are for the man.

I pick out a fluffy black sweater and matching black jeans and accessories. All black is one of my go-to looks.

Changing quickly, I examine myself in the mirror. I feel confident for the day ahead.

I add on a jacket just to be safe. Going outside with Fisher seems like it could be a fun plan.

This is it—my opportunity to tell Fisher how I feel.

"It's now or never, Ellie. You've got this."

I straighten my shoulders back and stand tall as I stroll out of my bedroom, my black military-style boots giving me an extra boost of confidence.

I stop in my tracks.

Fisher is waiting by the front door in a deep-green cashmere sweater and straight dark-washed denim jeans.

He doesn't know I'm out of the room yet. I watch as he coolly slips his arms into his jacket. I like that we both had the idea of going outside while it's barely snowing.

Fisher turns around, and a smile grows on his face.

"Great minds think alike," I say while showcasing my black puffer jacket.

"Indeed," he answers.

"Have anywhere in mind?"

"I saw a pond around the side of the house. I'm frankly surprised the hotel doesn't have it fenced off. Want to go take a look?"

He cocks one eyebrow, waiting to see if I will take him up on this risky offer.

"Go see a magical pond as the snow falls? I can't say no to that." I beam.

"I thought you might like the idea."

I walk up beside him and feel myself grinning ear to ear.

"Lead the way," I say while gesturing to the front door.

He laughs, "Let's go," and puts on a scarf before heading outside.

OUTSIDE, the cold air whips against my face. I can feel the sun beating on my skin as snowflakes land everywhere.

I shiver loudly.

"Cold?" Fisher asks, sounding concerned.

"I'll be fine."

"Are you sure? We can get you more layers or even just stay in."

"No, no, really, I'm good. It caught me off guard, that's all."

"The snowstorm we're trapped in caught you off guard?"

Is Fisher teasing me?

I feign annoyance as I bring my hand to my chest.

"Mr. Underwood, I don't think that's appropriate behavior."

He lets out a deep belly laugh, one I've never heard before, and extends his hand out to mine.

"Let's get going, shall we?"

I look down at the extended hand.

"Lead the way."

I place my hand in his, and we begin the walk to the pond, something I wouldn't have ever imagined I would be doing with Fisher. Maybe it's not North Carolina; maybe it's the magic of the holiday season. I can be cheesy and believe that, given everything that's happened.

Both of our boots sink into the snow that has grown overnight. Mine keep sinking in the more we walk. There's no way we can go much farther.

"It's right over here," Fisher says.

He looks down at me, and I bob my head up and down, and he squeezes my hand.

We may have gloves between us, but it's an intimate gesture, nonetheless.

We walk the remaining distance until I come to an immediate halt.

"Wow," I breathe out.

I can see my breath in the air swirling around the falling snow.

"I knew you'd like this," Fisher whispers, giving my hand another tight squeeze.

Looking out before me is the most breathtaking view I've seen in ages—a glistening pond with a light sheer of ice covering the top. The sun is beating down on it and casting a glimmering shimmer of light.

With the snow piled up all around it, it's almost as if we are the only ones who will get to see it like this. Any day now, it'll start to freeze over fully.

"Thank you."

"Look over there," Fisher says as he points across the pond.

"Where?" I ask as I look around.

"Oh, my goodness, it's them," I say in disbelief, bringing my free hand to my chest.

I squeal that I've spotted the family of deer.

"Looks like we're in their home," Fisher says with a light laugh.

"I've decided it's not a movie scene here."

"What is it then?"

"It's a fairy tale."

"A fairy tale?"

"No, you're right; that doesn't give the magic as much weight as it deserves," I say matter-of-factly.

He laughs heartily.

"What have you decided it is then?"

"It's a wonderland."

I look up at Fisher and see something new. Something different in his expression. Something more resolved.

I smile brightly up at him as the sun hits my face.

"That's perfect."

"Wonderland."

As we continue to stare at one another, I know this is my moment.

"Ellie..."

Lines crinkle around his eyes, and a lopsided grin appears.

"Am I imagining this?" I ask.

I lift our connected hands up to my chest.

"Is your heart beating as fast as mine?" I ask.

Fisher's chest rises and falls.

"You do this to me," I whisper.

"Ellie."

He moves our connected hands over to his chest.

"Do you feel this?"

"I do."

"You do the same to me."

I gasp. "I do?"

"You have for a long time. I just never imagined you would feel this way about me."

He moves our hands to the center in between us. As I look up at him, I know this is the moment everything has changed.

I lift up on my tiptoes as Fisher leans down. Our foreheads touch as the sun shines through us, and the warmth from our connection speaks volumes.

"I've wanted you for a long time too."

He pulls back slightly, so I do the same, giving him a hint of a warm smile.

Fisher leans forward and places a gentle, chaste kiss to my lips. I feel as if my entire body is lit up with fireworks, and the warmth I felt earlier spreads throughout my whole being. Then, slowly, he pulls away.

The family of deer darts off into the woods, capturing both of our attention.

I look away from the deer back to Fisher and find his eyes at the same time he finds mine.

"Let's get inside," he says.

THE AIR SURROUNDING us feels different, almost as if it's warm and settling instead of complicated and uneasy. That finally admitting our feelings for one another has broken the tension, and now we can relax in each other's presence.

"Ellie," Fisher starts as we linger in the entryway of the cabin.

He removes his coat, waiting for me to answer, and I mimic his actions.

"Fisher?"

"I meant it."

He takes my coat and hangs both up on the coat rack.

I step forward and take his hands in mine.

"I did too."

"We have a lot to discuss. But in the simplest terms, I want you."

I suck in a deep breath.

"I'm yours tonight."

He arches an eyebrow and gives me a smug smile that I want to devour with my mouth.

"Not the night. Give yourself to me while we're here, at least. Then we can talk about what this is outside of North Carolina."

I bite my bottom lip and nod my head bashfully.

"Okay," I whisper.

Fisher drops one of his hands and uses the other to lead us to the living room. He settles me onto the couch before leaving for the kitchen.

"Drink?" he asks.

"Yes, please."

I get off the sofa to turn on the fireplace, the sound of snow falling harder catching my attention. I think it'll continue to do this today, but hopefully, it will stop for good soon.

"Do you want to call and order us food? I'm good with anything," I shout.

"Of course," he answers.

I settle back onto the couch and decide to keep the television off. If I have this week with Fisher, I want to make the most of it. I don't know what any of this means or how far we can go, but I do know that I like that he wants me.

Yes, I want to lick every inch of his body, but tonight is for getting to know the man behind the myth. The cold and stoic man who lets down his guard for those he trusts and loves. I realize now he's always looked at me like that.

He has the business on his shoulders and no one to share it with. No one to support him. Maybe that could be me.

That kiss out there was different. He could have taken me right there on the snow, and I wouldn't have complained for a second about it. But he didn't. Instead, he placed a gentle kiss on my lips and gave my whole body a renewed sense of confidence.

"Ordered a slew of items to keep us covered for a while," Fisher says as he brings two wine glasses to the living room.

He settles down on the couch and hands me my wine glass.

"Thank you," I murmur before taking a sip.

I pull the wine glass away and set it on my lap.

"What now?" I can't help but ask.

Fisher laughs and then takes a sip of his own wine.

"Tell me more about you. I feel like I have a lot to learn."

I scoff.

"You know me."

"I do?"

"Okay, let's see," I say, taking a meaningful sip of my wine.

I've got it.

"What do I order from Rocco's Deli?"

"Cobb salad, no tomatoes or bacon, balsamic dressing on the side only. Why?"

Fisher's eyebrows furrow together.

I settle farther into the sofa with my legs tucked under me.

"When you and I are in a meeting, and Tony is going on and on about projections, instead of answering any questions you are actually asking him about, what do I do?"

His eyebrows tighten together once more.

"You give him a sports analogy, which I always wonder how he hasn't caught on after all these years," he says with a light laugh.

"When I was stuck in Charleston because of that hurricane, why did you send me a private plane?"

"I knew you'd be worried about your work, not that you needed to be. I wanted to make sure you were safe and not stressed."

I bite my lower lip, debating going even deeper.

"And when my mom died last year, what did you do?"

Fisher's expression softens, and he brings his hand to one of my knees.

"What did you do?" I repeat softly.

"We took the afternoon off and went whale watching on my boat."

"And why did you think of taking me whale watching?"

"Because it makes you happy."

"And did you do what everyone else does and give me a pity party?"

"No."

His thumb starts strumming along the length of my knee toward my upper thigh. It's the most comforting touch I've ever experienced.

As I look at Fisher staring so deeply back at me, how could I ever think that this man doesn't have feelings for me in return?

I place my hand over his hand on my leg.

"Why was that?" I finally ask.

"Because you're the strongest person I know. You wouldn't want that."

"Now, I'll say it one more time. You know me. You know me better than anyone ever has or will."

The tension is thick.

This isn't the North Carolina air or the magic of being in wonderland—this is raw and beautiful. This is us.

"Do you mean that?"

"I do."

A few moments pass us by.

"Why me? I'm all wrong for you."

"Because you see me."

TEN

Fisher

BECAUSE YOU SEE ME.

I never thought four words would penetrate my heart. The idea that this beautiful, wildly intelligent woman would want me is inconceivable. I'm speechless for the first time.

I graze my thumb against her upper thigh and watch how her breath hitches. Then I let my palm spread over her thigh and squeeze hard.

It elicits a small moan from her lips. The ones that are pouty and taut, begging for me to show her who I really am.

I continue to let my thumb move against her covered thigh.

"I want you, Ellie."

Looking at her angelic face with rosy cheeks and mouth parted, I patiently wait for a response.

She says I see her, and now I want her to see me. All of me.

"I want you too."

That's all the permission I need.

I had planned to go slowly… to get to know her better. There's time for that later on. Now, I want to take this woman as mine.

Rising from the couch, I stare down at Ellie and watch as her chest rises and falls rapidly. The way her chest presses against the sweater makes my cock twitch.

Seeing Ellie naked has always seemed like a far-off fantasy—one that, in recent months, I've found myself obsessing over.

I'll admit that I obsess over everything that has to do with her. An obsession that may turn into my new reality.

"I know we're complicated, but I want you more than anything right now," I say.

Her breath hitches as she stands and wraps her arms around my neck.

"Let's stay in our bubble while we can," she whispers against my mouth.

Ellie places a gentle kiss to my lips and lingers there. It feels natural to wrap my arms around her waist and pull her body closer to mine.

I take her lower lip and nibble at it, and her body becomes needy as she tries to grind against me in our embrace.

Looking down, I see plaid throw blankets in front of the roaring fireplace.

Ellie notices where my gaze lands and licks her lips.

"Yes," she whispers.

"Maybe we should go into my room," I murmur.

"No. I want you right here, right now."

I lead Ellie around the coffee table with her hand in mine. She breaks away first.

All I can do is stare as she immediately starts to take off her sweater, followed by her tank top.

I groan into my fist as I see her standing before me in a thin lacy black bra with the sweetest pebbled pink nipples poking through the lace.

She pulls off one boot and then the other. As she's about to shimmy out of her jeans, she stops midway through. I can see part of her ass sticking out.

"You do like watching me," she teases as she continues to pull off her jeans.

"Anyone who wouldn't is a fucking fool."

"Good thing I don't want just anyone."

She kicks her jeans to the side.

"Care to join me?"

I unbuckle my belt and shove my pants to the floor first, watching as Ellie stares at me, mesmerized. Pulling off my shirt, I throw it onto the couch.

Ellie licks her lips as her eyes dance wildly all over my body.

"Come here," I rasp.

She shakily steps forward.

"Don't go getting scared now, princess. Not when I finally have you in my arms."

She smirks.

"Princess? Really?"

"If you were really mine, that's how you would be treated day in and day out."

I start caressing the outside of her arms, causing goose-bumps to rise.

"And what if I wanted the opposite?" she asks.

"Then I'd fuck you like you're my whore."

A moan escapes her lips.

"Which is it? How do you want me to take you for the first time?"

"I... I..." she stammers.

"Is this too much?"

She smiles up at me.

"No, no! I've never really had either, but..."

She straightens.

"Fisher?"

"Yes?"

"I'd like you to lead the first time."

I smile.

"Then lie down, princess. Let me worship your body, starting by feasting on the cunt I've been craving."

She gasps, then slowly lowers herself down until she's almost lying on the flannel blankets. I kneel and spread her legs open, keeping my hands on her knees so she can't close them.

"Lie down fully, princess."

"Okay," she hesitantly agrees.

"Do you not want me to lick this pretty pink pussy?"

"No, it's not that. I just..."

"You can trust me."

Her shoulders visibly relax.

"I know I can. It's just not something I've ever done before. Everyone else has always acted like it's not necessary."

My body tenses as I let her words seep in.

Mother fucking boys.

"Anyone who isn't begging to lick you day and night isn't worth your time. Now let me feast."

She lies back completely.

"Anything you don't enjoy, just tell me. Communication is key here."

"I will, I promise."

I spread her legs farther apart and pull down her panties, tossing them to the side. I finally get to see her glistening bare pussy ready for the taking.

She starts to squirm in my hold. I lean down and let the hint of my breath tease her pussy.

I lick between her folds and let her body naturally settle as I continue the motion. While I lick and suck, I watch as her body vibrates.

I strum against her clit, causing her to start grinding against my mouth.

Thank fuck she's enjoying it like she should have been all this time. I love that I'm the first one to deliver this type of pleasure.

As I continue to strum against her pussy, I apply more pressure.

"I think I'm about to..."

She pants heavily as she tightly grips the blankets, and I feel her thighs clenching around my head.

"Come for me, princess," I say before putting my head back between her thighs.

Ellie breaks apart on my tongue.

Sitting up, I look at the sweat starting to glisten and the pieces of hair sticking against her body. This beauty is going to be my undoing.

"Oh my god, that was unlike anything I've ever experienced," she pants.

I grin as she tries to find the words. Ellie notices and giggles through her hitched breath.

"Yes, Mr. Underwood, you eat pussy fantastically."

My grin widens and then falls as I realize we have a situation on our hands.

"I don't have a condom with me," I confess.

I wasn't exactly planning on having sex at this retreat. Ellie isn't anything I saw coming.

She nervously chews on her lower lip.

"I'm clean and on the pill," she whispers.

"What are you saying?"

My heart beats wildly.

"I hope that's not all you have in store for me tonight," she declares more confidently.

"Oh, Ellie, you better spread those legs wide. In that case, I plan on burying my cock inside of this pretty pink pussy every chance I can get while we're here."

She gives me a beaming smile and spreads her legs completely open.

"Ready when you are."

RESTING in front of the fireplace with Ellie relaxing on my chest makes me feel like a new man. I delivered another two orgasms, which I'm proud of, given it's been a long time since I've been with someone.

Ellie has now fully seeped into my being. We were already complicated, but now that she has fully given herself over to me, it makes our situation even more tricky to navigate. The urge to keep her as mine has only grown.

Maybe there is a way that Ellie could still work at Rain Peak, and we could be together. I don't care what others will think about the situation, but Ellie might. We could always keep it under wraps to start if that's what she wants.

Calling her my princess felt so natural. It was unlike me to have the urge to use a pet name.

"What are you thinking about?" she asks.

I thought she had fallen asleep, given her even breathing against my chest.

"I like having you on me."

"Is that so?"

"It is."

I stroke the hair that's along the length of her back.

"Is that all?" she finally asks.

"Nothing for us to think about in this moment."

She stills.

"I like being on your chest too."

We both understand that now is not the time to have this discussion, not when we can bask in this moment.

This perfect girl is within my reach to keep. I just need to think about how we can make this work in the real world.

The buzzing of a cell phone finally steals Ellie's attention.

"Don't worry about it," I say.

"It's yours. It could be something important. We haven't had service all day."

Ellie peels her body off of mine and sits upright, bringing a blanket with her to cover her chest.

"I think I've seen every inch of you." I smirk.

She tilts her head and gives me an intense stare, and I can't help but laugh.

Standing and stretching out, I feel every bit of my age after having sex for the past few hours. I may be in shape, but a marathon like that wiped me out.

I grab my cell phone off the table and see it's Letty.

"You're right. It's Letty. I have to call her back."

"She cares about you."

I sigh.

"I know. I didn't ask her to."

Ellie smiles knowingly.

"No one has to be told to care about you."

"I know." I smile back.

I disappear into the bedroom and quickly call Letty.

"Mr. Underwood! Oh, thank heavens, the team and I have been worried sick about you and Ms. Robertson."

"Everything is under control."

"Well, thank goodness for that."

"Is there an emergency, Letty?"

"No emergency, but Ms. Avery, Mr. Knox, and a Mr. Sinclair have all called."

"Mr. Sinclair called?"

"Yes, he wanted me to let you know that he still plans to arrive but only needs a moment of your time."

"Thank you."

"Of course. Is there anything you need from me or any messages to relay?"

"No, that's all. Thank you."

Sitting on the couch inside of my bedroom, I sigh. Knox. Avery. Two people who will want answers if Ellie and I are to continue this.

Grant, on the other hand, I do wonder why he's still planning on coming up here. Next time Ellie and I make our way to the front desk, I'll have to find out what the conversation was between Russ and his assistant. Grant didn't mention anything to me when I called him about the retreat.

Walking back out into the living room, I find Ellie on the couch with the same blanket draped around her legs. The news is on, and it sounds like the storm is continuing throughout the night.

"Doesn't sound like good news," I say.

"That depends on how you look at the situation," she offers.

I close the distance between us.

"Coffee?"

Ellie looks over and up at me.

"Mr. Underwood, are you trying to keep me awake to seduce me?"

I chuckle.

"Is that a possibility?"

She grins.

"Why don't you test the waters, and we'll find out?"

"I like you like this," I remark.

"Like what?"

"Content."

The smile widens.

"I am, aren't I?"

"You are."

"That's because I'm waiting on that coffee."

"How the roles are reversed here."

"That they are."

ELEVEN

Ellie

WHEN FISHER SAID his cock was going to be buried inside of me for the next couple of days, he meant it. We've successfully had sex on every single surface inside of the cabin. When I say everywhere, I mean it.

On the kitchen counter, kitchen floor, dining room table, dining room floor, in front of the fireplace, on the coffee table, couch, while I'm leaning over the couch—it's been everywhere.

It's like my wildest dreams are coming true this week. Outside of the fantastic sex we've been having, I've equally been enjoying the more mundane moments. Frankly, more than I should be letting myself, given we haven't had a conversation about what any of this is yet.

Fisher and I are out on the front porch, watching the family of deer in the distance. We've named them Mae, Joe, Frank, and Bobbie Sue to honor the fictional farm they live on.

It's silly.

It's pretend.

It's perfect.

The only issue we are facing is that we both know time is running out at the cabin. The snow is no longer falling and sticking on the ground. Whenever we take our walks to the pond, we see more and more green patches appearing on the mountains.

I nestle farther into Fisher's side with my signature blanket around me, and he gently caresses along the length of my back.

I close my eyes and drink in the moment. We haven't discussed what comes next, but I hope this doesn't end here. We can figure out all of the obstacles that we'll face back in Washington. I know we can together.

"We should probably talk to Russ this morning. Get another update," Fisher whispers.

"That's probably a good idea. I bet everyone at work thinks we're dead."

I feel Fisher's chest vibrate from his light laugh.

"Thankfully, Russ is passing along our messages."

"Thankfully," I lie.

It's not that I'm not happy work is going well without us being more actively involved because I am. It's actually a sign of the environment that Fisher has built. My issue with it is it's another topic that puts our reality at the forefront of my mind. I know it must be the same for Fisher.

"Do you need to freshen up, or are you okay going over there like this?" he asks.

If this were a few days ago, there is no way I would have been caught dead in a man's flannel shirt in front of anyone but the deer, but at this point, we've all weathered the snowstorm.

"I'm good like this. Want to go now?"

I sense a hesitation.

"I think it's for the best."

For the best.

We both get up from the porch swing and stretch out. There's no delaying the inevitable.

I put my boots on, followed by my coat and watch Fisher do the same.

As I walk down the steps, I hear him padding across the porch. That's my cue. It's time to talk to Russ and find out if there is news on when we'll be returning to reality.

"Ready?" he asks.

"Yes, let's get going."

Walking along the snowy path toward the main lodge is different this time. We aren't in the safety net of boss and assistant, nor are we stuck in a cabin as lovers.

Fisher opens the door for me, and we remain silent.

It's not uncommon for us to feel comfortable being in silence with one another; however, this time feels different. Maybe I'm all in my head again.

"Mr. Underwood and Ms. Robertson, good morning to you both," Russ greets us.

"Good morning," we say in unison.

Back to business mode.

"What's the status of the resort opening and mountain clearing?"

Russ's face pales.

"I am so sorry no one notified you last night, but the resort roads have been cleared. We also have a Mr. Sinclair who has left a message for you as well."

I look over to Fisher and see an apathetic expression.

"Russ, while we understand most of this was clearly out

of your control, the lack of communication has been disappointing," I begin.

"Where is Mr. Sinclair now?" Fisher cuts in.

Russ looks frantically between the both of us, unsure of which issue to solve first. He makes the right decision by addressing Fisher.

"He's in the lobby, sir," he stammers.

"Thank you."

Fisher peers down at me.

"I have to speak to Grant. I'm not sure what he needs to discuss."

"What do you mean?"

"There's no reason for him to have left California to come to North Carolina unless it's something urgent."

"He's your friend, isn't he?"

"He is. I'll meet you back at the cabin."

Russ clears his throat, and we both look over.

"Mr. Underwood, he's right there, enjoying the scenery."

Russ points around us to where a set of tables is. We follow the line of sight and see a man who has to be Grant Sinclair.

The only way to describe him is dashing—a fitted designer suit and short-trimmed, mostly black hair reading a newspaper. Grant stands out in the sea of people dressed for the mountains.

"See you back there."

"Right," I say with a smile.

Fisher walks away toward Grant.

It is interesting that he came all this way. I wonder what the reason is.

Turning my attention back to Russ, I put back on my professional mask.

"Mr. Underwood and I will be checking out tomorrow morning."

"Of course, Ms. Robertson. I'll have a variety of breakfast items sent to the cabin shortly."

Russ can tell I'm still unhappy.

"And I will personally follow up with the additional ways that we can rectify the miscommunication that has happened in addition to what has already been discussed."

"Thank you."

As I head back to the cabin, I process what I was just told. The roads have been opened. That means we could leave today, but one more day in our bubble sounds nice. I get one more night with Fisher before we have to go back to reality.

We haven't talked about what comes next. I took Fisher in the moment, but I still have a crucial decision I have to make. With that, I need to know what he wants. It's time for me to tell him what I want too.

I need to get my answers before the clock runs out.

"WHAT DO you mean you're unsure of what you should do?" Harper draws out.

"Well, I know I'm going to ask him about what happens next, but I don't want to force anything."

"Ellie..."

"What? I know we've had a nice time together here, but maybe that's all it is."

"Why are you doing this to yourself? And what are you considering a nice time?"

I pause.

"You've been sleeping together."

"Yes."

"Why didn't you tell me?"

"You know I don't like to overshare."

"It's not oversharing when I'm one of your best friends."

"I know." I sigh.

"Look, I get this is all new for you to open up like this, especially since the last person you dated was Knox."

"I don't want to talk about dating Knox and Fisher in the same conversation."

"Don't you think you need to? It's going to come up at some point."

"I understand that, but Knox and I broke up years ago. We weren't a right fit; I think he and I both knew that."

"Yes, but it was for his music."

"And like I said, that was years ago. Water under the bridge, and we have barely spoken since then."

"I'm just saying it's going to come up."

I wince as I plop onto my bed.

"I know it will. Honestly, though, Knox was all wrong for me. I just…"

"You can tell me anything."

"Is it weird to think that I dated Knox so that I could meet his dad? Fisher is everything I want in a partner."

"I don't think it's weird per se…"

"But?"

Harper laughs.

"If this situation with Fisher does last past tonight, maybe don't word it like that to Knox when you end up telling him you're dating his dad."

I can't help but laugh at the absurdity of it all.

"Good thinking."

The sound of the cabin's front door opening catches my attention.

"Fisher's back, I'm going to go."

"Good luck, babe."

"Ellie?" Fisher calls out.

"Be out in a few minutes!" I shout.

I look at myself in the mirror and groan. After breakfast, I really need to shower and put myself back together. I fix my hair quickly and head out to the living room.

"How did everything go with Grant?" I ask as I adjust my sweater sleeves.

Looking up, I stop in my tracks.

"Oh, hello, Mr. Sinclair," I say, surprised.

Grant Sinclair just smirks.

"Good morning, Ellie. Please call me Grant. Fisher here invited me to join you both for breakfast. I hope that's not an intrusion."

My eyebrows furrow together momentarily. I regroup to try and maintain a blank expression.

"No, of course not. Russ said breakfast will be delivered soon," I say with a smile.

Looking over at Fisher, I see it's all business. Good, that's how it should be.

The doorbell rings.

Fisher starts to walk to get it, and I stop him.

"I'll get that, and it should be set up shortly."

"Thank you," Fisher responds.

Grant starts speaking to Fisher about the resort as I walk away.

As the server sets out the food on the table, I feel Fisher's gaze coming from behind me. My skin prickles every time he does; it's a new sensation I'm beginning to crave.

"Everything is ready," the server says.

"Perfect, thank you."

He nods and disappears through the front door.

"We're all set," I say through a plastered-on smile.

"The resort is doing well under the conditions," Fisher comments.

I hum in agreement as we take a seat.

"Ellie, what's a promising young woman like you sticking around Fisher here for so long? Surely, it's not his winning personality?" Grant taunts.

I can't help but turn the plastered-on smile into a genuine one.

"It's the long hours, seven days a week," I retort.

"Oh, I like her," Grant says through laughter.

Glancing over at Fisher, I notice a hint of a smile playing on his lips.

"How did you manage to make it to the resort so quickly?" I ask.

"Helicopter."

"Of course," I reply.

"As soon as the snow stopped, we got the go-ahead. Possibly special permission, but I'm sure you understand how that goes."

"I do."

We all start to eat breakfast.

I selected the eggs and avocado toast from the delivered options as it's my go-to meal. Something tells me we'll be back to normal soon enough.

"Ellie is such a beautiful name."

"Thank you."

"Ellie," Grant repeats as if testing it against his lips.

Fisher grunts as he cuts into a steak.

Keeping eye contact with Grant, I see a teasing smirk. He definitely knows something is happening between us, and he's enjoying poking the bear.

"Do you plan to stay up here long?" I ask.

"Yes, I'm sure Russ and the team have your room available," Fisher chimes in.

"They did, but I have to head out to Florida tomorrow," Grant answers.

"Why Florida?" Fisher asks.

Grant gives a tilt of his head and grins.

"An old friend is picking up something I left behind the last time I visited."

"Oh," I reply.

That's so cryptic.

"My friend likes to get to places ahead of me. I always have a way of catching up."

"Right, of course," I say through a smile as I dig into my avocado toast.

"Fisher, will you see me out after this?" Grant asks.

He agrees and then takes a bite out of his meal.

As I watch the egg drips down the length of Fisher's steak, my mind can't help but wander to what it is we really do for Grant Sinclair. It's probably not something I want to know about.

COZIED UP ON THE COUCH, I hear the door open as Fisher returns. It's been hours since he left with Grant. When he asked Fisher to see him out, I wasn't expecting it to take this long. And why wasn't I invited if the conversation was about work?

I let out a loud sigh to get Fisher's attention.

"Ellie..."

"It's fine."

I huff loudly.

"Where were you both?" I ask.

Fisher's steps get closer.

"We had a walk around the property and then resumed our conversations in the lobby."

"That's nice."

"Is something wrong?"

I don't answer.

"If something is wrong, just say it. I don't have time for these games. It's not like you."

I get up from the couch and stand with my arms crossed over my chest.

"Maybe you bring this side out in me," I taunt.

Fisher stalks closer, and a mischievous grin spreads on his expression.

He finally closes the distance, and the heat exuding from his body is suffocating. I don't know how he manages to make me feel this way. It's as if my body has become tuned to answer him even when I don't want it to.

Fisher lightly traces my collarbone. My nipples instantly pebble as goosebumps spread like wildfire simply from his touch.

"Maybe I like bringing out all different sides of you," he murmurs.

He removes his hand from my skin and gathers a fistful of my hair. It's not too rough but enough to show off my neck. I can feel my panties starting to dampen.

"I don't think so," I scoff.

I push playfully at his chest, and he immediately lets go of my hair, and I take a few large steps back.

I glare at him as a lopsided grin appears on his expression.

He left me alone for hours.

Now he can deal with my attitude.

TWELVE

Fisher

"I SHOULD HAVE KNOWN."

She steps forward, places her hands on her hips, and shoots an eyebrow up.

"What's that?"

"That you'd want to act like a brat in the bedroom too."

Ellie can't help but grin.

I've caught onto what this woman needs. It's becoming natural to decipher the many facets of her personality—ones that I don't even think she's aware of until I call her out on them. I can handle each and every one of them that emerges.

"We aren't in a bedroom, *Mr. Underwood.*"

I can't help but let my grin widen.

"That can be fixed."

I stalk forward.

"I think I need to do something to fix this attitude for you."

Ellie steps forward and runs her hands up and down my arms before setting them on my waistband. She shrugs one of her shoulders up and starts undoing my belt buckle. I cover one of my hands with hers.

She pauses.

"Do you think this is how it works?" I taunt.

She opens her mouth and snaps it close.

"That's my good girl. Now, tell me this."

Ellie tilts her head to the side. I can tell it's taking all of her energy to not say something back.

"Do you want me to play with my bad girl?"

"Bad girl?" She whimpers.

"Do you trust me?"

Ellie tilts her head back and grips my shoulders. Her beautiful honey-colored eyes are lit up with desire.

"I trust you."

Her body naturally tries to move closer to mine with that confession.

I start to nip at her ear roughly as she grinds her pussy into my thigh. I lick down the column of her neck and start to trail small kisses back up again, leading to the waiting mouth I want to consume. Reaching her lips, my tongue demands entry, which she instantly grants. She's the sweetest thing I've ever tasted.

Pulling away, I place a few small kisses against her now-closed mouth. I trail them all the way to her neck once again. She automatically tilts her head to the side and squeezes her arms around my neck roughly.

I pull her hair roughly in one of my hands to give myself better access.

"Goddamn," I murmur into her ear.

"Fisher," she whimpers, "I need more from you."

I nip back down along the length of her neck toward her collarbone.

"Yes, more."

As I pull away slightly, I see Ellie panting heavily. She's the most gorgeous woman I've ever laid eyes on, and she's in my arms.

She opens her eyes to see why I've stopped.

"What are you doing?" she whines.

"Admiring your beauty," I admit.

"If you don't do something about this ache right now, I'm going into my room to take care of it myself."

"Is that so?"

Her mouth twitches.

"Yes."

I cock an eyebrow.

Ellie giggles while trying to remain serious in our stare-off.

I bend down and scoop her up into my arms. She flays around momentarily and begins to laugh wildly.

"Fisher," she shouts as she holds around my neck once again.

"I think it's time I teach you a lesson for this behavior."

Her pussy grinds against my hip.

"A lesson?" she asks innocently.

"For acting like a brat."

"I can do whatever I want," she sasses.

I laugh darkly at her words as I head into the bedroom.

"What happened to me sucking your cock?" She continues to taunt me.

"We'll get to that eventually."

Back in my bedroom, I toss Ellie onto the bed. She springs to her feet instantly, and that's when I know she really loves this game that we've started.

My eyes darken as I sidestep around where she waits. She moves in tandem.

I slowly sit down on the edge of the bed, causing her to take a step backward. As silence takes over, her body gets needier from the lack of touch.

"Fine," she relents.

"Fine?"

She heaves a heavy sigh.

"Maybe I have been acting like a brat," she says as she fiddles with the end of her sweater.

I wait for her to give me the go-ahead.

"I think you need to teach me a lesson."

I spread my legs apart and fold my arms against my chest. She waits for my next move.

"Snowflake. That's your word if anything we are doing makes you uncomfortable, understood?"

"What is this dom and sub play? I don't think so," she scoffs.

"Get undressed," I demand.

I expect her to argue, but she does as I request. And now that she's fully naked, I know what I'll ask next.

"Turn around. Hands on the dresser."

Her head rears back, and then I see a twinkle appear as she does what I ask.

"I knew it. Such a dirty little brat, wanting to come out to play," I rasp.

She looks back at me with the same spark in her eyes as she pushes her bare ass out and smiles sweetly.

"I'm ready."

My cock twitches.

"Fuck. Say it again."

"I'm ready for my lesson, sir."

The only time I've ever wanted to hear *sir* fall from her lips.

I press my clothed body into her naked one. My hand skims her sides before one goes around to her front and slowly caresses her lower breast. I start to tease the pointy tip of her nipple by capturing it between my thumb and finger. She presses her ass into my cock as I continue to tweak it.

I trail my fingers around her breast, causing her to shiver.

I begin to knead at her tit roughly—my cock begging for relief as I continue to do so. I'm fondling the most perfect breast I've ever held. It'll never get old to me that I get to touch this woman; it's no wonder I already want to come.

"Your cock is so hard. I need it in me."

"With time, princess. I need to make you come first."

She moans right as she lets go of the dresser and leans her body back into mine. I can smell the scent of her drenched pussy.

"Wet for me?"

"Yes," she moans loudly.

I take her other breast in my hand and begin playing with her nipples and massaging her breasts repeatedly. Ellie's hands are in my hair as she tightens her hold.

"I planned to leave you needy and wanting," I whisper into her ear.

She whines as she continues to rock her ass against my cock. I remove my hands from her breasts and have her lean forward to hold onto the dresser once more.

With her bent over, I position the outline of my cock in between her ass cheeks and begin rocking.

"Take off your pants. I need to really feel you," she says breathily.

I need it too.

Stepping back for a moment, I kick off my shoes first and then pull down my pants and boxer briefs before finally removing my shirt. Focusing back on Ellie, I see she's looking back at me with her eyes on my weeping cock.

"All in due time, princess. Face forward."

She nods eagerly and does as I say.

I slip my cock between her luscious ass cheeks and hold onto her hips. I begin to thrust, and pre-cum starts to drip down, making me feral.

Removing one of my hands from her hips, I trail the length of her side down to her pussy. I feel it throbbing as I gently graze it.

"Let me take care of this ache," I rasp.

I start massaging her pussy slowly, thumbing at that one spot I know she loves. I could play Ellie's body easily.

"Fuck, this feels so good," she whimpers.

"I need to hear you break apart for me, princess."

She moans louder than before as she continues to rock against my cock. I slip a finger inside of her pussy.

"Fuck," she screams.

Ellie stills as she begins to come and I continue fingering her while thrusting my cock into her ass.

"Fuck," Ellie pants out.

I stop thrusting as I revel in watching her come down from her release.

Ellie turns around, wobbly with a lazy smile, and I wait for her direction this time.

"Fisher?"

"Yes, princess?"

"What happened to teaching me a lesson?"

"Does someone deserve a spanking?"

She giggles while trying to catch her breath.

"Maybe I do."

I consider the offer. I'm in far too deep at this point, and my plans all went out the window.

"Next time."

"I like the sound of that."

"Now it's time to fuck my girl."

"Your girl?"

"Yes. You're mine."

Ellie looks confused.

"I am?"

"Do you think I'll ever get enough of a fix? I've only had you for a few days, and I'm addicted."

Ellie's hand flies up to her mouth to stifle her gasp. We'll have to address this later.

"Get on the bed and let me fuck this pretty little hole."

She nods eagerly and then climbs onto the bed.

"Lie back and spread your legs."

Slowly, she rests on her elbows and then spreads her legs wide.

"Wider."

She continues to open them.

My cock is painfully hard as I see my new favorite sight, Ellie's glistening pussy, on display.

"Perfect," I whisper.

She spreads her legs even farther apart. I stalk closer to the edge of the bed as her eyes dance around my naked body.

I pull at her hips and jerk her to the edge, forcing her to lie back fully. I tease her entrance with my cock.

"Getting my cock nice and wet with your cum."

Ellie moans as I line up my cock and slowly push forward.

She yelps at the intrusion but immediately starts trying to pull me deeper inside.

"Easy. I don't want to hurt you."

"Fuck me harder."

"I plan to all goddamn night."

She pulls at the sheets behind her head as I tighten my grip on one of her hips and thrust inside. I've never felt better or stronger than fucking this woman right now, watching her tits bounce up and down as she tries to get my cock further inside.

"My filthy girl, begging for more of my cock."

"Make me sore. I want to feel you for days to come."

I begin thrusting harder, listening to the clap of our bodies meeting with each deeper thrust.

I pull out momentarily and flip her around.

"Ass up, princess."

She pushes her pert ass into the air.

Gripping her shoulder with one hand and her hip with the other, I slide my cock into her pussy once more.

I know I'm getting close to her coming again. This time, I won't be far behind when she does.

"Fuck, fuck," she whimpers.

"Come for me."

***

"I CAN'T BELIEVE this trip is finally coming to an end," Ellie murmurs against my chest.

"The best retreat I've been to."

She raises her head.

"What? It is," I say, doubling down.

I try to stifle my laughter. Ellie grins before placing her head against my chest once again.

"There is so much work to do back home." She sighs.

"There is," I agree.

I don't want to think about work when I have one more night with her in my arms. I meant what I said earlier—I want to make her mine. I get the feeling she doesn't want this to end either. Our connection is unlike anything I've ever experienced, and I don't think I'll ever get enough.

She lightly starts to trail her fingers against my chest as I pull her in closer to my side.

"Christmas is next week," I say, and I feel the way her breath hitches.

"I can't believe it."

I start to stroke the back of her hair.

"You mentioned that you aren't going to visit your dad because of travel, right?"

"That's right. Especially not now. Even if I do have an offer from a certain someone to stow away on his plane," she teases.

That's right, I did offer that.

"Won't you miss seeing your dad if you don't go?"

"I'll head to Florida soon. Besides, he'll have my sister there."

"How is your sister?"

Ellie sighs. One of her arms pulls me closer.

"Good. I miss her, but it's easier for her to go back."

We rest in a comfortable silence.

Ellie has had a complicated relationship with her dad and sister since her mom's passing. Part of me wonders if she used the retreat as an excuse.

"I'm sure they both miss you."

"I know they do."

We linger in more silence and strum our fingers across each other's naked bodies.

"It just hurts to be reminded of her when I'm with them."

"Take all the time you need. They both understand."

"One day, it won't hurt this much."

"It'll evolve. You'll always miss your mom, but you won't be as sad as time marches forward."

I feel wetness against my chest, so I continue to stroke her back in reassurance.

"I've been wanting to talk to you about what happens next between us."

She shoots upright and keeps the sheet around her chest to stay covered.

"Or not," I say with a chuckle.

"No, no. I mean, what did you want to talk about with it?"

"Since you aren't going to Florida, would you want to travel to Charleston with me for Christmas? I think it'd be nice if you and I tried to explore what this is."

Ellie's face lights up.

"I would love that."

THIRTEEN

Ellie

"WHY DON'T MORE people visit Charleston in the winter? This is gorgeous," I say.

"It is. I have to admit, I probably should have visited Avery during this time of year before now; the summer is a bit stifling," Fisher responds.

"Well, we're here now." I beam.

"No one I'd rather be spending the holiday with."

Fisher smiles down at me as we cross the busy main street of downtown Charleston, King Street. It's lined with dozens of high-end stores and restaurants, all lit up with twinkle lights for the holidays. It's a great destination for window-shopping or for punishing your bank account.

"Are you sure Avery doesn't mind that we are staying downtown and not at her home?"

"She definitely will mind, which is why she doesn't know we're here yet."

I stop in the street.

"What?"

My eyes practically pop out of my head. Fisher pulls me to the sidewalk.

This is not the impression I'm looking to make with Avery. Even though I've met her a dozen times before, it's never been like this. I want her to be happy for us exploring a relationship, not resentful that I'm keeping her pseudo-father from seeing her sooner.

"Avery isn't expecting us for a few days. I wanted this time just with you, where we aren't trapped in a snow-storm," Fisher says, squeezing my hand.

I can't help but melt under his touch. If Fisher thinks it'll be okay, I have to trust his intuition.

I never realized how much I wanted someone to give me reassurance like this. It's as if Fisher knows that I need him to slowly unravel our new dynamic for us. He's begun preempting my needs and satiating them in a way that only a true partner could.

"She'll be fine, I promise," he adds.

"Okay, I trust you."

He smiles widely.

"You have no idea what that means to me."

I squeeze Fisher's hand.

I'm seeing a sweeter and softer side to the man who usually holds the weight of the world on his shoulders. It's awakening a new part of me, one that I'm still coming to terms with. I can be a career-focused woman and still have a partner to help.

Now, if only Fisher were my partner for good.

"Where to first?" he asks.

"I'm not really that familiar with Charleston. I've only been here on that bachelorette trip, and we weren't exactly just roaming the streets."

"That's right; we'll have to stop at the Blue Marlin Lounge if we have time."

"Who owns it, by the way? I know you were able to get us in as VIPs, but you never shared much about the whole situation."

Fisher hesitates.

"You don't have to tell me if it's a big secret," I tease.

"No, it's fine. It's just you."

Maybe I should take offense to the "it's just you," but something about that makes me feel like I'm deeper into Fisher's world than I thought I was.

"It's actually Grant's."

My head rears back.

"Grant? As in Grant Sinclair?" I say, shocked.

"It's just one of his many investments. He's actually from this area."

"You learn something new every day."

Fisher grins. "That you do. Now, how about we do some shopping?"

"Do you like shopping?" I ask as we continue to stroll King Street.

"I like you."

Is this schoolgirl smile I keep getting ever going to go away? I certainly hope not.

"And I like shopping," I say with a laugh.

Fisher pulls me into the closest store, and I instantly realize I'm out of my depth here. I do have one credit card that I could make a few impulse purchases with. It's not like I ever go shopping like this, so it'll be fun to do something so off-brand.

A sales associate instantly greets us and offers complimentary champagne.

I start to browse the rows of clothes lining the walls.

"See anything you like?" Fisher asks as he trails behind me.

"I do, it's all so beautiful."

My fingers glide against the edges of the dresses, blouses, and sweaters.

I pause in front of a dress that looks like it'll flatter my figure nicely. As I hold it out in front of me, I feel Fisher get closer.

"Ellie, did you think when I called you my princess that meant I didn't want to spoil you?" he whispers into my ear.

It causes my body to naturally shiver. Right now, I'm thinking of something else entirely, and it's not shopping.

"I can't let you do that."

"I want to. Do this for me."

I turn around to face him, and his face is lit up with excitement.

"You're being serious, aren't you?"

"I am."

"I never thought you'd be one to call a woman you're sleeping with *princess*," I tease.

Fisher's grin turns downward.

"Don't reduce yourself to that."

I've hit a nerve, one that I didn't know he would have.

We haven't exactly discussed what it is we're doing here, just that we both are enjoying exploring what this could be. I know I need answers, but I'm not ready to ask the question yet. I like this stage.

"In that case," I say as I turn back around and start going through the rack of clothes.

I see Fisher's body vibrate with silent laughter as I pull out options.

"What do you think?" I ask as I hold out a midnight-blue dress that I'm unsure about.

Fisher studies it and then gets a wicked gleam in his eyes.

"It's nice, but..."

He looks around and waves for a sales associate. The woman from earlier comes running over quickly.

"How can I help you?"

"We need to get a dressing room started," he answers.

"Yes, of course," she begins.

The woman's stare lingers on Fisher a little too long for my liking. I've never been one to get jealous, but I've also never been with someone like him before. Someone who I want to claim as mine in front of everyone.

I clear my throat obnoxiously, causing the woman to take my handful of clothes. She gives me a brash smile and heads to start the dressing room.

Fisher cocks an eyebrow at me and smirks.

"Everything okay?" he draws out.

"Yes, peachy."

"Peachy? I don't know if I've heard you use that one before."

He steps forward and towers over me. I cross my arms and look to the side, trying to focus on anything but him with how I'm feeling.

I realize I'm being childish, but I just can't help it.

"Yes, everything is good," I say while trying to make even myself believe it.

"I see."

Fisher stretches his hand out and waits for me to take it. I eye it carefully, unsure of what his intentions are given the situation.

Finally, I place mine in his, and he starts to lead me back to the dressing room.

"MISS, right through here is your dressing room," the woman calls out.

I know she has to plaster on this smile to remain professional. I've had to fake a smile one too many times myself, including now.

"Thank you," I answer sincerely.

The woman steps away and leaves Fisher and me alone.

"I'll be right out then," I say and turn toward the dressing room.

This isn't a typical dressing room where you can see and hear anything around it because of the tops and bottoms being open. This is a fully closed door. We're in a designer store where they ensure their customers' comfort, including full privacy in a dressing room.

As I go to close the door, Fisher's hand catches it. He opens it up slightly more and sticks his head in. The way his eyes gleam and his mouth tilts upward makes me want him badly.

God, he's just so attractive. I hate it. I want to pout in private, but all I can see are two dreamy eyes and tattoos peeking through his button-up shirt that I want to devour.

I bite down on my lower lip as I try to contain what I'm feeling. Just one look at him, and heat is pooling between my thighs.

"I know that look," he rasps.

"I don't know what you mean," I whisper.

Even though I'm really trying not to, I can't help myself as I continue to stare at his tattoos coming through.

It's wintertime and very cold. There is no reason why his shirt should be unbuttoned like this other than he knows how it affects me.

"May I?" he asks, still wedged between the doorway.

"You may," I say as I open it wider for him to step inside.

Fisher enters the dressing room and quietly shuts the door, sealing us together in here.

I don't care if the store staff are around the corner. All of this is new with Fisher, and I want to know I'm the focus of his attention.

I slowly take off my camel coat and toss it onto a bench while Fisher drinks in every movement.

"Will you help undress me?" I ask innocently.

I turn around and face the wall with my arms lifted in the air. I feel the sensation of his large, warm hands pulling at the hem of my shirt.

He carefully lifts it up, and it drags along my body. I assist it going over my head and toss it onto the bench too. Fisher's warm body presses against my back. His arms cross over to my front, and he goes to unbutton my jeans.

He pops the button and pulls down the zipper.

My breath hitches at how sensual something so mundane can be.

His fingers tease the edge of my panties. Back and forth his finger goes, only causing the wetness to continue to pool in my panties.

"What are you doing?" I whisper.

The palm of his hand starts to dip into my panties and slowly travels down until he cups my most sensitive area. His breath teases the outside of my ear as I lean back into him. My arms naturally go around his neck as my eyes close.

One finger starts teasing my entrance. Still using a soft touch, it goes back and forth. The feeling is euphoric.

"Wet for me already," he rasps.

"Yes," I manage to mutter.

He finally dips the finger inside. The intrusion stings, but I love it all the same. I begin rocking against it as I try to stifle my moans.

He enters another finger, and I still.

"I feel so full." I moan.

Fisher's fingers are rather large, so I need to adjust to two of them being inside of me.

"Fuck my fingers," he groans out.

I start moving again as he uses his thumb to strum against my most sensitive spot.

"Yes, more," I practically beg.

He goes harder against my clit as I rock faster into his fingers, needing to find relief. It doesn't take long for my body to adjust; it never does.

"Does my princess like to be finger-fucked for anyone to hear?" he growls into my ear.

"I do." I moan.

"Be a good girl, Ellie. You can't let the blonde know that I'm about to make you come."

"And why not?" I can't help but ask.

He laughs darkly.

"You were jealous," he says.

"No," I lie.

I don't want to talk about this; I just want to come.

Fisher walks us forward. I naturally lean and brace my hands on the nearby wall. I don't need to lean forward too much, just enough to hold me up as I rock back and forth.

I can tell he's holding me back from coming.

"Why won't you let me come?" I whine.

"You know why."

"No, I don't. Please let me come. I need it."

He thrusts his fingers deeper inside of me, and I yelp in surprise.

"You were acting like a brat out there, and we can't have that."

"Why? Because you're worried what she might think?"

He chuckles.

"No, because you're all I want. Now, I need to hear you say it first, and then I'll let you come."

It is relieving to hear that I'm all he wants. I don't want to admit that I have been acting that way. What is happening to me with this man? I'm being jealous when he's not officially mine.

"If you won't..."

Fisher removes one finger and stills everything else.

He really isn't going to let me come until I say it out loud.

"Fine. I'm all you want," I admit.

"And why is that?"

"Because you like fucking your assistant?"

He chuckles and starts to pull out the last finger.

Wrong answer, apparently.

"Wait!" I shout loud enough for anyone else to hear.

"What's that?" he whispers into my ear.

"Because you see me."

"And you see me. You don't have to be worried about any other women."

He continues his previous motions as I melt into his touch, knowing exactly what I need to hear. The buildup is so close, I know I'm going to come any minute.

"Come all over my hand, princess."

I still as the orgasm starts to wash over me. It's an out-of-body experience I've never had before.

I'm left a panting mess as I keep bracing my slumped-over body onto the wall. I feel Fisher's back against mine as he begins placing small and deliberate kisses along my spine.

Loud knocks interrupt us.

"Excuse me," an unfamiliar woman's voice shrieks from outside of the dressing room.

More knocks follow immediately.

"I said excuse me. Please come out here at once."

I can feel Fisher's smile against my back.

"One moment," I shout weakly.

I slip back into my outfit and gather the clothes I intended to try on.

Fisher opens the door and gestures for me to go first.

I stop right outside the door and wait for him. He stands next to me and places his hand on my lower back in reassurance.

An older woman and the blonde associate are both standing outside of the dressing room waiting for us. The older woman's face is spewing pure venom, while the blonde looks more amused than anything.

"Excuse me, you can't do whatever it is you did in there in an establishment like this," the older woman says.

Fisher has a bored expression on his face, and he turns to the blonde woman.

"She'll take everything she's holding."

"Oh yes, yes, sir. Right away," she stammers before reaching forward to take the dozens of clothing items from my hold.

"Feel free to add a cleaning fee to my bill. We'll be back later this afternoon to pick up the bags."

"Yes, of course," the blonde woman responds.

He pulls out his wallet and hands her a black credit card.

"I'll be back in just a few minutes. Sheila, can you

please get our guests another round of champagne?" the woman asks.

The commission this woman is about to make is more than she probably made with every other order sold this week.

"Well, I never," Sheila starts before stomping away to get the champagne.

"Please have a seat," the blonde woman says before disappearing.

Once they are both out of sight, I interlock my arm with one of Fisher's and bury my head into his shoulder. I can feel the heat from embarrassment on my already flushed face.

"You're turning me into some kind of monster." I groan.

"And why is that?" he asks, amused.

"I would have never done that before."

"Which part? Come in a dressing room or spend twenty thousand dollars on clothes?"

My head shoots up.

"Fisher, are you serious? I can't let you do that for me."

"Yes, you can, and you know why?"

I try to wrack my brain with why I would possibly ever let him spend this much money on me for clothes.

I shake my head.

"Sorry, but this time, I am at a loss."

He smirks.

"What's that look for?"

I search his eyes for a sign.

"Really, you don't know?"

I think about it some more. This is silly; he needs to just tell me at this point.

"No, tell me. Please? Now I'm just curious where you're going with this."

Fisher gives me a rare broad smile.

"You're my brat and my princess, remember?"

I give him a pointed look.

"Oh, dear god, what have I become?" I fake cry out.

I bury my head back in his shoulder. I know he's amused by this.

"Excuse me, but here is your complimentary champagne," a male voice interrupts us.

We both look up to find it is indeed not the older woman who was sent to get it.

"Thank you."

The man leaves, and Fisher goes to toast me.

"What should we toast to?" he asks.

"To us."

I tilt my glass forward, inches away from his.

"To us."

We clink our glasses right as the blonde woman starts to come back.

FOURTEEN

Fisher

BACK IN OUR HOTEL SUITE, I have an entire weekend planned out for us. In a couple of days, we'll be over at Avery's home and won't be able to have this amount of time alone.

Avery is planning a few Christmas dinners with some of her local friends. I'm sure she'll use the time to have me get to know them. I'm glad to, but I also want to take advantage of these moments with only Ellie while we can.

Avery is always trying to get me out of my comfort zone of solitude. I know whenever I tell her about Ellie and me, she's going to be ecstatic. Not only that, but I anticipate a dozen questions will be coming my way.

She knows who Ellie is in the context of being my assistant and as Knox's ex-girlfriend—a category I haven't let myself give much thought to this week. I probably shouldn't have taken Ellie as mine like I did, but it's been unstoppable. At some point during the first moment when she said

I see her to finally feeling her pussy wrapped around my cock, she became mine. That's what she is. Now, I just have to get over the remaining hurdles so it can be official.

The first is showing Ellie what it would be like if we were to become partners. I have two nights to continue to spoil her the way she deserves. It makes my cock hard watching her light up from being spoiled. It's a selfish decision that is working out well for both of us.

"I'll be right back. Do you need anything?" I shout from the other side of the closed bathroom door.

"You can come in," she says through a set of giggles.

Pushing it open, I see Ellie lying in the large whirlpool bathtub with bubbles covering the body I've come to know as my personal playground.

"Care to join me?"

I stand mesmerized.

This woman is everything.

"I would, but I have to step out for a moment. I'll be back soon."

I walk over and press a kiss on top of her head.

Ellie pretends to pout in the bathtub.

I chuckle at my luck. This gorgeous, intelligent, and capable woman is on her Christmas holiday with me— someone who feels like an old man, one she can't get enough of.

"I promise I'll be right back. Relax. When I get back, we'll get ready for dinner."

"Okay." She beams.

The bubbles start to separate around her breasts as she reaches out of the water for me.

"A real one," she begs.

"How can I deny you?"

I lean down and let her soaked arms wrap around my

neck. Ellie presses a punishing kiss against my closed mouth.

I really like this side of her that is coming out for me.

Breaking away, I laugh.

"Enjoy yourself."

"Oh, I will. Do you see how nice this tub is?"

LEAVING THE HOTEL SUITE, I nearly trip over the bags from our earlier shopping trip. I better move these before we go out tonight.

It's been rather easy to pretend like the real world and work don't exist as much as we have been. If this were a week ago, I'd be locked in this same suite all weekend attached to my computer. Instead, I'm off to look at potential gifts at a store I researched online during the plane ride to Charleston.

When I told Ellie I wanted to treat her like a princess, the words flew out of my mouth, but the taste of it felt right. Even for a man my age, the first time you find the right person for you, it hits you hard.

I was comfortable living the day-to-day of my life. I may have been hoping for more out of it, but I certainly didn't expect anything like this to happen.

Whenever Ellie fell asleep in my arms, I began browsing what stores were on King Street. During my past visits, I never cared much for what was around. Always in and out for whatever purpose brought me to town.

That's when I spotted a jewelry store that my friend Grant had mentioned to me in passing the day prior. I didn't see anything that would be exactly right for Ellie, but I know they'll have something that showcases her beauty.

Heading out of the hotel doors, I feel a buzzing in my pocket. Pulling out my cell phone, I see it's Avery. I know I'll have to talk to her sooner or later about what I'm doing.

I answer it as I head in the direction of the jewelry store.

"Hello, Avery."

"Hi, Fisher. How are you?" she asks.

Avery is never this courteous with me; she's up to something.

"What's wrong?" Her laugh flows through the phone.

"When were you going to tell me?"

I furrow my eyebrows together in confusion.

"What's that?"

"That you're already in Charleston."

"Oh, that."

"Yes, that. I tried calling you yesterday, and you never answered. I called Letty to see if you were still planning to come to Charleston when she was just notified by your pilot you had safely landed."

Fuck. I do love the team I've put in place, but I can't do anything in private anymore without word spreading.

"I am."

"And..."

There's no better time than the present to tell Avery about Ellie.

"You know you're like a daughter to me," I start.

"I don't need to hear that. What's going on? Why didn't you come to Lachlan's and my home?"

"I'm staying downtown."

A pause.

"With whom?" she finally asks.

"Ellie."

"Ellie?" She squeals.

I sigh loudly again.

"Yes, Ellie."

"Oh. My. God. Fisher! I can't believe it. Wait, please don't tell me this isn't what I think it is. I'll be so disappointed if this is something to do with work for real," Avery finishes.

"It's not for work."

"I am so happy for you! When are you coming to see me? Are you still staying in the FROG for a few days?"

"Yes, and why do you call your guest house that again?"

"It's literally a freestanding room over a garage, so it fits," she answers.

"Right, well, yes, if you don't have an issue with it, then Ellie and I will be by Sunday as I originally planned."

"I am so excited to see you both. I'll text you my address again."

"See you then."

Hanging up the phone, I feel a weight lifted off my shoulders.

It feels good to tell someone about what's been happening between Ellie and me this week.

I head into the jewelry store.

"Good evening, sir. How can I help you?"

"Hello. I'm here to look at your diamond jewelry."

"Yes, of course. Right this way. Is there any piece in particular?"

"I'll know it when I see it."

"Understood. I'm Pierre, and I'll be assisting you today. One moment, and I'll have options ready for your perusal."

Pierre goes behind the counter and starts pulling out trays of diamond rings, bracelets, necklaces, and more. It'd be overwhelming if I didn't know Ellie so well.

"Please take your time, and if there is anything I can show you up close, please let me know."

"Thank you."

Pierre takes a step back to allow me room to browse.

As I go back and forth along the trays of diamond jewelry, I spot something that screams Ellie—a thin diamond necklace and matching tennis bracelet. I've never seen Ellie with much jewelry on, but I know she likes it, and I've seen the dainty sets she wears. All of them are understated yet powerful, just like this set. And just like the girl herself.

"Pierre?"

"Yes, sir," he says as he steps forward.

"I'll take this and this," I say, pointing to the jewelry.

"Of course."

"I'd also like options for two-carat diamond earrings as well."

"Can do, sir."

Pierre gets to work pulling out the pieces I've requested.

That's when I spot it. The gift that I'll save to give Ellie on Christmas morning. Something she won't expect after I surprise her with these presents soon.

I can't wait to see Ellie's expression when she opens it all.

I OPEN the hotel suite door to find Ellie lounging like a model on the couch, ready for dinner. In a fitted navy-blue dress, tights, and sky-high heels, she looks perfect.

"A dress from today?"

"I had to show off your purchases," she says with a grin.

"Worth every penny." I smile back.

"I didn't want to start without you, but the hotel sent up a bottle of champagne. Interested in a glass before dinner?"

"I'd like to have you before dinner instead," I rasp.

She blushes into the side of her hair.

"We can't. Someone took a little longer than I anticipated."

"I did. Let me change, and I'll be right out."

Ellie nods and gives me a shy smile.

As I head into the room, I hear her shout, "I'll pour a round of champagne!"

Discarding my jacket and outfit, I quickly change into a navy-blue suit to match what Ellie's wearing. This is another part that's coming too naturally for me. I want to match with the beautiful girl who's going to be on my arm tonight.

I wonder what her reaction is going to be whenever I show her the jewelry I purchased. I know she's curious about what my errand was, but I appreciate that she didn't ask. That's just Ellie though.

I look through my bag to find my watch box. I quickly pull it out and put on my matching watch before finding my black suede shoes and putting those on next.

Adjusting my suit coat, I give myself one final look in the mirror. I pick up the jewelry store bag with her items nicely wrapped in it and head back into the main living room space.

"Here you are," Ellie says as she approaches me with two flutes of champagne.

I take one and clink my glass to hers.

"Thank you. Why don't we have a seat since we have a few minutes before we have to go."

"Okay."

She hasn't noticed the bag in my hand.

I smirk.

Ellie rounds the coffee table and takes a seat on the

large cream sofa. I sit as close to her as possible on it, and she looks up at me curiously.

"I have a surprise for you," I say.

"What's that?"

I show her the bag I'm holding.

"For you."

She gasps, and her hands fling up to her cheeks.

"What did you do? You already bought me enough today. I can't accept this," she starts to ramble.

I see a blush creeping up on Ellie's skin as she gets more flustered.

"Take it."

She tilts her head to the side and finally relents.

Pulling out the first box, she unwraps the blue bow and then slowly opens the velvet box.

"Fisher," she gasps again.

It's the tennis bracelet.

She holds it out to inspect it in awe.

"You shouldn't have."

"I wanted to."

She smiles sweetly over at me.

"Will you help me put it on?"

"Here," I say, gesturing for her to hand me the bracelet. I slip it on her wrist and can feel her trembling.

"There are two more."

"What?" she practically shouts, and I chuckle at her confusion.

"Yes. Two more. Open. We're going to be late if you keep gasping like this," I tease.

"Very funny."

She pretends to gives me a cutting stare, which only makes me laugh more.

"Come on, princess."

She opens the next box to find the necklace. We follow the same routine, and I put it around her neck. It fits perfectly. I watch as she holds onto it at the front.

"Last one."

Ellie turns around, and her hair falls below her neckline naturally. The wavy curls span down her back.

"I don't even know what to say to all of this."

"Say thank you," I tease.

She pretends to shoot daggers at me as she opens up the smallest box. As she looks from me down to it, she gasps again.

"Fisher. I just... I don't know what to say. Seriously. This is all too much. Thank you."

"No, it's not. Do you need help putting those in?"

She shakes her head with her smile in place.

"I'll be right back. Thank you."

Ellie gets off the sofa and places a small kiss to my cheek before disappearing into the bathroom.

That's when it finally hits me.

None of this is my typical behavior—from calling her princess to the shopping trips to not spending every moment thinking about work.

There's a reason why I'm acting this way.

Love.

I'm falling in love with Ellie Robertson.

"WHAT DID you think of the steak?" I ask Ellie as the server takes our plates away.

"Seriously, the best I've ever had. Good choice for the restaurant."

"It was a recommendation from Avery."

"I'm not surprised. She has the best taste in restaurants."

Ellie pauses before taking a sip of her martini.

"Is something wrong?" I ask.

"No, not at all. I was just thinking about Avery. Does she know I'm actually going to be with you yet?"

I smile.

"Yes, she actually called me earlier today. She knows we will be over there Sunday morning."

"Okay, that's great," she answers, but I still sense the hesitation.

"Is there something else?"

"Well..." She trails off.

"Avery is going to be very welcoming. She loves you."

"Oh no, Avery is wonderful. Really."

"But?"

"Does she think I'm here only as your assistant?"

Ah. That's it. I hadn't considered this yet.

"No, she put it together after talking to Letty."

Ellie's shoulders visibly relax as she goes to take another sip of her martini.

"Good, I'm glad."

"Is there anything else?"

I see her pause before shaking her head no. That's interesting; is there something she's keeping from me?

No, she wouldn't.

"No, really, that was it."

"Good. Are you ready to get out of here?"

"I thought you'd never ask."

FIFTEEN

Ellie

"THIS WHOLE NIGHT HAS BEEN AMAZING," I say as we walk into the hotel room.

"I'm glad you enjoyed it."

"Did you not?"

"I have you; I'll be happy anywhere."

I blush into my shoulder as the door to the suite closes behind us. The curtains are pulled back to the sides of the windows, giving us the most amazing view of the Charleston cityscape lit up with holiday lights.

"Thank you. This has been so special. I'm glad we did this."

I pop off one heel, followed by the next, and walk over to the window to look outside.

"I'd do anything to make you happy."

I pause and turn to face him.

"Come join me?"

He nods and walks over to the same spot by the window, and we take a few small steps to reach it together.

"It's so beautiful here."

"This city has nothing on your beauty."

I blush as I tilt my head into my shoulder once more.

"Such a charmer. I had no idea," I tease.

Fisher wraps his arms around my waist from behind. I lean my back on his chest and rest my head on his shoulder.

"What a whirlwind week," I murmur.

"Unexpected, to say the least, but I'm glad it happened," he says.

"Me too."

He places a small kiss on the top of my head. I smile, thinking about how this small act means so much.

He places another small kiss on my ear, making my body tingle from the contact.

Then places another on the top of my shoulder. This one is more wet than the others. Another tingling sensation ripples throughout my body.

"This is a beautiful dress," he whispers into my shoulder and lightly kisses the same spot.

"A super attractive man bought it for me," I say breathily. I'm already anticipating what's to come.

"Is that so?"

Fisher starts to trail his fingers down the length of my arms.

"He likes to worship my body too. Quite the catch if you ask me."

I stifle a giggle.

"If he bought the dress, that means he can do what he wants to it."

It's not a question.

"That's true," I whimper.

He bends down and reaches for the bottom of the dress hem, slowly lifting it inch by inch.

"What are you doing?" I moan.

I don't recognize my tone; it comes out more sultry than I've ever heard before. The sensual feeling of his fingers barely touching my skin is lighting me on fire.

"Taking what's mine."

I arch my back as he finishes lifting the dress up and over my breasts. Raising my arms in the air, I give him ample space to lift it fully. Once it's off, he tosses it to the ground.

"What are you going to do with me?" I moan out.

"I'd like to fuck you in front of this entire city," he whispers.

Fisher takes a large step back. I twirl around in my bra, panties, and black tights.

"Beautiful," he murmurs as he looks me up and down.

"Fuck me in front of the city?"

"That's the goal." He smirks.

With the curtains open and lights on, technically, anyone could see into the room and what we're doing.

Fisher backs up and sits down in the nearby accent chair. I laugh as I pull my tights off and add them to the pile with my dress.

"Now you're almost exactly as I wanted you."

I sashay a bit closer to where he sits.

"What else would you like me to remove?"

I jut out my hip and raise an arm to put my body on display.

"Bra first."

I smirk as I unclasp my bra and slip it off. It gets added to the pile too.

"Fuck." He groans.

"What's next?"

"Take your panties off."

I grin as I pull them down my hips and slide them off. I leave them where they've pooled on the ground.

"I think that's about it," I say with a giggle.

I go to take off my diamond bracelet so it doesn't snag on anything when Fisher stops me.

"Keep it on," he commands.

I look up to find him rising from the chair.

"I want to fuck my princess in her new diamonds."

I cock my head to the side as wetness shamelessly gathers low.

He stalks closer until he's mere inches away from me, causing my nipples to turn into tiny peaks from his proximity.

He leans close to my ear.

"I bet if I were to touch this pretty pussy, you'd be drenched, wouldn't you?" he rasps.

The feeling of his hot breath dances on my skin, eliciting goosebumps to rise.

I nod my head eagerly.

Fisher laughs darkly as his finger plays with one of my hard nipples. I moan as I try to lean into the touch for more. His finger slowly travels away from my breast and along the length of my stomach before it finally reaches where I'm now desperate for his touch.

"Please," I beg.

His hand dips low and begins relieving the needy ache.

"Fuck," I pant out.

He works vigorously against my clit while his other hand begins massaging one of my breasts. The roughness of him pushing it in every direction makes me want to beg for him to finish me off already.

"I like you panting like this for me," he rasps.

Suddenly, I feel him walk us forward toward the window. He turns me around so my naked body is really on display for the city to see. I'm nervous someone will actually see us like this.

"The curtains are still open," I manage to get out.

"Worried?"

I hesitate.

"A little."

I feel his smile against my shoulder.

He gently pushes me the final inches forward, and my breasts are now flush against the window as he continues to work my clit.

"Fisher," I yelp.

"We're up high."

"But," I stammer.

"Don't you want someone to see you dripping wet while dripping in diamonds?"

"Fuck." I moan.

I do like the thought of that. Anyone can see me being finger-fucked.

Fisher finally gives me what I need as his finger goes inside of me. He's learning my body so well already.

"I'm so close."

He lets go and flips my body around to face him.

My ass and back are flush against the glass window now. I pant as I wait for what's to come.

"I need you to come on my tongue."

He falls to his knees, and his mouth captures my budding orgasm right before I detonate.

"Fuck."

I fall to pieces as light bursts around me.

THE NEXT MORNING, Fisher has a call that he needs to take for work, so I head downstairs to find a coffee shop to bring him back his espresso.

I know I need to call Harper. She doesn't even know I'm in her town.

Finding a cute coffee shop near the hotel, I order my coffee first so I can drink it slowly while chatting with Harper.

An oat milk cinnamon latte. Absolute perfection. Tis the season and all.

Once seated, I pull out my cell phone and find Harper's contact information, taking a sip of my iced coffee as it rings.

"Hey there!" Harper says as she answers the call.

"Hi," I say through a small laugh.

"How are you? Back in Seattle?"

So much to unpack.

"Not exactly..."

"What does that mean?"

I can sense Harper's hesitation.

"Well, I have a surprise."

"What is it?"

"I'm actually in Charleston," I say before taking another sip of my coffee.

Another long pause.

"What?" Harper says, dragging out the word.

"Fisher and I are spending the holiday in Charleston."

"What are you saying right now?"

I can't help but giggle at her confusion. A lot has changed since she and I last spoke.

"Fisher and I are still exploring our relationship. We're visiting his friend's daughter for Christmas."

"What?"

These revelations dumbfound Harper.

"Harper, girl. I'm in Charleston. I would love to see you if I can."

"Um, you better! Where are you now? Give me all the details!"

I laugh as I down the rest of the iced coffee.

"Well, we are currently staying downtown so that we could have a few days for just us," I start.

"Makes sense."

"And then tomorrow, we are actually going to Daniel Island."

"Oh, nice! Everyone calls it DI. It's a super cute part of Charleston."

"Good to know."

"Anyway, I'm actually going to be on DI for Christmas, weirdly enough."

"What a coincidence! What are your plans?"

"Grayson and I will probably have an easy morning, and then we're heading to his friend Lachlan's for Christmas dinner. I've told you about Lachlan before, right? He and his wife, Avery, are the best. I actually doubt they would care if you stopped by for a drink. Want me to ask?"

Wait. Wait a second.

Lachlan.

Avery.

Daniel Island.

Oh my god. How have I never put this together before?

"Harper."

"Yeah?"

"Avery is Fisher's friend's daughter," I admit in disbelief.

"No way," she shouts.

"Yes way. I literally don't know why I never thought about it before!"

"Stop! I'm going to have Grayson confirm," she starts.

Harper must move the phone away from her mouth because I hear her ask Grayson, but it doesn't hurt my ears. Then, she returns to the conversation.

"He's texting Lachlan now."

"Well, surprise. This is a good thing, right?"

"Such a good thing."

"THE WEEKEND JUST FLEW PAST US," I murmur.

"We can have more opportunities like this."

I look around the hotel suite to make sure we have everything. I'm usually not a messy person, but clothes have flown more times than even I expected this weekend. You never know where they could have ended up at this rate.

"Have everything?" Fisher asks.

I see him glancing around the living room area too.

"I think so."

"If they find anything, they'll mail it back."

"If you say so."

I grab the handle of my bag right as Fisher goes to take it.

"I can get that for you."

"We may be entering into a new dynamic, but I am still me. I can roll my own bag," I retort.

"Fair enough. After you then," he says while gesturing to the door.

I roll my suitcase out of the door and into the hallway, waiting as Fisher follows behind me.

"I'm so glad we were able to find such unique gifts downtown on short notice."

"Avery especially will love what we managed to do."

I feel relieved we were able to get presents for Avery and Lachlan.

"Thankfully, you were able to talk to Lachlan."

I laugh as we head toward the elevators.

"It'll all be good," he says.

I really feel like it will. Regardless of how anxious I am about it all, I know that this is shaping up to be a wonderful holiday with our Charleston friends.

"Let's head to... What did you call it? DI?" Fisher asks as we walk into the elevator.

"Yes, that's what Harper called it, at least."

"Small world," he says.

"I know. What are the odds?"

"Too small. I still don't know if I believe it."

"I know, right? It's crazy."

"Who else is going to be there?"

"Avery said they have basically the same group coming over for Christmas Eve and Christmas Day."

"Who are they?"

The elevator doors open, and we head to the valet.

"Outside of your friends, there's Emily and Noah. They aren't together, from my understanding. I'm not sure who is coming to what or when."

Of course he doesn't. These aren't the type of details Fisher would bother to ask. In fact, it's something that I normally would have asked if I wasn't so stunned by what's been happening.

The valet hands Fisher the keys to our rental car. Well,

luxury rental car. This isn't your run-of-the-mill vehicle. I'm surprised he didn't hire a driver. Did he actually rent this car himself? This is also something I normally would have done.

I try to shake out of these thoughts. It's Christmas, and I need to focus on how special this time together is.

Fisher opens my car door, and I slide into the convertible. He rounds the corner to get in himself, and then we are off.

Phase two of the Charleston vacation has commenced.

SIXTEEN

Fisher

THE DRIVE from the Charleston peninsula to Daniel Island is an easy one this Sunday morning. I glance over to see Ellie looking like a goddess with the sun reflecting brightly against her complexion. The wind is blowing in her hair, making it fly around wildly.

Normally, I wouldn't have rented a convertible, but when it was one of the only options available, I thought we should try it. It was a risky move that paid off. We could have kept the roof on, but Ellie didn't want to put the top up when she saw it.

Watching her with a small smile and eyes shut, it's taking everything in me to focus on the road and not just stay entranced. It's an accident waiting to happen, and I know I have to look away.

"You're staring," she says.

I look back to the front of the car and out at the road.

"You're gorgeous."

"I never knew," she says with a light laugh, still not looking over at me.

"Knew what?"

"That this is how you would be when..." she starts.

Ellie pauses.

"When you're dating someone."

She still won't look over at me. It's as if this is a confession more so meant for her than for me. I understand where she's coming from with it. We know that there is a lot to discuss and many steps to take if we are going to be together.

It feels so natural, and yet not.

I reach across the center console and take her hand in mine, keeping it on her thigh. Watching her squirm slightly was the confirmation I needed.

She likes it when I'm touching her at all times. I've come to learn that she isn't one to just voice what she wants or any of her feelings, for that matter. She's reserved and tactful. All of what I know about her professionally makes so much sense in this context too.

Then there is the other side of her that I've been coaxing out, which is sassy and jealous. I love that version of her as well.

There are two topics we have been doing our best to avoid—one is work, and the other is Knox.

Work is the easier problem of the two. I'm planning on telling her about the promotion soon. I have to, but it feels like it's actually the best-case scenario with these recent developments.

I may not get Ellie in my day-to-day once she's promoted, but she would still be working at Rain Peak. I'll still be able to see her daily.

Then it leaves telling Knox. Whenever we figure out a

way to explain to him what has happened, she'll officially be mine for good. I can have her in my life permanently.

Even though Knox and Ellie weren't right for each other, I know he'll find the situation strange. Let's face the facts here, he's been traveling the world trying to make it as a musician and hasn't exactly been regretting his decision to end their relationship all those years ago. And I don't think that Ellie is with me as a substitute for Knox. She doesn't have daddy issues or ex-boyfriend concerns; she simply likes me.

"What are you thinking about?" she asks.

I have been in my own head for a while now.

"You."

That perks up her attention.

"Really?"

She finally looks at me, and I wink before focusing back on the road.

"Of course, you know how to wink all sexy," she says with a groan.

I roar with laughter.

"Sorry if that upsets you."

I look over to see her grinning.

She gives my hand a reassuring squeeze and leans back with her eyes shut.

"Let's see what this baby can do," I say.

I hit the pedal, and we're flying down the road.

"Fisher," she shouts through a laugh.

Her eyes pop open and over to me.

"Don't worry, just had to get your attention."

"You have it."

"Good."

She squeezes my hand again. I'm beginning to think I also need to be touching Ellie at all times.

I KNOCK on Avery's front door. On her front porch, I notice the haint-blue ceilings and porch swing with a wooden rolling bar cart next to it.

Children running down the sidewalks wrapped in sweaters make me realize this is what Avery has always wanted—a life like this, one with security, neighbors, and somewhere she can eventually raise a family.

I'm proud of her for making the life she wants. She deserves it.

Ellie fidgets with the end of her jacket as we wait for Avery to answer the door.

"You look gorgeous," I whisper.

"Thank you."

"You have nothing to be nervous about. You know Avery."

"I know, it's just different."

"It is." I sigh knowingly.

I wouldn't steer Ellie wrong. Avery is excited to see her like this. She would have told me if she had any concerns, for Ellie more so than me.

The front door swings open and standing before us is Avery's husband, Lachlan.

"Fisher, great to you see," Lachlan says.

We shake hands before he turns his attention to the woman by my side.

"And you must be Ellie. It's great to finally meet you."

Lachlan puts out his hand to shake hers too.

"Thank you for having me join," she says as she takes his hand.

"Of course. We're both thrilled to have you here."

Lachlan motions for us to both go through the large wooden doors. We walk into the foyer with our bags in tow.

"Avery, they're here," Lachlan shouts.

Their home is exactly as I would have pictured Avery would do. With gold, white, and blue patterns throughout, she really has made this her home.

"Oh my god! Hi! Sorry, be right there," she shouts frantically from a different room.

Ellie laughs.

"Right. Well, let me show you where you'll be staying, and then whenever you're ready, you can come back here?"

"Thank you." Ellie beams.

Lachlan walks us to the back of the house, and I spot the guest house we'll be staying in through the large open windows.

"Right this way," Lachlan says as he unlocks the guest house's front door.

We step inside, and it really is a two-bedroom home.

The space is decorated similarly to the main house. In one direction are the bedrooms, and in the other are the living room and kitchen spaces.

"Take your time. I'm sure Avery will be out prepping for this evening whenever you want to come back over."

"Tell Avery we'll be quick," I say.

Lachlan's shoulders relax slightly.

"You know how she is."

"I do. She'll want to come back here and start seeing how it's all going right away."

"She's been excited," Lachlan says with a small laugh.

"I'll have to apologize for being early."

"No, no, she'll love it."

Lachlan looks around and then gives us a small nod.

"See you back in the main house whenever you're ready."

"Thank you."

When the door closes behind him, I notice Ellie slightly relax too.

"Everything okay?"

"Yes, it's just different. I'll be fine."

I wait to see if she'll elaborate further.

"If you're sure."

Ellie walks around the home and starts looking at everything. I pick up our bags to bring them into the bedroom we'll be using.

"I like this," Ellie says as she comes into the primary bedroom.

"It is a beautiful place to live."

"Charleston, I mean. It's all so picturesque."

I pause as I take in what she's saying. I hadn't considered that Ellie may want to leave Seattle one day.

"It is. I really need to visit Avery more often."

Ellie sits down on the bed and stares over at me. I see her mouth twitch, almost as if she's in debate about what she wants to say.

Normally, I would press her to express herself. Only, after all of the uneasiness about being at Avery's, I don't want to pressure her if she's not ready to share.

"Would you ever leave Seattle?" she finally asks.

I take a seat down beside her on the bed.

"I've thought about it."

Another lingering pause.

"And?"

I settle the palms of my hands on top of my knees.

"Seattle was never meant to be permanent for me. I met

Avery's dad, and he took me under his wing. Now, here I am, running his company. And..."

How do I explain the complexity of what I feel about it all? Did I originally see this path as the right one? Not initially. Now, I don't exactly know how I would do things differently. I don't have regrets, but I do wonder what else is in store.

Being in my forties isn't a death sentence. I still have a lot of life to live. It's just difficult to see how or why I would change it all.

"And I have. I don't know if I could. But that's a lot to unpack a different day."

She seems to understand without me needing to lay all of my cards out there today—Christmas Eve.

"Do you want to leave Seattle?" I have to ask.

If she did, everything would be different.

"No, I don't think so. I'm happy with where I'm at," she answers.

I try to study her expression to find the lie.

Her smile isn't reaching her eyes, and I don't see any true sign of happiness in that decision. There's more she's not sharing—a truth for a different day as well.

Maybe as we go, we'll figure it all out. One day, we'll tell each other our truths.

"Are you happy you still came with me here for Christmas?"

"I am."

She pauses.

"I am glad to be out of the snowstorm with you."

She bumps her shoulder into mine.

"It is a bit nicer, isn't it?" I tease.

We both look at each other and smile knowingly. While

it is nice to not be trapped on a mountain, the snowstorm was the catalyst for this relationship forming.

"HI!" Avery beams as we enter through the back door.

She rushes over and embraces Ellie first. Then she pulls back and keeps a hold of the tops of her shoulders.

"I am so happy to see you here."

"Thank you for having me. You have a beautiful home," Ellie says.

"And you," Avery replies, turning her attention to me.

Lachlan chuckles in the background.

"Come here," Avery says as she opens her arms wide.

"Hello, Avery," I drag out as I pull her into a hug.

We break apart, and I laugh.

"Oh, come on, we're only here for a few days. Don't give me a hard time."

"Well, that may be difficult. First, you barely return my calls, and then you are trapped on a mountain! But now, you've brought me Ellie, so you are forgiven," Avery teases.

"Happy to be of service," Ellie says with a laugh.

"Anyone want a drink?" Lachlan asks.

"I'd love one," I answer as I walk over to Lachlan.

"Let's head to the bar then."

"Are you okay?" I ask Ellie.

"Is she okay? You cannot be serious. She's with me. We'll be in the living room," Avery answers on her behalf.

Ellie raises her eyebrows, but I can see the shy smile.

"In that case, we'll bring drinks over to you ladies shortly."

"Thank you, Fisher," Ellie sing-songs as she's pulled by Avery toward the living room.

I catch up to Lachlan, who's already in the lounge-like area.

"Is this your work?" I ask as I watch him behind the wood-crafted bar. It's an architectural beauty.

"It is. I made a couple of bars for my friend Grayson and decided to do the same for the home. They were the largest projects I've done."

"How long does it take you?"

"Months, but it helps me decompress."

I nod as he slides over a whiskey, Lachlan's drink of choice. He knows I'm a fan of it as well.

"How has everything been going for you? Avery's non-profit has really taken off," I say.

"It has; I've been working on it with her for so many months. I'm glad it's going so well for her. It was important."

"I knew it would."

Lachlan pours two glasses of champagne and slides one over to me for Ellie. We leave the bar and head in the direction of the living room.

"Grayson and Harper should be over soon."

"What a small world."

"Fuck, right? I couldn't believe it. But it's good—the more the merrier."

Walking into the living room, the women barely notice our presence until we hand them their drinks.

"Thank you," Ellie says with another small smile.

"You boys get out of here. It's still girl-talk time," Avery instructs.

Lachlan and I laugh as we return to the lounge with the bar.

"No one else stopping by tonight?"

"No, tomorrow a few of our friends are going to be coming by. Grayson and Harper will be back too."

"No one is going to visit family?" I ask as I settle into a brown leather chair.

Lachlan's eyes go vacant, almost as if he's seen a ghost.

"No. Grayson, Harper, and I are from a small town outside of Boston. I'm sure we'll go back soon together."

I don't pry any further. I know there is something dark about Lachlan's past. Avery hasn't shared much, but I know it has to do with the death of a friend. Something that I'll let him hold onto in private.

We both drink from our whiskeys as we settle in.

"Hello?" A man's voice booms through the house.

"Fucker just lets himself in," Lachlan jokes.

"Grayson?"

"That's the one. I'll be right back."

I take another sip of my whiskey.

In the distance, I hear laughter between Lachlan, Grayson, Avery, Ellie, and who has to be Harper. I get up to go greet them too.

Coming around the hallway, I see Ellie is in a tight squeeze in Harper's arms.

"Harper," she barely breathes out.

Harper lets go and looks confused until she finds me.

Watching this group together makes me wish that this could be permanent. That we could have this year-round.

"Oh!" Harper chirps.

"Don't," Grayson tries to whisper.

Ellie looks up at him, confused.

"Don't what?" Ellie asks.

Grayson swipes a hand through his hair.

"I'm Grayson; I've heard a lot about you," he says as he walks the few steps toward me.

"Same as you. It's great to meet you both," I answer as we shake hands.

"And you must be Harper. Ellie speaks so highly of you," I say.

"She does, does she?" Harper says with a grin.

Ellie still has a confused look at this interaction.

"I'm so excited to meet you finally too. Daddy Fisher in the flesh!" Harper shouts with a laugh.

Grayson hangs his head back and sighs loudly.

Ellie's face pales.

"Harper!" she shrieks.

I laugh.

"Daddy Fisher?" I have to repeat.

"That's right. That's what we've called you for years," Harper teases.

I chuckle.

"Well, glad to meet you officially."

"Back at you..." Harper starts, and I know what's coming.

"Daddy Fisher," she repeats, almost in disbelief.

"Red," Grayson mumbles as Avery and Lachlan laugh in the background.

"ALRIGHT, let's go get the man another drink and you a beer. Anything for you, Harper?" Lachlan asks.

"White wine, please."

"White wine it is," Lachlan confirms.

Ellie pulls me to the side as Harper and Avery head into the kitchen. Avery pulls out prepared appetizers, and Harper starts to take off the coverings.

"I am so, so sorry about that," Ellie confesses.

I can feel the secondhand embarrassment.

"She's just having a good time. It's fine," I try to say reassuringly.

I caress the sides of her shoulders and let her sink into my touch.

"Daddy Fisher, though? Interesting," I whisper.

"I want to die." She groans.

"Don't be silly. It is a good one," I admit.

"You know how it is with the girls."

"It's fine. Why don't you join them, and I'll refill your champagne."

I take her flute from her hands and wait for her answer.

"I'll be out there then."

I smirk and give her a wink before heading to the bar where Lachlan and Grayson are.

In the lounge area, I see Lachlan behind the bar getting to work on the drinks.

"Another champagne for Ellie, please."

"I should bring Avery one too."

He pulls out a new flute and then the champagne, and Grayson sheepishly looks on.

"You knew it was coming from a mile away," I say to break the tension.

"All weekend, she's been Daddy Fisher this and Daddy Fisher that," he admits.

"I'll have to get the full story on the nickname eventually."

"I'm sure Harper will share it tonight," he says through a laugh.

"I look forward to it."

"There's never a dull moment around here," Lachlan says.

That's something that I want—a change from the mundane in Seattle.

SEVENTEEN

Ellie

"OKAY, SPILL," Avery whispers across the living room to me.

"She never spills," Harper chimes in.

"Hey now," I try to feign as if I'm offended.

I'm not really one to share the details of what's going on in my personal life, especially where Fisher is concerned. It was always such a pipe dream that anything would happen between the two of us that I still want to protect it.

We haven't even defined what it is we're doing, so what do I have to spill? I'd really like to know what the future will hold between us first.

"Well, I mean..." I stammer.

"Take your time," Avery tries to reassure me.

"Well, we spend all of our time together."

"You do," Avery comments.

"And I've felt this way about him for a long time. I just never thought he would feel the same way."

"And he clearly does," Avery adds.

Harper laughs right as the men enter the room.

"What's so funny?" Grayson asks.

"Oh nothing, Captain," Harper sing-songs.

Fisher hands me my champagne flute and gives me a skeptical gaze.

I mouth to him that everything's good. He gives me a wry smile and nods.

"Alright, I'm going to give the caterer a call. He should have been here by now to start with dinner prep," Lachlan adds.

He turns to Grayson and Fisher. "See you back in the lounge?"

The men agree and go their separate ways.

"I was nervous they were going to interrupt story time! Okay, we're ready," Avery says while getting cozy in her seat.

I can't help but smile.

"Well, Harper here convinced me to finally just admit my feelings. Being trapped in a cabin does help," I admit.

"And looked at what happened," Harper has to add.

"Well, we'll see. It's all so fresh, and we've been out of our normal comfort zones. We haven't exactly talked about what will happen when we go back to Seattle."

"You haven't?" Avery and Harper ask in unison.

I shake my head no.

"That doesn't mean anything though," Avery starts.

"Yeah, I mean, it is Christmas. You never know," Harper adds.

"I'm not worried about it. Seriously. We said we'll talk about it after Christmas."

"Exactly! Nothing to be worried about," Avery declares and pops up off her spot on the sofa.

"Who wants to come with me to the bar and get Lachlan to make us some festive drinks? I need something with cinnamon, cranberry, or something!" Avery says excitedly.

"Love that for us. Great idea," Harper says.

"Lead the way," I answer.

She starts clapping excitedly.

"The next few days are going to be so fun!" Avery chirps.

"Why does my liver hate me every time I come to Charleston?" I groan.

"Last time really worked out for me. Maybe it'll help you," Harper says with a laugh.

"Don't worry, I already thought there was something in the North Carolina air. I'm sure it's traveled here too."

"I have no idea what that means, but I love it," Harper says as she pulls at my arm.

THE DAY and night have gone by in such a blur. The ease of being with this group has been unmatched. I don't want to think about this being my reality because I just don't see how it's possible.

Fisher has his walls down around Grayson and Harper because of how close he is to Avery and Lachlan. It's nice to watch him like this—feeling calm and even personable, unlike his usual demeanor in Seattle. He doesn't get the opportunity to have this back there either, just relaxing with friends.

I know he must have friends there or something akin to that, but he spends so much time working I really haven't taken note of anyone significant during the years I've been his assistant.

When I asked him if he could see himself leaving Seattle, it felt like he wanted the answer to be yes, but then reality came crashing down.

What I do know is that I want to be with Fisher. I want this week to turn into a reality, one that means staying in Seattle and trying to make a life with this man there. I want that, and I'll do whatever it takes to be with him.

Fisher looks around the room, searching for me. I left to use the restroom and have been lingering in the hallway, watching everyone relaxing post-dinner.

He spots me and signals for me to come back and join them.

The way he's resting casually in his chair makes my heart flutter. This is a life. A possibility of what could be.

Why can't we be career driven and also have this type of comfort by being so close to the people we value and love? If only we could make that happen.

I walk up to him slowly. The sound of Christmas music plays loudly as Harper and Avery take turns picking out the music.

"Happy?" I ask.

"Very," Fisher answers.

"Good."

"Are you?"

"Very."

"Good."

We both grin.

"Alright, love birds. Who wants another Avery Christmas Cocktail?" Harper shouts.

"Is that what we're going with?" Lachlan teases.

"You made it for your lovely wife. I think so," Harper doubles down.

"Another round coming right up."

"I'll go with you," Grayson chimes in.

"Sit with me?" Fisher asks.

I look around to see where he's referencing.

"You're in an accent chair," I say.

"On my lap."

I raise my eyebrow.

"Isn't that a little risqué?"

"It's just my lap."

The way my whole body shivers when he uses his authoritative voice is entirely unfair. He knows that he just got to me.

"Don't be so smug."

He grins widely as I sit in his lap and lean into his shoulder.

"This is nice," I murmur.

"See."

"I like it here," I admit.

"I do too. We'll have to make more of an effort to do this."

I don't want to give away that this crumb of planning for the future has me swooning.

"Alright, you two, it's time to bake cookies for tomorrow! Fisher, go join the boys. Let us girls go pretend like we're really baking," Avery declares.

Fisher chuckles.

"Alright, Avery."

"Thank you very much."

"Back in Seattle, I want to keep you locked away for myself," Fisher murmurs into my ear.

"I like the sound of that."

"Then it's a plan."

"We do have work though," I say through a giggle.

"Don't remind me." He groans and gives me a small kiss on my cheek.

It's another sign that maybe this is real and just how things will be back in Seattle.

I get off his lap and head into the kitchen, where Avery and Harper are. Baking is not something I enjoy, or ever will, but I'll happily keep them company as I wait for another Avery Christmas Cocktail.

I'M DREAMING of Fisher's mouth on me. I have to be. I know there is a reason I should be waking up soon, but I just can't ruin this perfect dream.

In this dream, his tongue is lapping up my wetness, and my body is coming alive. I feel the buildup bubbling inside of me as I beg him for more.

Just keep going. I'm so close. I'm almost there.

"Be quiet, princess. I'm eating my breakfast," Fisher murmurs against my wetness.

"What?" I groggily respond.

I feel pressure being applied to the spot I love for him to touch. My hips naturally rock up and down.

"Fisher?" I whimper.

I twist in the bed as I start to come out of the fog-like state of not quite awake.

I look down to see that his head is beneath the sheets. I watch as it bobs up and down.

"Oh fuck," I moan out.

I continue to grind my hips into his mouth, and my face is beginning to flush as I eagerly chase my release.

Gripping at the pillows behind me, I revel in the feeling I know is inevitable.

"Right there. I'm so close," I say as I twist in the sheets.

"I know, princess. I know," he murmurs.

He applies more pressure with his tongue, finally setting me off into euphoria. I grab the pillow I've been holding onto and cover my face with it as I scream into the abyss.

Moments go by, and I toss it to the side where it was.

Well, good morning to me.

"Merry Christmas, my princess."

"Merry Christmas to me."

Fisher chuckles as he slides back up and lies next to me. Naturally, I roll over and into his arms, and he begins stroking the length of my arm resting on his chest.

"What a way to wake up." I pant, still out of breath.

"You liked it?"

"Um, I clearly loved it," I say with a small laugh.

He chuckles again.

Continuing to pant, I finally feel like I'm coming down from this unexpected high.

"I can't believe that's how you woke me up."

"Happy to do it again."

I lazily trace the lines of the tattoos on his chest and arms, one of my new favorite pastimes.

We let a few moments go by as my breathing steadies, both still awake as we rest comfortably in bed.

"I can't believe today is Christmas."

"Best Christmas I've ever had," he says.

"I doubt that," I retort.

"It's true. Nothing better than waking up beside you."

It is nice. It's perfect. Almost as if we're meant to do this every day for the rest of our lives.

The warmth of his body is like a security blanket I didn't know I needed.

My hand starts to dip down beneath the sheets.

"What are you doing?" he growls.

"Now it's my turn."

"You don't have to reciprocate."

I can see his chest rising and falling as my hand travels below the blanket and sheet.

"It makes me wet knowing I get to be the one to make you come," I admit.

I dip my hand underneath his waistband and find his hard cock, ready and weeping for me to play with it.

"Looks like you may be happy for me to reciprocate."

I grin, pleased with myself that I make this devilishly handsome man hard and wanting.

"I'd be a madman if I didn't love the feeling of your hand wrapped around my cock."

"I love that I make you feel this way," I murmur.

My hair starts to fall wildly around me as I pump up and down along the length of his shaft. My thumb plays with the head as pre-cum appears.

My panties already begin to get wet again. I love that I get to feel his cock come to life like this.

"Do you like this?" I whisper.

"I love the way you touch me."

"Let's see what my mouth can do then."

"Fuck, Ellie."

I dip down below the sheets and smirk before putting my head lower. My mouth instantly wraps around his shaft. I add my hand to it and start pumping in tandem.

Fisher grunts as he thrusts his cock deep into my mouth. I know he loves the way the warmth encases it.

I want to be his undoing.

I need to be the fix and the reason why he comes alive.

"That's it, princess." He groans as his hips buck upward.

"Suck my cock just like that."

I hum in response.

"God, I want to keep you," he murmurs.

I want that too, more than ever.

I pick up the pace and feel him getting close.

"I'm about to come."

I suck deeper and cup his balls. Slowly, I start to lightly massage them. Then suddenly, I feel him still.

The rush of his cum going deep into my throat is overwhelming.

"Is my princess going to swallow?"

I eagerly nod my head as his cum continues to fill my mouth.

I want to say, *I'll do whatever you want*, but that's a feeling I'll unpack a different day.

"MERRY CHRISTMAS," I shout, coming through the back door of the main house.

"Merry Christmas!" Avery shouts back.

The aroma of what has to be bacon, sausage, biscuits, and more wafts through the room.

"Whatever you're making smells fantastic."

"Thank you! Please relax. Breakfast will be ready soon. It'll be just the four of us this morning."

"Morning," Fisher greets as he comes in with our presents.

"Morning," Lachlan answers.

Lachlan is pouring coffee into four mugs in the kitchen. He finishes up and hands us each a cup.

"Please help yourself to however you like it best," Lachlan says, gesturing to the variety of milk, creamers, and sugars out on the counter.

"Thank you," Fisher and I both respond.

Fisher sets his mug down on the counter and then heads to the Christmas tree to add our presents to the mix. I get to work making our coffees the way we both like them.

"Merry Christmas," I say to Lachlan.

"Merry Christmas. It's a beautiful day, isn't it?"

"It is. I love the weather here."

"Just don't come in the summer," he says with a chuckle.

"It's brutal," Avery adds.

"Not like now," Lachlan finishes.

"No, this is beautiful," I say warmly.

"Alright, so who is ready for breakfast?" Avery cheerfully asks.

"Let me help," I offer.

"Thanks, girl."

Avery gets me to work right away, plating different dishes that she's prepared. Fisher offered to set the table. As I'm bringing dishes out to the table, I realize this is what Christmas is meant to be like.

I need to be better about going to visit my dad and sister. I can't waste the time we have with one another, not when it could be like this or even better.

***

"AVERY, YOU ARE A CULINARY GENIUS," I say.

Biscuits and gravy, fluffy scrambled eggs, and so much

more. I don't care how basic it might be to some, but these biscuits and gravy just changed my whole outlook on Southern food. I get the hype.

"Thank you. I was never like this. But there's something about being out here in this community that makes me want to try to get into all the clichés."

"Like making the best biscuits and gravy?" I offer.

"Exactly! I mean, it's not like Lachlan cares," she starts.

"Excuse me, wife, but I happen to also be a huge fan of your biscuits... and gravy."

Avery giggles into her mimosa.

"Alright, so who is ready to open a few presents?" Avery asks.

I managed to sneak one for Fisher undetected while we were shopping. I know he's going to be surprised when he sees it.

When we were in a leather goods store, we went in because of a travel bag he was eyeing. He debated if he should splurge on something like that for himself. I know he buys himself whatever he needs, no matter the cost, but this seemed like a want. Which is why I went back in and bought it.

"Here, this one is for you."

I hand Avery the gift, and she excitedly takes it. She starts to undo the gift wrapping eagerly.

She pulls out a framed plaque with her non-profit details listed.

"Lachlan helped us," I add in.

Avery studies it and then looks back and forth between me and Fisher.

"This is amazing," she says as she holds it against her chest.

She pulls it away and closely studies it.

"I told Lachlan the other day how much I wish I had focused on the small wins at the beginning of all of this. I can't believe you guys got this done so quickly."

Fisher and Avery have a silent exchange—one that I know has everything to do with how proud he is of what she has accomplished.

Avery was married to someone before Lachlan, whom Fisher didn't approve of. She ended up divorcing him around the same time she met Lachlan. They were always meant to be, Fisher said. I should have known then what a romantic Fisher was. There are a lot of small signs I feel like I missed while being in my own head about our strictly professional relationship.

"Us next. This is for both of you," Avery says as she hands us the package.

Fisher encourages me to open it.

It's small and paper-like. I'm curious about what Avery is bouncing in her seat proudly over.

I tear off the wrapping to find a printed-out paper that looks like a receipt. As I study it, I gasp as realization dawns on me. Tears start to prick, and Fisher takes the paper from my hands.

"Oh my god, I swear I thought this would be a good gift. I am so sorry," Avery says frantically.

"No, no. It is. Thank you, Avery. Thank you, Lachlan. This is perfect."

Fisher squeezes my thigh and gives me the reassurance that I need.

Avery got Fisher and me a one-week stay at the same mountain resort, the one we were just stranded in. It's for the same time next year.

I was overwhelmed with the thought that someone as close to Fisher as Avery is assumes that we'll still be together next year. That what's happening between us is more than just a holiday fling between two people who shouldn't be together.

"Sincerely. Thank you. Only hopefully, if we go back next year, we won't get trapped."

Everyone laughs.

Fisher hands Lachlan his gift from us, and I realize I'm in so deep here. Deeper than I even thought.

EIGHTEEN

Fisher

"I STILL CAN'T BELIEVE you went back for this," Fisher says in disbelief.

Back in the guest house, we're changing into new attire for Christmas dinner. Avery and Lachlan's friends are coming over, and it'll be our last night here in Charleston.

Originally, Ellie and I planned to spend one more night, but we thought it was best to get back to Seattle after checking our email. Work awaits, even though we both don't want to return to reality sooner than we had planned.

"You loved it," she says through a giggle.

Ellie's sorting through her new outfits that we purchased the other day.

"Go with the red dress; it'll be beautiful on you."

She turns around and blushes.

"Sold."

She pulls the dress off the hanger and tosses it onto the

nearby bed. She slips her shirt overhead and pulls down her shorts, leaving her in nothing but her bra and panties.

I inhale deeply. Seeing her like this will never get old.

How did I get so lucky to be who Ellie wants? It remains a goddamn mystery to me and probably always will.

"If we didn't have to get going," I muse.

She perks up and sees me watching her undress.

"If only." She sighs.

Ellie slips on the dress and heads back to the full-length mirror to examine it.

"Are you sure this is okay? It is chilly outside."

I consider her question.

"Wear the jacket you bought. It's only to go in and out of the house. Plus, I'll be there to keep you warm," I say with a waggle of eyebrows.

Ellie laughs as she sees me through the mirror.

"Speaking of gifts," she says.

Ellie goes to her Christmas gift and unboxes a matching diamond-encrusted watch.

"Will you help me clasp this?"

"Of course."

She hands me the watch, and I clasp it against her dainty wrist.

Holding onto it, I pull her to me. Ellie has to use her hand to brace herself on my chest.

"I thought you said we didn't have time," she whimpers.

"A kiss isn't going to take much time at all."

"I don't believe you for a second," she teases.

Ellie lifts up and places a gentle kiss on my mouth. I pull her into me as I wrap my arm around her waist.

She pulls back, and I see a twinkle in her eyes.

"I think you may be the one getting the bad ideas," I rasp.

"Me? Never," she says.

She leans up and presses another gentle kiss to my lips.

"You're perfect," I mutter.

"No, I'm not."

I lean my forehead down, and we stay like this for a moment.

"Want to try that again, princess?"

She grumbles and starts to pull away.

"I mean it. You're better than I imagined."

"Thank you."

Ellie presses another quick kiss to my lips. I watch as she busies herself with pretend last-minute tasks.

"Ready for Christmas dinner?" she asks as she fumbles with a bag.

I hadn't realized it, but Ellie has a hard time accepting compliments. I've noticed over this week that she gets bashful or wants to pull away anytime I pay her one. That's something that will have to change.

"Ready if you are."

"THIS IS ALL SO GORGEOUS," Ellie says to Avery.

Avery has her house transformed into a Christmas spectacular. I'm not sure how she managed to find the time to do all of this between breakfast and this evening, but it looks like we may be in the North Pole and not Charleston.

There are Santa statues, nutcrackers, candy canes, and more everywhere you look. Somehow, it doesn't look cheap or overdone. It's exactly right.

There were decorations already out, but nothing to this level.

"Thank you! I wanted something special for tonight," Avery says.

"She's right, this is wonderful. Well done," I agree.

"Thank you. I think Lachlan is with our friend Noah in the lounge."

"I'll head that way. Can I grab you ladies anything?"

"We need two Avery Christmas Cocktails!" Avery exclaims.

Ellie laughs at her enthusiasm.

"Two it is. I'll be right back."

I can't help but smile that I'm with the two most important women in my life, and they are both beaming on Christmas.

I place a kiss on top of Ellie's head before heading to find Lachlan.

I haven't met Noah yet, but I respect him for all of the work he did for Avery. Noah was Avery's divorce attorney when she was trying to leave her first husband. He was instrumental when it came to all of the ins and outs that she had to work through—outside of just the divorce. His team of legal experts came through and really helped her out.

Her ex-husband, Kevin, is currently in jail. Avery had discovered that he was cheating on her and began investigating. That's when she met Lachlan at her church. It was also when she found out that Kevin was in a money-laundering scheme with the head of the local church she attended. It was all so over-the-top.

His trial is meant to happen sometime next year, and there's no way he's getting out anytime soon with how many charges he has.

Turning down the hallway, I hear Lachlan's laughter.

"Merry Christmas," I say as I enter the lounge.

"It certainly is. Avery has made this place into Santa's workshop. Brilliant, isn't it?" Lachlan says as he shakes my hand.

"How could I forget, Christmas is your holiday too."

Lachlan chuckles and then takes a sip of his whiskey.

"That's right. Since I met Avery, at least."

I look over to see who Noah must be.

"Noah, Fisher Underwood. It's nice to finally meet you," I greet.

"You as well. Avery has talked so highly about you."

We shake hands, and he goes back to sipping his beer.

"You too. Who would have thought you all would have turned into friends?"

"Avery wasn't going to have it any other way." Lachlan chuckles.

"I can see that," I add.

"What can I get you to drink?"

"I'll take an old-fashioned. Avery and Ellie requested one of the cocktails you created last night. What's it called again? An Avery Christmas Cocktail?"

"What's that?" Noah asks.

"Maybe we should have come up with something more original, but we did have a few drinks at that point," Lachlan says.

"Indeed," I say.

Lachlan heads behind the bar to start making the cocktails.

"I'll share the recipe with you before you leave. Want me to make you one?" Lachlan asks Noah.

"I'll stick to the beer."

"Where are Grayson and Harper?" I ask.

"On the way. The car service was delayed." Lachlan sighs as he finishes up the drinks.

"It is the holidays," I say.

"Tis the season," Lachlan says with a grin, and I hum in response.

"Is Emily still coming?" Noah asks.

"She is, but I haven't gotten a recent update from Avery on where she is."

"Is she bringing the new guy?" Noah asks.

"Doubtful. No one has met him. He's a big fucking mystery," Lachlan answers as he slides my drink over to me.

I take a meaningful sip and place it down on a coaster. Lachlan slides the other two cocktails next to mine.

"I'll take these drinks to the girls," I say.

"Thanks, man," Lachlan answers.

Picking up the two drinks, I head back to the main living room and kitchen space. Avery had tonight catered, but I'm sure they have to be somewhere over there still.

"Wait, are you serious?" I hear Avery whispering.

I pause in the hallway.

"Please don't say anything," Ellie whispers back.

"I won't, of course not. That is yours to share."

"Thank you," Ellie says, sounding relieved.

What did she tell Avery that she hasn't shared with me? It's not like they are friends, really.

I wait to see what else is being shared.

"I have to ask," Avery starts.

I feel as though she's looking around so no one else hears.

Fuck, and here I am, hiding in the hallway, listening in, exactly what I shouldn't be doing right now. I should be giving them privacy to have this conversation, yet I can't walk away.

"Go ahead," Ellie offers.

"Why not see what would happen if you did?"

"It's not important to me. It's something that was an option, but things are different now. I really am happy with my decision."

I can feel the weight of the pause in the air.

"That's all that matters."

I start walking toward them and do a fake cough to alert them of my presence.

Whatever the secret is, Ellie is happy with her decision. That's all that matters. Part of me wants to bring it up immediately, but I won't do that. If Ellie wants me to know, she'll tell me. If anything, I hope she knows that she can come to me and that I would be here for her no matter what the issue may be.

Rounding the corner, I hold the two cocktails in the air.

"Two Avery Christmas Cocktails," I announce.

"Thank you!" Avery exclaims.

"Thank you," Ellie says sweetly as she takes the drink from my hand, and Avery takes hers as well.

"These are still so good. I'm so glad they were created last night. A new Christmas tradition!"

Ellie laughs as she takes a sip of her drink.

"Everything okay?" I ask Ellie softly, rubbing my hand down the length of her back. I want her to feel comfortable with me about anything that may arise.

She frowns before collecting herself.

"Everything is perfect."

She smiles up at me. I know it's genuine, at least.

"Okay, if it's not, you can talk to me."

The doorbell rings.

"Don't worry, I know."

We both turn our attention toward the front door.

"Who knows who this will be! I'll be right back," Avery shouts.

It gives Ellie the needed opportunity to go back into her poised mode. Then, we hear an unknown woman's voice mixed with Avery's.

"That must be her friend, Emily," Ellie says.

"I haven't met her before."

"Oh, okay. How was meeting Noah?"

"He's nice. You'll have to come meet him. When you're done with this one, why don't you come join me in there?"

She gives me a small nod.

"Fisher, Ellie, this is my dear friend, Emily," Avery announces as she rounds the corner with her friend in tow.

Ellie and I both introduce ourselves, and the women all settle on the sofa.

"Emily, can I get you a drink?" Avery asks.

"No, thank you. I have to head to a friend's house after this."

Avery sighs.

"We still can't know who he is?"

"Not yet," Emily says with a shake of her head.

"Alright, you can keep your secrets for now."

Avery looks up at me still lingering.

"Fisher, why don't you be the best and get Lachlan and Noah?"

"Can do."

Emily's face looks flushed.

"Noah's here?" she stammers.

"He is! It's been ages since the two of you have seen each other, right?" Avery asks.

"It has," Emily weakly answers.

"Isn't it a small world? Noah and Emily grew up together," Avery shares.

"That is. And you aren't friendly anymore?" Ellie asks.

She must be getting the same feeling from the way Emily reacted.

"Oh no, of course we are. Just busy," Emily quickly adds.

"I'll be back out," I say, and Emily smiles weakly.

I walk back down the same hallway to the lounge. As I'm walking, I hear the door open and Grayson and Harper's voices in the distance.

Everyone's here.

"Emily, Grayson, and Harper all just arrived," I share as I reenter the lounge.

Noah and Lachlan both perk up.

"Let's head out there," Lachlan says.

I nod and head back to where I came from.

"Look who it is, Daddy Fisher," Harper teases as she watches me come into the room.

"Merry Christmas, Harper. Grayson," I say with a chuckle.

Harper walks over and pulls me into a hug. Grayson follows behind her and shakes my hand.

"Where's Emily?" Lachlan asks as he searches the room.

"Oh, she had to run off; she was just stopping by," Avery answers.

"Oh, okay," Lachlan responds.

I look over to Noah, who is fidgeting with his watch.

Is it possible no one else knows that something is going on between these two? Ellie glances over to me with the same taken-aback expression.

"Alright, I'm going to get the hors d'oeuvres ready! Please, everyone, take a seat. Lachlan, if you can set the vibe and handle any more drinks?"

"On it."

They both go their separate ways, and I see a sheen of sweat on Noah's forehead.

"THAT WAS FUN," Ellie whispers into my chest.

We're cuddling in our bedroom.

The rest of the night went off without a hitch. It's probably the best Christmas I've experienced in a while, possibly ever.

"I'm glad I had you with me here."

I kiss the side of her hair.

"Thank you, Fisher. This week has been the best of my life. I can't believe what's been happening, but I'm so glad for what we have."

"I am too, princess."

She snuggles closer into me as I rub the outside of her back.

"Ellie?"

She hums.

"When we're back in Seattle, I want you to stay with me."

"What do you mean?"

"Let's keep exploring what this is. I don't want this to become nothing. You're far too important to me. Stay with me through New Year's so we can get to know each other more."

I can feel her smile against my chest.

"I would like that. A lot. I'm not done with you yet either."

"Then it's settled. I'll send someone to fetch some of your belongings and bring them over for us."

"You know, I could do that."

"I want you to myself, so let me have someone else do it for you."

"It's going to take some getting used to."

"Someone taking care of you?"

"Yes, it's not easy when I'm used to being in control."

"You still are. I want to do nice things for you because it makes me happy to see you happy."

NINETEEN

Ellie

"GOOD MORNING, Mr. Underwood and Ms. Robertson. I'm Mia, and I'll be your flight attendant today," Mia greets us as we walk onto the private plane.

"Good morning," Fisher curtly responds.

I give her a small smile, and she gives me a sweet look back. Her eyes travel the length of my body, causing me to pause. Mia must notice because her eyes widen before she focuses on Fisher and away from me.

Fisher isn't one to look at attractive women when he's with me. I've realized that now; however, Mia is breathtaking. She looks like a doll come to life, and even I can appreciate her appearance.

I search his face, and there is no sign of whether he's really noticed Mia at all. We both walk past her and settle into seats right next to one another.

Less than two weeks ago, I was debating uprooting my whole life for a job opportunity without ever confessing how I felt to Fisher. Now, I'm returning from a holiday vacation with him to spend more time together. We'll be bringing in the new year and deciding if we want to continue. I'm confident we will and then can determine how we want to share it with everyone else we know in Seattle.

I do know that I eventually have to talk to Fisher about my career. I just don't want it to come across as something I'm expecting now that we are exploring a relationship together. We've had some serious conversations, but they all have danced around the reality of our situation.

Last night, when Fisher asked if I was willing to stay with him at his home, it was another confession that we still are treading lightly with what's happening between us. I'm not sure whether it's because he's unsure about how it'll be perceived or because he's nervous about me not wanting to make this permanent.

Being snowed in and then having a magical long weekend together isn't exactly what life would be like for us. We both work too hard and into the night far too frequently. Usually, it's because we have the other one there. That won't always be the case. Everything has to evolve, including our professional relationship.

Change is natural. It's a way to keep working on yourself and your goals. Hopefully, that's what's in store and not our demise.

"Everything okay?" Fisher asks as he reaches for my hand across the armrests.

"Yes, just thinking about the clients I'll have to reach out to again," I lie.

Now is not the time to unpack what I've been thinking about. Although, I probably should be thinking about the clients.

"After New Year's. No one is worried about the retreat."

"True."

I stare out the window and realize I need to get out of my head.

"Can I get either of you anything?" Mia asks.

"I'll take an espresso," Fisher answers.

"Water is fine for me, thank you."

Mia gives me a wide smile as she nods.

"I'll be right back," she says.

"No coffee today?" Fisher asks.

"No, I'm good, for now at least. It is a long flight."

Fisher's eyes darken, and I see a wicked gleam appear. He smirks as realization dawns on me.

I rear my head back and shake it.

"Oh no," I start.

A mischievous look fully takes over.

"We can't!" I squeal.

He looks down at me.

"Why is that?" he rasps.

Mia brings over the coffee and water before heading back to the galley.

"Mia, for one."

I mean, she is a whole other person on this plane with us. It's unavoidable.

"Works for me."

I give him a pointed stare, and his grin widens.

"And so do I."

Fisher gives a small shrug.

"Fine, but we can't with Mia around."

He smirks. The man is a smirker now. What have the Carolinas done to this man?

He reaches up and hits the button for Mia, and she comes over quickly from the galley.

"Is everything okay?" she asks hesitantly.

"Ms. Robertson and I need privacy for the next hour or so to review confidential materials."

Mia licks her lips and nods. It's almost as if she knows what he has planned.

I'm sure as a flight attendant for private aircraft, she gets this all the time, but it's still somewhat embarrassing to be part of.

I don't normally do things like this. Fisher has a way of getting me to do things that I want but don't feel like I should do.

"Of course. I'll be in the galley if you need anything."

"Thank you for your discretion."

Mia scurries away, and without looking back at us, she closes the curtain to the galley.

Well, looks like this is definitely not Mia's first time hearing this request.

"Problem solved," Fisher says nonchalantly.

"Don't be so smug," I huff out.

He cocks his head to the side, and a lopsided grin appears. Then he pulls off his glasses, sets them on the table across the way, and methodically rolls up his sleeves.

A dirty tactic. He knows I'll do whatever he wants like this.

I stay firm in my resolve, crossing my legs and folding my arms across my chest. I stay put. It's difficult to stop my body from squirming in my seat, but I think I'm mostly accomplishing it.

Fisher gets up from his seat and stands with his hands on his hips.

"Yes?" I ask.

"I see someone is feeling a bit bratty again."

I roll my eyes and bite down on my lower lip. Okay,

maybe I am; maybe I do like this side of our newly founded dynamic.

"Up," he commands. My body instantly replies, and I do what he says.

"Turn around."

I huff more, but I do that too.

Fisher's hands softly caress down the center of my back.

"I like this," he rasps, and my body shivers in response.

"I like that too," he murmurs.

I'm too relaxed with him like this. It's so easy to give myself over to him. I like the way he controls my body, but more than that, I want it. I need someone like Fisher to finally give me the chance to relax and not feel like I need to be so in control of everything.

"I like it too," I whisper.

"I know you do. Now, are you going to be my good girl and do as I say?"

I nod up and down eagerly.

"Take this off."

Immediately, I pull up my sweater and toss it to the side.

"Jeans too."

Reaching down, I pull my jeans off and put them in the same pile with my sweater. Having my clothes taken off and tossed aside is starting to become a recurring theme.

"Lean forward."

I bend over and place both of my hands on the top of the seat. As soon as I do, I feel Fisher's hands roaming all over. He places small kisses down the center of my back as he begins to massage my breasts. His hands travel to the back of my bra, where he unclasps it.

"Adding it to the pile too?" I taunt.

"It's not the last addition," he gives right back to me, so I pretend to pout.

"I thought you were going to be my good girl, princess, or are we still feeling needy?"

Wetness is pooling low. I do feel needy all over my body, and he's barely touched me.

Fisher's chest is against my back as I resume my original position with my hands on the airplane seat.

He roughly pulls at my breasts and begins massaging them together. I moan as he begins plucking at my nipples, and my thighs instantly go together to try and get any relief.

"Tell me, which are you going to be?"

I huff.

Fisher starts to remove his hands from my chest.

"Wait! Wait."

I sigh.

"I'll be... good."

He laughs darkly.

"Spread your legs apart."

I do immediately, and his hand dips low beneath the front of my thong.

"Already dripping wet for me."

"Yes." I moan.

Fisher's palm begins roughly caressing my ache. He's barely gotten started, but my body has already become accustomed to his touch. The way he knows what to do to make me come quickly is frightening.

He removes his hand, and I feel the loss immediately. Gripping both sides of my hips, he pulls down my panties and lets them fall around my feet.

Right then, I hear a noise coming from the back of the plane.

"Does the thought of Mia seeing you bent over the seat

for me turn you on or frighten you?" he whispers into my ear.

The way his breath lingers goes right down to my core.

I bite my lip, not wanting to tell the truth.

"Tell me, princess, if Mia came out here and saw my cock deep inside of you, would you want that?"

I hear Fisher undoing his belt buckle, followed by the sound of his pants and boxer briefs coming down.

"Fisher..."

"Did you see the way she looked at you?" he asks.

"She was interested in you."

He chuckles. "I don't think so, princess. Her eyes roamed every inch of you."

Looking back around, I lick my lips as my eyes see Fisher rubbing the length of his cock.

"I don't think so..."

Fisher's eyes darken as I watch on.

"Play with yourself. Get your pussy nice and ready to take me."

I move my hand to start rubbing myself as I watch him continue to stroke his cock.

"Face forward," he commands, and I do as he says.

He grips my hip, and slowly, the intrusion starts. I feel his cock stretching me apart as he inches inside.

"You're doing so well for me, princess."

I moan loudly.

"Fuck, I need more," I whisper.

"Should we invite Mia in here to see you like this? I bet her pussy would be drenched after hearing the way you're begging for my cock."

Fisher begins thrusting repeatedly into me. I try to stifle my moans but can't contain them.

"Bend down lower," he whispers, and I do as he says once again.

Realization dawns on me. Technically, I'm not visible to anyone but Fisher right now, and his dress shirt is still on.

"Tell me, princess. Do you want her to see you come undone?"

I debate what I want and what it feels like I should do. In normal society, people don't just invite flight attendants over to watch them being taken by their boss.

"Yes," I admit.

"Ellie, you can let go with me. Don't be afraid to ask me for what you want."

Another thrust.

"I won't."

I'm learning that maybe there is another side to myself I never realized I had in me.

"Remember, this is all about you. You want to stop? We stop."

"I want her to watch if she wants to."

Fisher continues to ram his cock deeper inside, and my breasts are bouncing wildly from this angle.

"Mia?" Fisher calls out.

"Yes, Mr. Underwood? How can I be of service?" Her voice comes out huskier than earlier. Maybe she has been listening in and likes what she was hearing.

"Mia, I need you to be truthful with me. I don't want to put you in an uncomfortable position."

Only the sound of Fisher's cock pulling in and out of me sounds throughout the plane.

"You could never make me feel uncomfortable, sir," Mia answers.

"Do you find Ms. Robertson attractive?"

Another pause.

"Yes," she says confidently back.

"If I were to tell you I'm deep inside of her wet pussy, how would that make you feel?"

Another pause.

"Turned on."

I gasp.

"Would you be interested in watching Ms. Robertson being fucked right now?"

The sound of the curtain whipping open catches my attention.

Fisher stills.

"I'd be very interested, Mr. Underwood."

I pop my head up and hold onto the original spot I was gripping earlier.

"Hi," I chirp.

"Hi," Mia says with a wide smile.

She walks to us, and I see a gleam in her eyes.

"Mia, this is all new for me, but I want to make sure you know you don't have to participate, watch, whatever," I stumble.

"Ms. Robertson, I'd love to watch you. You're gorgeous."

"Ellie. Please call me Ellie."

"Ellie, if I may, you have perfect tits."

I gasp as Fisher starts to thrust.

"Is it okay with you both if I sit down?" she asks.

"Play with yourself, Mia. You're a voyeur, aren't you?"

She begins to sit down in a nearby seat. Watching as she nods her head in confirmation is a turn-on.

"I am. I love to watch."

Fisher leans down against my back.

"Don't be shy, princess. Show her what these pretty tits look like as they bounce while my cock is buried deep inside of you."

I groan as I move my position.

"Fuck," I moan out.

Fisher grips my hips and continues to thrust hard into me, harder than before.

Mia may like to watch, but I'm learning I like to put on a show.

MIA HANDS me her signed NDA and gives me a flirty wink.

"Any flight you want me on, please feel free to request me."

"We will."

Small talk with a stranger who just watched me have sex for an hour and then continue to operate as normal is a strange experience. I know I'm not acting naturally. Mia is acting indifferent, like that happens all the time.

Walking off the flight hand in hand with Fisher, I feel as if I was just born anew. I can't believe I did that.

Time with Fisher feels like a fever dream.

I don't come undone.

I don't get called brat and princess.

I don't let pretty flight attendants watch me being fucked by my boss.

I'm polished.

I'm together.

I'm focused.

"Are you okay with what happened?" Fisher asks.

The chauffeur opens the car door, and I slide in.

"I don't know what it is you're doing to me, but yes, I liked it. No regrets."

"Good. I just want you to feel free to be yourself. What-ever that means."

"I know."

"I'm making you feel safe, and you're breaking open my heart, see? We're both coming to life," he says.

His play at trying to make this lighthearted is the truth. We're becoming each other's undoing. Only I think I like seeing us both come a little undone because of the other.

"Where to?" I ask.

"Back home. With me. Unless you've changed your mind?"

I see the hesitation. What happened on the plane was unexpected, but it hasn't made me change my mind about Fisher. If anything, it makes me trust him even more.

"I can't wait."

I lean against his shoulder and shut my eyes.

While I don't know what's going to happen from here, what I do know is that there is no going back. I like this new me that's emerging. I just hope it's with Fisher by my side for good.

"Darin, take us to the penthouse, please."

"Will do, sir," he says and puts up the privacy screen.

Fisher squeezes my thigh, and I like the way his hand looks on top of me. I'm becoming needy for his touch at all times. Work is going to be impossible if we keep at it like this.

"What do you say?" he whispers.

"Oh no, no, you don't," I say through a laugh.

"Darin can't see or hear anything," he counters.

"Nope. Keep your hands to yourself until we get to your place."

I playfully remove his hand from my thigh and place it

on his, already wishing I didn't because I long for his warmth.

"We'll always play by your rules... for now."

TWENTY

Fisher

LETTY GREETS Ellie and me as we walk through the door. She's not surprised at all when I tell her that Ellie will be staying at the penthouse. Somehow, I think Ellie and I were the last ones to catch up with the way the other person feels about the other.

I grip Ellie's hand tightly as I lead her to my bedroom.

As I go to open the door, she breaks away. I study her expression to try and gauge how she's feeling about this.

"Darin will be back with the list of belongings you asked for. Anything else, we can go by your place during the week to pick up."

She nods her head as she continues to explore the room.

"I've always wondered what your bedroom would be like," she murmurs.

She looks around the space, and I do the same to take it in from her perspective. Everything is black and sleek. I don't like chaos, and a room should be the most orderly place in the house. It's meant to be used for sex and sleep, that's all. Having piles of extras disturbs that peace that I relish.

"It's very..." she starts.

I cock my eyebrow and wait. This should be interesting.

"Clean," she finishes.

"It's a bedroom," I retort.

That elicits a small smile as she runs her hand along my bedspread.

"It's very you."

I chuckle.

"I'm not sure how to take that."

She stops at the foot of the bed and smiles widely.

"You may have let your guard down in wonderland, but this is very you. I like it. Maybe a little dark," she teases.

I walk over to where she is.

"But I like that it feels like I'm in your secret space."

Leaning up on her tiptoes, she presses a small kiss to my lips.

"Well, now that you have me here, what do you plan to do with me?"

My hands tangle in her hair, and I pull it back, keeping her steady in my arms. Leaning down, I start to nip at her neck, then lick the same spot to soften the sting. I've come to learn that she loves when I do this.

Ellie's hands start to go for my belt buckle, but I stop her from continuing and place a small kiss to her ear.

"If you're mine, that means I need to take care of you in all ways. Tonight, we eat and rest," I whisper.

"Fisher."

"I mean it. Tomorrow is a different story."

Ellie sighs loudly.

"What about wanting to have sex in the car?"

I chuckle.

"Tomorrow."

"Fine," she whines.

I watch as disappointment washes over her expression. She tries to collect herself, but it's not working, not when I've been getting to know this side of her in the Carolinas.

"Don't be disappointed."

"I'm not. This is all just new to me, remember?"

"That's why you have *me*."

I do remember. All of her ex-boyfriends didn't know how to treat someone like Ellie, and that includes my son. They didn't see what she needed to be fulfilled or when she needed someone to simply take care of her instead of putting their wants first.

What my girl wants is to be taken seriously and climb the corporate ladder while also being treated softly and with care. For someone to understand what mood she's in and to give her what she needs for it.

It's been a long and unexpected travel day. Tonight is for care.

I lead Ellie out to the dining area. The new chef Letty found is preparing dinner in the distance.

"What's on the menu tonight?" I ask Letty.

"Chef Diego is making Ms. Robertson's favorites this evening to welcome her to the house."

"What?" Ellie asks, startled.

"Tomato soup, a lovely chicken alfredo pasta, and cheesecake for dessert."

Ellie's head goes back in alarm, and she looks back and forth between Letty and me in confusion.

It's cute the way she's surprised that everyone on my staff already knows what she likes. She's been here time and time again. Like I said, everyone had to have known how special she was to me even before this.

"Nice touch, Letty. Thank you," I say.

Ellie still looks shocked as she takes a seat at the dining room table.

"Is red wine okay with you both this evening?"

Ellie doesn't respond.

"Ellie?"

She shakes her head and comes out of the fog-like state.

"Yes. That would be lovely. Thank you."

"I'll be right back," Letty says before disappearing.

"Fisher..."

"Yes?"

"How does Chef Diego know what my favorite foods are?"

"Everyone on my team is the best at what they do. It makes perfect sense that Letty would have picked up on what you like throughout the years."

"Yes, I suppose that's a good point."

"And when I informed Letty that you would be staying with me, she also had to have picked up on what that implied."

"Yes, that makes sense..."

"If anything is ever overwhelming to you, just say the word. You know that this is what my life is like back here. I don't have time for anyone to not be able to do their jobs effectively."

She finally focuses on me.

"It's not overwhelming, it's just unexpected."

Letty returns with a bottle of my favorite red wine and pours us each a glass.

"Thank you," I say.

"I'll be back out. Should I leave this here?" Letty asks as she holds the wine bottle out.

"That would be great."

Letty nods and sets it down, then heads back into the kitchen where Chef Diego is preparing the soup.

"Fisher, I have to ask. I can't take the suspense anymore."

"What's wrong?"

Ellie takes a deep breath and straightens her shoulders back. Conviction is the only thing swirling in her eyes. This is the Ellie I'm all too familiar with and see on a daily basis.

"What is it that we're doing, exactly?"

"Having dinner?"

"Don't act like you don't know what I'm really asking."

My eyes shoot back in confusion, and she sighs.

"I can't keep dragging this out week by week. Are we trying to be together, officially? Is this real, or is this just some game?"

"You aren't a game to me."

"Then tell me."

"I want you as mine. I thought I'd made that clear."

"No, I mean, not really. Right now, we are exploring what happens until New Year's week. I don't know if I can keep doing this without the commitment that it could be real one day."

"I see."

"Do you?"

I get up from my seat and walk over to where she sits. Crouching down, I come face-to-face with the woman who has stolen my heart and needs to hear me say it once and for all.

"I want you, Ellie. I want you here in my home. I want you at work. I want you always. If you need to hear me say it again, I will. I want you. I intend to give this a real shot. I know we have a lot to work through, and you and I both know what that is."

She nods and reaches out for my hands.

"I want you to be it for me. Do you feel the same?" I ask.

"Yes. This is what I've wanted for a long time. I just needed to hear you tell me we're on the same page. That this isn't just a fling to you."

I crush my mouth to her supple lips. My tongue demands entry, which is immediately granted. Biting down on her lower lip roughly, I taste a sweet tang of copper. I lick the wound immediately before consuming her mouth once more.

Ellie steadies herself by wrapping her arms around my neck, encouraging me to keep going.

The sound of dishes being set down breaks us out of our trance.

"Soup is served," Letty says, and then the sound of her footsteps leaving follows.

"We're going to have to be more discreet," Ellie pants out.

Our foreheads are touching one another as we come back to reality.

"Letty is discreet. Don't mind her presence."

"We'll see. But for now, I think we should get to this soup," she says through ragged breath.

"Right. I believe I was the one to say tonight was for care."

"I'LL HEAD IN FIRST," Ellie says.

"Your car isn't here."

"Well, we surely can't go in together."

"Why not? We have before."

Ellie and I are in the back of my car, about to pull into the office.

"It's different now."

I wait for her to collect her thoughts.

"I don't want anyone to think I get special treatment because we are in a relationship."

Special treatment. Of course, I hadn't thought about that.

"Fine. Darin will park in the garage. You can get out first, and I'll follow a few minutes later. Remember, we're the only two usually in this early."

She relaxes slightly in her seat.

"Thank you."

I lower the divider between Darin and us.

"Darin, park in the garage. Ms. Robertson will be getting out ahead of me."

"Can do, sir."

Darin rounds the final block to the office and pulls into the parking garage, taking my spot. Not as discreet as I'm sure Ellie would have wanted, but it is what it is.

"I'll see you up there," she says.

"Don't I get a kiss goodbye?"

She gives me a pointed look and then relents. With a roll of her eyes, I see the spark coming through.

"See you up there," she repeats as she leans in to give me a chaste kiss on the lips.

Ellie pulls away and hops out of the car quickly, and I watch as she heads toward the elevator bank.

This is going to get tricky.

I've meant every word I said to her, but working together is going to be more challenging than I imagined it would be. All I want to do is kiss her all day long.

"Heading in, Darin. I'll call for tonight."

"Have a good day, sir."

I HEAD into the office through the same bank of elevators and winding hallways. Ellie is seated at her desk in front of my office, already working.

"Good morning, Mr. Underwood."

"Good morning, Ellie."

"I'm preparing the follow-up for the retreat. I've also scheduled a debrief for today to share. You are free after lunch. Does that work?"

She finally looks up at me through her long eyelashes and bats them as if nothing is different. I hate this feeling. She's not just my assistant anymore.

"Cancel whatever I had before lunch and plan to see me then. If you can order us lunch, we can work through it."

"Well, sir, your eleven a.m. is actually with Doug. He already sent me an email this morning confirming it and saying it was of priority."

Doug. Perfect timing.

"Working lunch then."

"Your nine a.m. confirmed and should be here shortly. Coffee is waiting on your desk."

"Thank you."

She turns her attention back to her computer and acts like everything is as it was prior to the retreat.

Shutting my office door behind me, I already want this day to be over with if this is how she's going to act.

Professional.

I don't think I'm a fan of the term any longer.

A KNOCK on my door interrupts me from the figures I've been working through all morning. Since being back, there are new projections for the first quarter.

The numbers show it will be a great start to the year. We're finalizing the end-of-year financials, too, but I still have to sift through those.

Another knock on the door.

"What is it?" I shout.

"Doug is here to see you," Ellie says through the door.

I didn't mean to come across as rude. I know Ellie can handle my demeanor, but I don't want it to cause any issues between us as our relationship continues to evolve.

Thankfully, Doug is here to follow up with me on Ellie and the new role he's desperate to have her fill.

"Send him in."

The door opens seconds later, and Doug comes through it, walking more casually than normal.

"What has you in a good mood?" I ask, perplexed.

"Well, I've come here hoping we can finally tell her the news."

I tent my fingers against my mouth pensively.

"It's time. She's ready for the next step, and it's the new year."

I can tell he's been prepping this whole situation for days, from his casual exterior to the pleading tone. He's right, though, regardless.

"I know."

"And I need her. You know the team needs her. I'm

spread so thin, and everyone I've interviewed isn't as good as she is."

"You're right."

Doug looks confused that I've given in so easily. The truth of the matter is that he *is* right. I've been trying to keep her for myself, but it's best for her career and our relationship if I simply let her take this new role.

I pick up the office phone and dial her extension.

"Mr. Underwood?" she asks hesitantly.

"Please join Doug and me in my office."

"Can do."

The line clicks, and I replace the phone right as she comes through the doorway.

Ellie lingers there, and I can see she's anxious since this is unplanned.

"Is there something I can help you with?" she asks as she holds her hands in front of her and waits.

"Yes, please join us. Take a seat."

Ellie takes the empty seat next to Doug in front of my desk. I wait until she's settled in to continue, then give a slight nod in Doug's direction.

"Doug, would you like to be the one to do the honors?"

"Of course."

Doug turns to face Ellie.

"Fisher and I have been discussing this for a long time. We both think you have a lot of potential. You've done so much for the organization and know the ins and outs better than almost anyone."

"Thank you," she replies.

I can tell she's nervous but is trying to stay composed. Playing it cool is the way to go, and she's succeeding.

"It's time," I say.

Ellie shoots her head in my direction, and her mouth parts as she stares at me, confused.

"I'd like to offer you the open operations manager role on my team. You have the experience and knowledge. It's yours."

Ellie looks flabbergasted as she goes back and forth between the two of us.

"You want this?" she asks me.

I laugh casually.

"No. I don't. But Doug here has been asking me about it for weeks, and he's right. You can't be my assistant forever; you want more growth. This is your opportunity. Doug here can meet with you to go over the role, pay, and those details."

"We can head over to my office?" Doug offers.

"Thank you. Yes! I'm excited for the opportunity." Ellie beams.

"Now remember, Doug, I get two more weeks with her here."

"Don't worry, sir. I know."

Ellie's smile is contagious as she sits, waiting for the next step. Doug gets up from his seat and gestures to the door.

"Ready when you are."

"I'm ready."

TWENTY-ONE

Ellie

"I CAN'T BELIEVE how this week has gone," I say.

He's holding me tightly as we cuddle in bed.

"You deserve it," he murmurs against my hair while my nails dance along the lines of his tattoos.

I sigh happily at the new routine we've gotten into.

This past week at work went by in a whirlwind. I never expected that a promotion was in the works. Part of me did wonder if the story was true about them talking about it for weeks, but I know Fisher wouldn't lie to me about it.

Then there's Doug. I know he's needed someone in the role. Doug looked like the weight of the world was lifted off his shoulders when I accepted.

I already was going to email the recruiter at Troy Medical Company to tell her that I wasn't going to take the offer in Charleston, but this made the decision icing on the cake. I get the man of my dreams and a promotion.

"What do you want to do today?" Fisher asks.

"You mean, you don't want to go into work on a Saturday?" I tease.

"Not anymore."

"I like that."

He kisses the top of my head and continues to stroke my back.

"I do have an idea if you're up for it," he says.

"What's that?"

I perk up and lean my head in my hand.

"Tomorrow is New Year's Eve, and the office is closed Monday."

"Yes," I cautiously acknowledge.

"Up for an adventure?" he asks with a sly grin.

"Always."

He chuckles.

"Get dressed and pack your bags for the cold. I'm going to make a quick call."

"You aren't going to tell me where we're off to?"

"No, princess. I'm going to surprise you."

He gives me a flirty wink before hopping out of bed. Grabbing his cell phone on his way, he leaves the bedroom and closes the door behind him.

"I wonder what he's up to," I mutter.

I hop out of bed and turn on the shower.

Scrolling through my cell phone, it rings. It's Harper.

"Hi there," I answer.

I test the water temperature. It's too cold for me to get in so soon.

"Why, hello there, I haven't heard from you in days," she says.

"Well, I think I have good reason. You know, with my entire life changing," I say with a laugh, and she joins in.

It's true. Everything is finally happening.

"What else has been happening?"

"Well, Fisher and I are officially in a relationship. He wants to see where this will go."

"That's great. I know how much you wanted this."

I can sense the hesitation in her tone.

"Yeah, it really is great. Oh! I got a promotion. And not because of this Fisher situation," I add.

"Really? I'm so happy for you! What is it?"

"Operations manager. I think I've told you about Doug, right? He's the one who quizzes me on what's happening all the time. Turns out he's been asking Fisher if he could offer me the role for weeks."

"And you aren't upset he just agreed to it?"

"I don't know if that's the case, but no, I'm not. I've been planning the retreat. It wouldn't have been good timing for me to switch roles."

"I'm really happy for you."

I pause.

"But what?"

"I just want to make sure this is all really what you want. I know you and Fisher have been inseparable, but I thought you really wanted to move away from Seattle. Won't this prevent you from doing that in the future?"

"I do. It's not set in stone. It's just for now."

"Have you told him that?"

"Not exactly. I promise we're on the same page. I want all of this."

"Just remember, if you aren't honest with yourself, you can't be honest with him. You never know how he'll feel unless you can do that."

I'm getting annoyed by what she's implying. Getting this promotion and being with Fisher is everything coming together.

"I have to run. Fisher is taking me on a surprise trip for New Year's," I snap.

"I'm not trying to hurt your feelings. Just be careful and make sure you are doing what's right for you."

"Thank you, but I know what I'm doing. I really have to go."

Fisher comes through the bedroom door and leans against the wall. He's frowning, and I know he must have heard me.

Roughly turning off my phone, I toss it onto a nearby table and walk toward Fisher with a smile.

"I'm hopping in the shower. Want to join me?" I waggle my eyebrows.

He studies me for a moment.

"Are you okay?"

I straighten my posture and flash him a wide smile.

"Oh, yeah, I'm fine. It was just Harper."

Fisher's stare is unnerving. I know he sees through my act, but it's nothing I'm ready to share. Harper's simply wrong this time.

"Are you sure?"

I bop my head up and down.

"Yes, I promise."

He rubs the outside of my shoulders and arms. It's almost as if he's waiting for me to come up with a different answer, so I flash him a beaming smile.

"Shower time?" I sing-song.

Finally, I get him to relax.

"You head in first. I'm waiting for a call. Wheels up in two hours."

"Two hours?" I exclaim.

Darting back toward the shower, I feel the temperature. It's hot enough for me to get in.

Wait a second. Wheels up? Does that mean we'll be seeing a certain flight attendant soon?

"Did you request Mia?"

Part of me hopes he did, while the other part of me doesn't. Really, I hope he didn't. Not this time. It would be too soon.

Fisher has unlocked a part of me that desires to be watched. I just don't want to form a relationship with anyone else outside of Fisher while he and I are still getting to know one another this way.

He chuckles.

"No, I know my girl better than that."

His girl.

Heat spreads through my chest.

I hope it stays this way forever.

ARRIVING IN BEAVER CREEK, Colorado, for a two-night stay at a luxury mountain resort was not something I would have thought I'd be doing for New Year's Eve if you asked me a month ago.

"Right this way, sir, madam." The bellhop guides us into the hotel.

Fisher places his hand on my lower back as we walk through the resort entrance and up to the front desk together to be checked into the hotel.

He steps up and talks to the receptionist to get us checked in while I take a step to the side for him to handle it.

A few minutes go by before he's back to focusing on me.

"All set."

He holds up a room key and leads me in the opposite direction of where I thought the rooms were.

"Where are we going?"

"I got us a villa."

"Oh," I say surprised.

"A little extra privacy while we're here."

"I love it."

I reach for his hand and squeeze it excitedly. Life with Fisher is anything but boring.

We take the long walk down the hallway and reach the end, where there are three different paths we can take.

"We're straight ahead," he says.

"Lead the way."

Fisher leads us once again until we're finally there.

When the door opens, we are, in fact, in a villa. It's gorgeous inside, with all of the typical fixtures for a mountain resort.

"This is beautiful."

"I had a feeling you'd like it here. It reminds me of the North Carolina resort," he starts.

I see a sheepish grin.

"Only hopefully, we aren't going to get snowed in. I'd like to take you back to Seattle and get my last week in with you as my assistant."

"Maybe I'll have to pay you a special visit next week."

"Is that so?" he rasps.

"Yes," I practically moan.

I trail my fingers along the glass shelving as I tour the villa.

"I just might need a preview."

"I think that can be arranged, Mr. Underwood."

Fisher looks down at his watch.

"If I didn't have a reservation planned for you," he says.

"Can we skip it?"

He laughs darkly.

"I think this is a surprise you'll like, princess."

"What is it?"

"You'll see."

I'M BEGINNING to love this man's surprises.

"This is beyond words," I gasp.

We're having dinner in an igloo-esque dining bubble. With the snow lightly falling and the lights twinkling all around us, this is hands down the best holiday season I've ever had.

"The last of the season," he murmurs.

I look to my side and find Fisher staring.

"Yes, but then we get to start the next chapter of our lives."

He squeezes my hand for a moment.

"Together."

He lets go and picks up the drink menu from the center of the table.

"Now, what would my princess like as we take it all in?"

"You pick."

Fisher peers up at me.

"I think my girl likes champagne."

"That's true," I say with a giggle.

The server appears and welcomes us to the restaurant. Fisher orders a bottle of champagne and a variety of appetizers to taste test.

"How did I get so lucky and find someone as wonderful as you are?" I start.

We both freeze.

I awkwardly laugh and begin looking around the other clear tents.

The server comes back almost immediately with the champagne. Fisher gives his approval, and then it's being poured.

The main obstacle we still haven't discussed is the one I just accidentally brought up—Knox. We know we have to, but I don't want to talk about him now, not on this trip. I'll bring it up soon after we've settled back into the day-to-day of work.

"Ellie."

Finally, I look over to Fisher to see him handing me a champagne flute.

"Thank you," I say while trying to act casual.

"To new beginnings," Fisher says.

"To new beginnings. I'm liking the start of this one."

That earns me a genuine smile back from him, and we both take a sip of our champagne.

"I know we haven't talked about Knox. And I'm okay with that for the time being," he says.

"I know. We're just getting to know each other this way. It's been really nice."

"It has been."

"Let's talk about Knox soon, after I'm done being your assistant and all."

His eyes darken, and I see a twitch of his lips.

"My assistant," he rasps.

I may have been his assistant for years, but my role has always been professional.

I blush into my side.

Fisher lifts my hand to his lips and places a small kiss on the back of it. He keeps it intertwined with his as he sets it down on the table.

The server brings out the appetizers.

"Is there anything else you need at the moment?" the server asks.

"That'll do," Fisher answers.

The server nods and disappears to assist another party.

"This really is another magical spot," I say.

"Ellie, we don't have to talk about it here. I understand your point, but we will have to talk about Knox eventually. I'm sure he'll understand when he finds out."

"Maybe," I offer.

"He will. I won't hide you or keep you a secret, but I can't lose him. Not after everything he and I have been through to get here."

My heart melts at both confessions.

"When we're back and in a new routine, we can figure out how to tell him," I say.

He nods in agreement and takes another sip of his champagne.

I know we can't pretend like we aren't together for much longer, not after how clear it is that we both want to be on this path.

My concern is how Knox will take it. I'm not as confident as Fisher that he'll get over it so easily. The version of Knox I knew barely tolerated his dad. I know they've grown past that, but I can see how Knox resorts back to that behavior to make Fisher feel guilty.

I just hope he won't do that when it comes to his dad and me being together. That's one obstacle I don't know how we'd move past.

THE NEXT MORNING, New Year's Eve Day, had a beautiful start. I was woken up with Fisher down below the sheets. It's possibly my new favorite way to wake up—that and receiving a latte hand-delivered by the same man delivering said morning orgasms.

We went skiing, which is a favorite pastime of mine. Surprisingly, it's not one of Fisher's strong suits. As he told me, "He never had time to ski."

Now, I'm preparing for our special New Year's Eve night. It'll be just the two of us with views of the snow-capped mountains to round out the holiday season.

I'm slipping into the bikini I brought. Thankfully, Fisher told me to do so when I was packing my bag. Otherwise, I would have never thought to bring one on a mountain trip where there is snow.

Since we are in a villa, we have a private hot tub, and Fisher ordered room service to be delivered later tonight.

Relaxing like this is an entirely different world. I have to refocus on work being a priority after this is over. I can't live as if those career aspirations of mine are nonexistent now that I'm in a new relationship. A girl can enjoy the downtime though.

Eyeing myself in the mirror, I size up the black string bikini I'm wearing as I sip this glass of champagne. I'm confident that Fisher will like it.

"Don't you look gorgeous?"

I turn slightly around to see Fisher in his matching black swim shorts. My mouth waters as I drink him in. I'll never get over the fact that I get this man. All secret swirls of tattoos and rippling muscles under the stoic demeanor, and he's all mine.

Fisher chuckles as he stalks toward where I am.

"You're making me want to forget about the hot tub

plan altogether," he rasps as he plays with the ends of the strings of the bikini top. The way his cool fingers touch me makes me feel like my skin is on fire.

This is what it's supposed to be like when you're with someone. The butterflies in my stomach, the heat pooling low, and the goosebumps pricking up, it's all because of this man.

"I think we have plenty of time to do anything we want." My voice comes out sultry and needy, which I definitely am.

"Come on, princess. I think you'll like what I have planned for you."

I spin fully around and wrap my arms around his neck.

"I like everything you do to me," I whisper.

I reach up as he bends down so we can kiss each other. He takes a nibble of my lip before opening the seam with his tongue. This kiss makes the neediness I already feel worse than before. I need more contact, friction, anything already. He breaks away first, leaving me a panting mess.

Taking my hand, he leads me out to the living room area and hands me a robe to put on.

"Wear this until we get out there. I don't want you to feel colder than needed."

I place it on, and he does the same with his robe. Immediately his hand is intertwined with mine again as we head out to the hot tub.

It's cold outside, but it's no longer snowing like it had been the night before. The hotel staff cleared our patio deck, but you can still see the snow piled up along the property.

String lights are up, twinkling in the night sky. Thankfully, tall hedges line around the patio deck to give us a secluded feeling.

We both pull off our robes and place them on a nearby table.

"I'll be right back... I forgot our champagnes," Fisher says as he helps me into the hot tub.

"Do you need any help?"

"No, enjoy yourself. Get warm."

He heads back inside, and I do as requested.

The warmth of being in the hot tub is nice, so I close my eyes and get situated.

The opening of the sliding glass door distracts me when Fisher comes out with our drinks and a champagne bottle.

I smirk as he gets closer.

"It's cold out here, so this will stay chilled," he says with a boyish grin.

"Fair enough." I laugh and move to the other side of the hot tub to give him space to get in.

"How is it?" he asks as he steps in with our glasses in hand.

"You'll get used to it."

He hands me my champagne glass as he settles into the warmth, arching an eyebrow as he takes a sip of his champagne. I follow suit. Then we set them both down on the tables around us.

"Come here," he growls.

I instantly do and straddle his lap.

"What plans do you have for me in here?" I ask, grinding my hips on his cock.

"My exhibitionist is ready to play," he murmurs.

Fisher pulls me roughly into him as I hold onto his shoulders. My nails dig deep into them as he starts to slide my hips back and forth along his already-hardened cock.

"Is that what you think I am?" I whimper.

"Everyone has a kink, princess. I like seeing you break

apart when you think someone else could be watching you come."

He winks as he pulls me harshly against his swim trunks. My head falls back naturally as I go with the pace he's setting for me. One of his hands reaches up the back of my swimsuit, and I feel the string around my neck unravel, exposing my breasts.

"Fuck," he mutters.

He reaches for the next string as he leans into my chest and puts one breast, followed by the other, into his mouth, sucking and blowing on my nipples. It drives me wild as he continues. I can barely feel the cold air on my skin because of how ablaze I am.

My bikini top falls into the water, leaving me topless.

"I love you naked and wanting," he rasps.

He pops me off him slightly and proceeds to pull my bikini bottoms off, followed by his own.

"Are you sure we should do this?" I ask.

"It'll be fine, princess."

Gripping my waist, he lowers me onto his shaft.

"That's my girl, easy."

I lower onto him and, after a few moments, finally adjust.

"I'm ready." I moan.

My hips start to rock slowly.

"Does my princess like that she's naked and on display out here?"

I bounce up and down on his cock while panting and moaning, pressing both of my breasts into his face.

"Fucking smother me," he murmurs.

Fisher licks and sucks them like it's his dying breath. I'm his ragdoll as he pulls me back and forth, and I know I'm about to come already.

"Fuck," I groan out.

I continue to ride his shaft as I begin to let the orgasm wash over me.

"Fucking beautiful," he murmurs.

I still with his cock buried deep inside of me.

Slowly, he pops me off and positions me almost fully out of the hot tub. I can nearly see over the hedges like this. The distant lights from other villas shine through. He lifts me up and sets me on the edge, making my nipples harden from being brought out into the cold.

He stands in the water, and I spread my legs open. I don't even care at this point how cold it is. I need to feel his cock inside me again.

Fisher lines up his cock with my entrance and thrusts in, pulling at my body to get deeper.

"Come on, princess. Let the neighbors hear how much you like to be fucked by your boss. Scream for me."

The role-playing ignites something within me again.

Fuck, he's so goddamn hot.

I start to moan loudly as I roughly palm my breasts. I'm already about to come again, and it's only been minutes.

"That's it, gorgeous. Play with those pretty tits as I fuck this pretty pussy."

"Fuck. I'm so close again."

He picks up his speed as he continues going in and out of me.

"Where do you want my cum, princess? Can I come on the pretty tits you're playing with?"

"Yes, please. Come on my tits. Come on me."

A few more hard pumps and I'm coming around his cock once more. As soon as I do, Fisher starts pulling out and then comes on my breasts.

"Don't worry, I'm not done with you yet."

I give him an almost-drunk smile.

"I figured you weren't."

"Let's get you inside where I can make you come into the new year."

I laugh.

"That's hours away."

He grins.

"Perfect. Sounds like a Happy New Year to me."

TWENTY-TWO

Ellie

"DO you have the final set of plans to share?"

Fisher is all business this morning. After New Year's, we returned to Seattle and settled into a routine. I've been staying exclusively at his penthouse for the past few weeks and have started my new role at the company. My last order of business working with Fisher is the redo of the company retreat we had planned in December.

It was rescheduled for Presidents' Day weekend in February. It's only one week away, which means it's crunch mode to get this up and running successfully. All of the clients who had committed to coming in December are planning to attend in February.

This holiday weekend is ideal for them to bring their families to ski and relax in the snow. Only this time, hopefully without a snowstorm causing the mountain to shut down.

"Yes, here is the final attendee list."

I slide the list over to Fisher across his desk. He picks it up and begins reviewing the document.

"Everyone is coming. This is excellent."

I hum in agreement.

"And everything is finalized with Russ at the resort?"

"Yes, I just got off the phone with him. Everything is accounted for this time."

"That's good. Excellent work."

"Thank you, sir."

Fisher's eyes flash up to mine, and I see a hint of amusement in his expression.

"Let's review the new itinerary you created," he says.

As we review each day thoroughly, it makes me miss working with him like this. It's amazing to witness Fisher in action. It's natural for him to know what decision to make next, and he explains his reasoning to try and teach me.

Watching him run through the impact on the revenue projections next, I realize he's been my mentor all along. He's wanted me to succeed this whole time.

It makes me understand that I have been ready for this next phase of my career, and it's thanks to this man in front of me.

As he adjusts his glasses, I remember there is one thing we never did when we got back after the new year—one thing I want to do right now as my thighs rub together. We never got to officially role-play in the office.

I get up from my seat and walk over to his door. Flicking the lock closed, I turn back around to see the same desire I'm feeling swirling in his eyes.

"Mr. Underwood, I think I've been a bad, *bad* assistant."

He stretches out in his desk chair, and I see the indecision. It's all fun and games to talk about but entirely something else to act on it.

"Ellie," he whispers.

"Yes?"

He exhales deeply and grips the end of the armrests.

"Ms. Robertson, what have you done? Come sit on my lap and tell me."

I beam and then get back into character. He's going to play along. It's after five p.m., and most of the office clears out by now. It'll only be certain employees staying late.

"I've misplaced all of the documents you needed for your trip. How ever will I make it up to you?"

I saunter over to where he's seated and climb into his lap, giving him my most innocent expression. The intensity of his stare has me questioning my confidence.

"Why don't you be a good girl and get under this desk to make it up to me."

I slide down his body and position myself on my knees. Fisher widens his legs to make room for my frame.

I go for the belt buckle first and then pull down his zipper. The bulge I'm greeted with is not a surprise. I pull out his cock but keep his clothes on him just in case.

"What are you going to do with that?" he asks.

I squeeze his cock in my hands and start to rub along its length.

"Should I put it in my mouth, sir?"

He lets out a guttural groan that makes me feel achy. This isn't about me today though; it's a fantasy of Fisher's that I plan to see through.

Licking my lips, I open my mouth wide and encase his cock, wrapping my hand around the base.

Sucking eagerly, I want to please him.

"That's it, princess. You're doing so well."

I keep going as I continue to suck and pull simultaneously.

"Best fucking mouth," Fisher murmurs.

He reaches forward and plays with the back of my hair. In tandem, I keep bobbing back and forth with his encouragement. I love the sting of him pulling my hair when I take his length deep into my mouth.

"Perfect, fucking perfect."

My hands go to his upper thighs as I try to take his cock fully into my mouth. Deeper and deeper I go, and it finally hits the back of my throat.

Fisher spasms, and I know his cum will be dripping down it soon enough.

It starts to seep out.

"Swallow," he commands.

Ripples of cum start to burst into my mouth. I try to swallow it all as it keeps coating my throat.

After it stops, I lean back on my heels and wipe my mouth with the back of my hand. My lipstick has to be smeared everywhere.

Fisher pants and leans back in his chair. I can tell he's trying to come down from his high. He reaches forward and places my chin in his hand, and I purr into the touch.

"You are perfect."

"Thank—" I start.

A loud knock on the door rings throughout the office.

"Dad?" a voice shouts out, and a series of loud knocks follows.

I stiffen.

It's him. Knox is here.

Panicked, I move away from Fisher and farther back into the desk I'm under. It was all part of the role I was playing, but now I'm suddenly very grateful that I chose this scenario out of everywhere we could have done this.

"Fisher? Dad? Are you in there?"

Fisher places a finger over his lips and signals for me to wait.

"He can't find out about you like this," he whispers, and I nod in agreement.

"Coming," Fisher shouts out to Knox.

This is definitely not how I planned for him to find out about Fisher and me, and it could be a disaster. I realize I need to stay hidden and quiet.

"Why is your door locked?" Knox asks, sounding perplexed.

Fisher never locks his door; he doesn't need to. It's not like anyone would just come barging in here. No one but Knox, it seems.

Fisher's new assistant starts next week, and he's had temporary employees filling in until then. Each of them has left right at five p.m. on the dot, so there's no one here to stop Knox or tell him anything at all.

"Force of habit," Fisher lies.

Fisher fixes his attire and walks to the door. I hear it open and am frozen underneath his desk.

Don't make a sound, Ellie.

We can't have Knox questioning that someone is in the office with Fisher.

"What are you doing here?"

"I just got back into town. Since when are you locking your office door? Where's Ellie?"

I hear shuffling as Fisher walks back toward his desk chair, and Knox has to be pulling out a seat across the way.

Stay still, Ellie. Just stay still.

Easier said than done.

Maybe I shouldn't be sitting on my stilettos like this. I wasn't thinking when I was positioning myself farther under the desk.

"Ellie was promoted a few weeks ago," Fisher answers.

I see his legs sitting down finally, and he moves his chair carefully in toward me.

"Ellie? Promoted. Wow, that's great. I'm glad it's happening for her after all this time."

Huh. That's unexpected but nice.

Maybe there's hope that he will be fine when he finds out that Fisher and I are dating. Probably not the best idea to break the news while I'm under a desk but still refreshing to hear.

"She's been doing wonderfully. Doug was begging me to reassign her to operations."

"That's great."

An awkward silence.

"What brings you back to Seattle? I thought you were in Nashville?"

"I was, and I'm going back, eventually."

"What's that mean?" I hear the confusion in Fisher's tone.

"I'm officially with the band. Our tour starts soon, and it kicks off here in Seattle. I want you to come to the show."

"Wow. That's..."

Fisher pauses and stands. I watch as he heads over to Knox's side, and the sound of a chair being pushed back scrapes against the floor.

"I'm proud of you. I'd love to come."

This is what Fisher has always wanted. Knox is finally getting his footing, and even part of me is proud of Knox. He's doing what he's dreamed of.

"Thanks, Dad."

My heart flutters with happiness for Fisher.

"I have to head out, but dinner this week? I'm not exactly sure when since we have rehearsals."

"That'd be great, just call me," Fisher answers.

"Will do."

The door opens, and I anxiously wait for it to close.

"Hey, Dad?"

"Yeah, son?"

"Think Ellie will want to come?"

Fisher hesitates.

"Possibly. Why?"

"Just thinking about inviting her, that's all."

Oh no. I hear the fake casualness he's trying to exude. It may be years since we've been together, but I know Knox well. Does he have suspicions? There's no way. He can't assume I was in the room with them.

"See you later," Knox calls out.

The closing of the door finally sounds, followed by the click of the lock.

I slowly climb out from under the desk and find Fisher leaning against the door. Normally, I wouldn't be concerned, but his face looks pale.

"Are you okay? That sounded like great news."

He finally looks up at me.

"Why would he want to invite you? It's been years, hasn't it?"

I swallow thickly.

"It has."

Fisher nods his head and folds his arms across his chest.

"Ready to head home?" I ask.

"That's a good plan."

The sound of Fisher's voice is cracked.

It's impossible that Knox wants me back. It's been years. He knows there's no way that would ever happen between us. I don't know why he asked if I would want to go to his show—it doesn't add up.

I pack up the retreat documentation and put it into my work tote.

"This is good news," I say, but Fisher looks completely distracted.

I wait for an answer.

Finally, Fisher looks over to me and shakes his head. He pinches the bridge between his eyebrows.

"Sorry," he says apologetically and sighs.

I offer a weak smile.

"Don't worry about it. Let's head home."

"Okay," he breathes out.

FISHER IS quiet back at the penthouse. Letty notices immediately as well but doesn't ask. Instead, she has Chef Diego start preparing one of Fisher's favorite easy dinners—he calls it zucchini surprise. It's delicious, and the surprise is that it's a random casserole that no chef would have ordinarily thrown together if it wasn't for a happy accident one day.

Fisher was alone and started pulling out ingredients that he liked, and that's how we now have zucchini surprise.

As I sit here next to a silent Fisher, I have to witness his mostly full plate being tossed around with his fork.

"Fisher, can we talk?"

He looks up at me.

"Of course, princess. What about?"

He reaches for my hand across the table and places his on top of mine.

"You know you can talk to me."

A smile that doesn't reach his eyes appears.

"I do."

I take a deep breath. I have to do this. Address it head-on.

"I don't think Knox has any interest in trying to get back together with me. It's been so long, and we have barely spoken in all this time. I really think it's because I was brought up minutes earlier."

"Ellie." He sighs with his eyes closed.

"I'm serious. He doesn't have feelings for me," I practically whine.

Getting up from my seat, I gesture for Fisher to do the same.

"Please believe me. I know what I'm talking about."

He rises, and I lead him over to the sectional sofa, and we collapse onto it. Folding my legs under myself, I reach for a blanket to cover us.

Gently, Fisher starts caressing my legs.

We knew that we'd have to tell Knox eventually. I don't understand why he's not talking to me about this.

"Why does this feel so much heavier than what we both thought it would be?"

"What do you mean?" I whisper.

"I don't want to lose what we have," he admits.

"We won't. It'll be fine. I know it will."

My eyes start to well with tears.

Please, don't let this be the end when we've only just begun.

I keep my eyes shut to prevent tears from spilling out as Fisher continues to stroke my legs.

"WHAT THE FUCK is she doing sleeping here? Fucking tell me! Just fucking admit it!"

I'm feeling groggy as I stretch on the sofa.

Wait. I'm still on the sofa. I must have fallen asleep after dinner.

"Don't shout," Fisher answers.

I peer up from where I was lying down to see Knox throwing his arms in the air. He places his hands on his hips and starts pacing around.

"I can't fucking believe it," Knox mutters.

He pauses, face-to-face with Fisher again.

I don't know what to do. I'm out of sight right now, but do I get up? Do I help Fisher explain what's happening?

"I fucking knew someone was in the office with you earlier with the door locked. I may not know you that well, but I knew something was up."

"Please, let me explain," Fisher says.

His tone is even, and it feels like we're in a meeting with the board of directors. He's showing no sign of emotion, just trying to stay collected.

"Okay, fine. Explain. Explain why my ex-girlfriend and your assistant—who is basically two decades younger than you—is fake sleeping on the couch right now?"

Decision made.

I sit up and see both Fisher and Knox looking over at me, although they both have entirely different expressions. Fisher looks hopeless and worried, while Knox is shooting venom back and forth between his dad and me.

"Look," I start.

"Stay out of it," Knox yells.

"Don't yell at Ellie," Fisher interjects.

"Oh, for fuck's sake. Now you pick her over me. Great. Fucking great."

"That's not what I said, but you cannot yell at her like that."

Knox throws his hands in the air again.

"Fuck it. You two deserve each other. Don't fucking bother reaching out."

Knox turns on his heels and storms out of the penthouse.

I stay frozen on the sofa as Fisher stares at the slammed door.

The light coming through the window soon fades. Finally, Fisher comes over and sits with me and hangs his head low in his hands.

I reach out and begin rubbing a shoulder, and he flinches.

Fuck. This hurts. The tears I was previously holding in begin coming out.

"Wait. I'm sorry. I didn't mean to do that," Fisher starts.

I hold up my hand to stop him from continuing and slowly get up from his couch. I know what I have to do. He looks up at me through red-rimmed eyes, and I'm sure they match mine. As tears start to prick through, I have to get this out.

"Fisher, I love you. I didn't want to tell you like this, but I do. I love you so much it hurts. That's why when I ask you this next question, I need you to answer truthfully. Can you promise me that?"

He starts to stand, and I shake my head no. He collapses back onto the sofa, with his arms hanging by his sides and his hair a mess. I want to comfort him, only I can't. The man I love is about to break my heart.

"Promise me," I demand.

"I promise." His voice cracks.

"We can make Knox understand. I know we can. He just needs time, which is something we'll give him. I know he doesn't care about me like that anymore," I start.

Fisher looks hopeless.

"I would never ask you to give up Knox, but if he asks you to give me up, what will you say?"

Fisher leans forward and hangs his head low once again. He scratches at the back of his head as he sighs loudly.

I nod to no one but myself.

I knew it.

"Say it."

He won't look up at me. We both know what I'm getting at.

"Say it," I cry out.

The man I'm in love with finally looks up at me, and all I see is sadness and remorse for what's about to come out.

"Okay," I answer for him.

I start to turn around when I feel a pull on one of my arms.

"Please wait," he begs.

"Just answer the question," I croak.

"I don't know. I just don't know. I'm sorry. I'm just so in my head; that was a disaster."

I pull away and out of his reach.

"That's the problem. I'm so sure of you, and you've never fully been mine, have you?"

He looks confused and shakes his head no.

"What are you talking about? Of course I've been yours."

"No, you haven't been this whole time."

Bending forward, I place a kiss on top of his head.

"Don't leave. Not like this."

All the energy has been drained out of my body.

"I have to."

My heart has been broken by the only man I've truly ever loved.

TWENTY-THREE

Fisher

FUCK.

I've messed up beyond words.

I was completely caught off guard when Knox stormed into my home demanding answers. I tried to diffuse any concerns he had, and that's when he saw Ellie.

My princess was sleeping peacefully on the sofa when all hell broke loose.

I tried to calm him down so we could talk like men in the other room, but he just wasn't having it. Then, when Ellie woke up, I couldn't control his reaction. It all happened so fast.

I was devastated by how Knox was reacting.

Then when Ellie began asking me how I was feeling, I was a fucking mess. I was confused and sad, unsure of what was transpiring.

What I should have said is that I agree with her, that

Knox will get over it. That she and I could work through the situation and come out on the other side still together.

The shock just hadn't worn off yet. I wasn't processing anything she was saying. I own that, but now I just need a chance to make it right with both of them.

Here lies the problem I'm now faced with—Knox and Ellie won't return my calls. I've tried reaching out repeatedly to both of them. Knox sends me to voicemail almost immediately, whereas I get no reaction from Ellie at all.

It's been all weekend and nothing.

Darin was able to drop off a few of Ellie's essentials that I know she uses daily. I couldn't be selfish and hold them hostage.

Although that's exactly what I wanted to do, I couldn't say no to Letty when she arranged the whole drop-off between Ellie and Darin. At least, that means I know Ellie is alive and well.

Walking into work, I have to act like I'm not dying inside. I don't even care how fucking pathetic I seem; all I care about is demanding Ellie's attention. I need to get her to listen to my side of what happened.

I plan to remind her exactly who I am when we are back in North Carolina this upcoming weekend at the retreat. I'll cancel her cabin with the resort, and she'll have no choice but to hear me out and let me apologize repeatedly all weekend. I'm willing to take drastic measures to get her to just listen to me.

Doug is planning on attending now to see how the retreats can fold into the revenue operations team. It's part of his new strategy for revising teams and responsibilities. He reminds me a lot of myself—someone who wants to make Rain Peak better with his fresh ideas and high spirits.

"Good morning, Mr. Underwood," a soft voice speaks.

Getting out of my head, I remember that my new assistant starts today. Someone with an impressive background working for company leaders for years, and most importantly, someone picked by Ellie.

"Good morning, Jan."

"Sir, I am very happy to be working for you. I added time to your calendar to review my full responsibilities. In the meantime, how do you like your coffee?"

She folds her arms in front of her with her hands and waits patiently. No matter how permanent I know this is, she's not Ellie.

"I'll get it today. Thank you," I curtly answer and head into my office.

Shutting the door behind me, I slink over to my office chair. It's after nine in the morning. Surely, Ellie is here already.

I make my double espresso and down it quickly. It burns going down my throat, but I'm now a glutton for punishment. I'll gladly take it if it means a path toward redemption and Ellie.

I quickly leave my office, scaring Jan as I do, and head toward the operations department on the same floor. It was meant to be another upside to the whole position change.

I find Ellie's office, only it's empty. Scanning the department, there is no trace of her anywhere.

"Morning, boss," Doug calls out.

"Doug, do you know where Ellie is? It's after nine," I ask, turning around to face him.

"She had an emergency and is working remotely," he starts.

I'm about to interject when he continues.

"Don't worry, she has reassured me that everything is together for the retreat."

My shoulders sag in disappointment. I really don't care about the retreat right now or if I look like a sad mess in front of Doug.

He appears worried but isn't daring to say anything. Straightening up, I head back to my office.

She's not coming in this week. It may seem concerning to anyone else, given Ellie's dedication to Rain Peak, but I know why. She's avoiding me.

She can have this week to think, but on Friday, I'm getting my girl back.

THIS WEEK HAS BEEN MISERABLE, and I don't care if I'm resorting to dramatics. A week without Ellie by my side is far too long.

Now, as I'm driving up this familiar mountain, all I feel is anxious about what she'll do when she finally has to face me. She has no choice but to let her boss talk to her while we're here.

Doug confirmed earlier today that she had already arrived. This is my opportunity to explain and apologize like I've been trying to. He did seem concerned, but I didn't press why over email. I'll find out when I'm finally there.

My cell phone rings in my jacket pocket. Pulling it out, I see it's Avery, and I debate answering or not. She is well aware of this week.

On Tuesday, she called me pissed off because she had to find out from Harper that I broke Ellie's heart. I tried explaining what happened, and it didn't help the situation.

"Avery."

"What are you going to say to her when you get there?"

I stretch my neck from side to side as I weigh my options.

"My plan is to beg. Grovel. Get down on my knees in the snow if I have to. Anything to get her to just listen to why I was like that."

"That's a good start."

I do feel relieved to hear that, at least.

"But?" I have to ask.

The car is almost at the top of the mountain where the resort is. I don't want to lose cell phone reception in these woods before finishing this conversation, but I also can't tell the driver to stop since he's bringing me to Ellie.

"What are you going to say when she asks you again about Knox? It's been over a week, and he hasn't answered your calls, right?"

"Yes," I confess.

"She's going to need more from you. Think about it. Call me when you've talked to her."

Avery hangs up without giving me a chance to say anything more.

All week, I've been thinking of how to make this right. I really don't know what it'll take, but I want to be with Ellie. I'm hoping when I see her, it'll all come to me.

Let's hope that's the case.

"We're here, sir," the driver says.

The memories come flooding back as I see the resort welcome sign.

The car comes to a stop, and the driver quickly rounds the corner and attempts to open my door. I beat him to it, so he quickly retrieves my bags while I scan everywhere for a glimpse of Ellie.

I don't see anyone from Rain Peak or our clients yet.

Some of them have to be here, but I'll find them later. They aren't important today.

"Thank you," I say as I take the bags and hand the man a tip.

"Thank you, sir."

Quickly, I check in and am led to my cabin, the very same one where Ellie's and my relationship started.

My chest feels a deep pain as it comes into view.

The bellhop helps drop my bags off into the cabin, and I'm out the door at the same time as he is.

I head back into the main lodge and find Russ.

"Good afternoon, Mr. Underwood. It's a pleasure to have you back here."

"Thank you, Russ. Do you know where Ms. Robertson might be? Poor phone reception," I lie.

"Yes, she's actually in the main ballroom preparing for the welcome reception with my team."

"Thank you."

I don't give him a chance for small talk as I dash down the lodge to the main dining hall where the reception is being held.

Scanning the nameplates outside of each room, I finally find the one I'm looking for—the welcome reception sign is set up by the open front doors.

And there she is.

My princess.

My best friend.

My love.

My Ellie.

I finally feel like a small weight has been lifted off my chest. There is so much to do and say, but seeing her with my own two eyes is much different than the secondhand accounts I've been getting.

She looks polished, with my favorite black sweater of hers on and black leather pants and boots; she's the image of perfection.

Ellie is the only one in the room right now, so I try not to scare her as I slowly inch forward. With her back to me, as she's arranging something on the table, I see her suddenly stop. She knows I'm here.

"Ellie," I whisper.

She stays still, so I stop walking.

"Ellie. Please. Please hear me out."

She won't face me yet.

"That day was the worst day of my life, and not because Knox found out about us but because I lost you. Please talk to me. Let me explain."

Ellie hangs her head low for a moment before finally facing me. Red splotchy marks are around her eyes, and I see she hasn't been doing well either.

I go to reach out for her, and she shakes her head.

"I'm here to complete my job duties, so please don't make this harder than it has to be."

She puts on her black puffer jacket without looking me in the eye.

"Ellie. Please. I didn't mean what I said that day. I was shocked and confused. Please understand that's not how I feel."

She scoffs.

"Stop."

Ellie darts right past me and bumps into my shoulder along the way.

"Fuck," I shout into the empty room.

Tears were streaming down her face. I fucking did that. I've done this to her, and it was all a mistake.

I chase after where she goes. Looking both ways, I see

the blur of black almost out the double doors. Jogging as quickly as I can, I reach the double doors in no time. Ellie is nowhere to be seen as I look everywhere outside.

Fuck me.

She can't be gone.

I pace around the outside of the double doors like a madman.

What should I do? I could ask what cabin she's in; that's a start, at least. Maybe they'll tell me what she has left to do. Then, if she isn't in the cabin, I can go check those places too. I didn't cancel her cabin reservation—that wasn't going to go over well.

Wait.

I know where she is.

I TREK around my cabin in hopes that I'm right. When we were here two months ago, this is where everything changed between us.

My boots clunk through the snow as I finally get to where I'm meant to be.

Ellie's here. She's standing still, looking out at the pond that is now frozen over. A family of deer is on the opposite side, only this time, their hoof prints are more noticeable in the snow, quite possibly because my eyes are finally more aware than they were in the past.

The crunch of my boots coming up behind Ellie is loud. She knows it's me as she stays looking out at the icy pond. I'm mere inches away, but I just wait this time. I need her to be ready.

Minutes go by, and it feels like I'm left waiting for a lifetime. Finally, she turns around and faces me. Her face is rosy because of the cold, and her head is covered with a black hat.

My mouth tightens into a thin line while I try desperately to take the right approach. I'll surely beg for another chance, but I need to let Ellie lead this conversation.

She studies me, and I know she can see my sadness by the way her face softens momentarily. Almost as if she knows I saw it, the same indifferent wall builds back up.

I have to try.

I tried to give her the first chance this time.

"You'll never understand how sorry I am for that day. For how I reacted. I hope you can see how stunned I was by Knox's behavior. My mind went blank after he stormed out. I'm not proud of it; in fact, I regret it deeply," I say.

Ellie's eyes shut close, and I take it as my signal to keep going.

"I love you. I'm sorry I didn't say it over Christmas or New Year's or hell—any of the other more romantic times where it was just you and me. I'm sorry. I should have claimed you as mine and promised to make you happy every day for the rest of my life."

Tears start to stream down her cheeks. I want to wipe them away, but I continue,

"I would never let Knox say I couldn't be with you. My initial reaction was wrong. I love you, Ellie. You are the love of my life, and I am begging you for another chance."

Her eyes open, and I see the same conviction from earlier shining through.

"I told you that I loved you that day because I meant it. My love hasn't gone away in a week. That would be impossible to do," she starts.

My eyes light up with hope that she's about to say yes to giving me one more chance.

"But I can't," she finishes.

My eyebrows come together as I stand here, confused as to what's happening.

"What? What are you saying?" I stammer.

"My love for you came with all of the complications that I knew were coming to us. My love for you has never been deniable."

"Wait," I interject.

"No, I won't wait any longer. I can't make sacrifices for you when there is nothing you are willing to do for me. I told you that day I would never ask you to give up your relationship with your son, and I meant it. That would be insanity to ask you to do. But I won't allow you to treat me like I'm only optional in your life."

"That's not how I feel at all," I begin.

"Isn't it?"

She walks closer to me. So close that I can see her breath.

Ellie stares at my mouth for a second before turning her gaze to mine.

"Prove it."

"How? Tell me how," I plead.

She steps back and walks around me.

"Please, Ellie," I shout.

She stops in her tracks and turns back.

"Prove to me that you mean what you say. That your words and actions hold truth and the love you claim you have for me. If you can do that, then..." She trails off.

"Then what?"

She throws her hands up in the air.

"If you can show me that you mean what you say, then come back to me. We have the vacation up here scheduled in December, thanks to Avery."

She pauses to regroup.

"Meet me in wonderland. I'll be here waiting if you can do that."

I'm stunned by what she's saying.

Ellie turns her back to me once more and starts heading up the pathway back to the resort.

I don't know what she wants me to do. I already explained how much I love her and how terrible I feel about what happened. How can I prove to her that it's true?

A wind gust has me snapping out of my confused state.

I head up to the resort to try and talk to her about all of this. As I reach the main doors, I head back to the welcome reception area. There's no sign of Ellie, but I see that Doug has now arrived.

"Fisher, how was your travel in?"

"Fine, fine. Have you seen Ellie?"

Doug looks perplexed by my question.

"I didn't," he draws out.

"Why? Where is she?" I spit out.

His face pales as realization dawns.

"I'm so sorry. She told me she wanted to tell you herself."

"What's that?"

"She's gone."

"Gone? What does that mean? Where?"

I search the room for any sign of where she ran off to in order to avoid this conversation with me.

"No, I mean she quit."

"What the hell are you talking about?" I yell.

"Fisher."

"Sorry, Doug. What do you mean she quit?"

"Earlier this week, she called me and told me she had an emergency that required her full attention. She thanked me for the opportunity but said she couldn't in good conscience keep the position."

My world spins on its axis.

"She didn't say a word," I manage to spit out.

"I'm really sorry. She said she wanted to tell you today since she had worked for you for so long. I wasn't expecting to see her today when I arrived."

This can't be happening.

She quit Rain Peak.

She's left the resort.

My girl is gone.

TWENTY-FOUR

Ellie

I HAD to get out of there as soon as possible after finally having a raw and honest conversation with Fisher. He just didn't get it. I'm not upset with him just because of how he initially reacted to the Knox situation.

I'm upset with myself. The job opportunity I originally had in Charleston was a better career move. If I hadn't been so wrapped up in Fisher, I would have taken it. I don't regret my decision because I do want Fisher. I did then, and I do now. That will never change, no matter how much time and distance is between us.

My problem is that Fisher couldn't just say we would get through this. That we could weather the storm together.

Whenever it all came crashing down, I realized that Fisher didn't see how much I was changing and growing. All of my growth was because of him. That he was opening up an entirely different side of me that I was embracing with open arms. I thought the same was happening for him, but I was wrong.

As soon as the first sign of trouble came, he did what the old version of Fisher would do—give up his own happiness. I know it's because he's a parent, no matter how bad of a son Knox is. I understand I don't get that relationship. What I do know is that Knox is almost a thirty-year-old man. He shouldn't be throwing fits like a child because he doesn't like how something goes. He's not a teenager.

What should have happened in that situation is we all talked about it like adults. Knox should have given his dad that much.

That's the thing about life, it just doesn't always go according to plan.

"We're here, miss," the rideshare driver shouts.

We've arrived at the airport. It's time for me to get out of North Carolina and away from Fisher completely.

"Thank you."

Hopping out of the rideshare, I get my own bags out of the trunk and start rolling them to the doors. It's very different than life with Fisher, but this is what I need to do for me. I can't help Fisher until I start putting myself first.

I look back and stare up at the mountains.

"Bye," I whisper.

Through the double doors I go to start my new life.

"YOU'RE HERE!" Harper squeals as she opens the front door.

I sigh in relief. It's nice to be with one of my best friends and able to just sulk.

"I am. Thank you so much for letting me stay with you," I offer as I walk in.

Harper waves me off.

"Hi there!" I shout to Grayson.

"Grayson. Grab her bags," Harper scolds, and he just laughs.

"I can get them," I say.

"Don't be ridiculous. I didn't even hear the doorbell ring. Harper's been staring out the window like a lost puppy waiting for her owner to return home."

Harper gives him a pointed look.

"Someone is being sassy," she sing-songs.

I just laugh at these two. It's nice to be here—somewhere familiar and normal with people I trust.

"Seriously, thank you both so much for having me. I'm really not sure what my plan is going to be."

"Stay as long as you like. We have this gigantic house for only two people," Harper answers.

As nice as that is, I'll eventually need some boundaries to ensure our friendship stays intact. Plus, I happen to know way too much about their sex life, thanks to Harper, and I really don't know if I want to sit on any piece of furniture more than I have to, even with all of the deep cleaning they get done.

"Seriously, stay as long as you like," Grayson says.

"Thank you. I appreciate it."

We're standing around their kitchen island. It's not awkward, but I know Harper is dying for me to give her the update on whether or not I talked to Fisher up in North Carolina.

I tap my nails on the island as I look around.

"This place is really nice, you guys," I say.

"Oh yeah, you haven't seen it in person yet!"

"No, not yet. It's great."

"Thanks. There is so much more to do, but at least we were able to move in," Harper chirps.

"You'll have to show me around," I say.

"Totally."

More somewhat uncomfortable silence.

I sigh and relent.

"Harper, get the drinks. Where are we sitting while I tell you what happened with me and Fisher today?"

Harper jumps up and down and claps. Then she settles since it's not actually something to celebrate.

"Grayson," she calls out.

"Yeah, Red?"

"Can you get some drinks for us? We're going out on the deck around the fire."

He just laughs and nods okay.

Harper takes my hand and starts to pull me out back. I let my tote bag slide down my arm and onto the floor near where we were.

She sits cross-legged on the plush black outdoor sofa. Naturally, she pulls a coordinating blanket out of a basket and tosses it to me as I'm sitting down and takes another one out for herself.

"Well, I did end up seeing him."

Harper tightens her mouth, surely trying to wait for me to continue. I'm just not one to usually divulge all of my personal details, but these are special circumstances.

Grayson appears with wine and hands us each one.

"I tried to be quick when I was there so that I could get out as soon as possible, but it wasn't fast enough. He came and tried to apologize. I think you would call it groveling."

Harper leans her head forward and shoots her eyebrows up, waiting for more.

"I did listen," I continue.

I stretch my neck and lean back fully in the chair.

"But I told him it wasn't enough. I get all of his points. I really do. But I wasn't the person he wanted to go to for help. Instead, he considered the possibility of me no longer being in his life."

Harper's mouth twitches as she weighs what to say.

"Look, girl, before I say anything, what exactly are *you* saying?"

She takes a big gulp of the wine.

"I told him no."

"You what?" she practically shrieks and rears her head back as her eyes widen.

"I told him I needed more. I need him to show me what I mean to him."

"So, you just left?"

"I get that it may not make sense. I need him to really show me how I can fit into his future. It has to be a partnership."

"Yeah, but you barely had time together?"

I sigh and take a sip of my wine.

"I know it might not make sense, but I believe it will to him eventually. And if it doesn't, then I'll never regret my time with Fisher. He brought out a whole new side of me that I never would have thought possible."

Harper smirks into her glass.

I toss a pillow at her, and she falls over laughing.

"You definitely meant sexually, right?"

"No. But yes, sexually too."

"I fucking knew Daddy Fisher was going to be a beast in the bedroom."

"Oh my god, Harper!"

I fall forward into my lap.

"Can I come out now?" Grayson hollers from inside.

"Yeah, Captain! We just found out she broke things off, but Daddy Fisher was packing the heat!"

"You are not helping." I groan.

"Well, hopefully this separation isn't permanent, and he'll be back in all of our lives soon enough," she says.

I sit upright.

"Wait. What about Avery?"

"What about her?" Harper asks as she cuddles into Grayson.

"I mean, won't this be a terrible position I'm putting her in? I can't exactly hang out with the four of you."

"Avery is on your side," Harper declares.

"I don't want there to be sides."

She waves me off as she takes another sip of her drink.

"Well, speaking of... Avery suggested we all go out tonight to distract you. What do you think?"

"I don't think I'm up for it tonight, but you guys should go. There are a few things I need to take care of."

"We definitely aren't leaving you, but why don't I show you to your room, and you can get situated? Then come back down here and join us when you're ready to just hang?"

"That sounds nice."

LYING on the guest room bed, I keep staring at this one contact in my cell phone. It may not be the best idea, but I just want to talk to him one more time.

I toss it down and shut my eyes.

It's still really early, but I can't hide away in here

forever. And maybe if I do this, it'll make the weight I still feel on my shoulders a little lighter.

I pick my phone back up and stare at the contact. I've got to just do it. One time only.

I hit call.

The phone rings.

And rings.

And rings.

It finally goes to voicemail.

I had a feeling he wouldn't answer. It's time I get this off my chest.

"This is Knox. Leave a message," the voicemail sounds.

"Knox, hey, it's me. Ellie. Look, I don't know if you'll actually listen to this, but I hope you do," I start.

I pause and take a deep, steadying breath.

"I know what a shock this may have been to you, but I promise neither of us ever wanted to hurt you. What you and I had was so long ago, and you've been doing remarkable things. Your dad is so proud of you."

Make this about me, not defending Fisher.

"Your dad makes me feel loved. I know you don't want to hear that, but it's true. I won't speak for him, just myself. What happened just started over Christmas, and we were still figuring out what it all was, which is why we were waiting to tell you until it made sense."

I pause.

"I'm sorry. I'm sorry if I hurt you because of my part in this. But I'm not sorry for loving your dad. He's been alone for a long time, Knox. You know this. And he completes me. I love him so much it hurts. And I'm sorry you had to find out this way. Please don't hate your dad. I know how much he loves you. I hope you take care of yourself."

I hang up the phone, feeling relieved that I said what I needed to say.

Someone knocks on the door.

"Hey, just checking on you," Harper whispers.

"Coming out now, just a few!" I feign happiness.

"Okay, take your time."

Time is all I have now.

———

"YOU LOOK FANTASTIC!" Harper exclaims.

"It's just my first day."

"First day as a new boss at a new company, totally worth being excited over!"

Grayson just smiles at me as he slides a hot cup of coffee my way.

"Thank you." I sigh.

I take in the scent of the coffee beans and let myself feel relaxed.

"I'm excited about today. I think it's good I started on a four-day workweek to ease myself in."

"You're going to do great!" Harper exclaims.

"I can admit, you're doing a fantastic job being my hype woman, but I'm good, I promise."

"Okay, Ms. Client Relations Manager. Such a change of pace, but I love this for you so much."

"I know, right? I loved working with clients the most at Rain Peak."

Harper and Grayson both pause in place.

"Guys, I will have to mention it from time to time, you know," I say through a laugh.

Harper tries to act natural, but she's failing miserably at it.

At least Grayson starts to resume pouring their coffees to busy himself.

"Have you heard from Fisher?" Harper asks.

"I blocked him everywhere."

"Oh."

"You think that was a bad idea?"

"No?"

She shifts her weight.

"But I mean, how is he supposed to contact you when he might get whatever little mind game you're playing?"

I sigh and set my mug down on the counter.

"It's not a mind game. I'm doing this to prove to myself that I can. Fisher needs time to figure out himself too."

She bobs her head wildly.

"Right, of course."

"Come on, Red. We have to get ready to go into the office today," Grayson says.

"Why do I have to go in?" she counters.

"You get bored to tears working on an article when you're alone in the house and have to meet a deadline."

"Well, that's awfully rude of you to say out loud in front of a guest," she mutters.

"Alright, you two, I'll be back tonight. Thank you again for letting me stay here. I think next weekend, I'll finally start looking for a place."

"Take all the time you need," Grayson responds.

They both disappear into their bedroom. Finally having another moment to myself, I look at my cell phone. Maybe I should unblock Fisher. I just wanted to do this without wondering about him at all, not that I'm doing a good job of that.

I fiddle with it as I weigh my decision.

No. It was the right one. For now, at least. I can always change my mind later on.

I grab the keys to one of Grayson's cars that I'm temporarily using and hit the road for my new job.

The company is the same one that I gave up the operations manager role at in the new year. When I called my contact and explained I was moving to Charleston, South Carolina, now and not staying in Seattle, she quickly informed me of the new role and how perfect she thought I'd be for it.

A few quick interviews later, and the job was mine. Now, I'm about to start the first concrete step I have for building this new life of mine—one where I make decisions for myself.

New Ellie, here we go.

TWENTY-FIVE

Fisher

Six months later

WHEN ELLIE TOLD me that I needed to prove my feelings, I kept going through the motions of my day-to-day. I thought I had been all along. For a while, I was left heartbroken and confused.

Every time I tried to take her stress away, press her to deliver more, be the version of herself she was too afraid to be, all of that to me was showing her my feelings.

It wasn't until Avery finally talked to me after everything happened that I learned more of Ellie's truth. She had been offered a job around the same time as the December retreat. It was an offer that would have really helped the trajectory of her career. Instead of taking it, she chose to stay in Seattle at Rain Peak because of me. She did that without any idea that I was holding back a job offer for her to advance within Rain Peak.

She was willing to stay on as my assistant and would

have given up that career advancement all for me. Apparently, when we confessed our feelings for one another, that was all the answer she needed.

Meanwhile, I was the asshole debating giving her the new job because I wanted her all to myself. Now Doug is down a manager, I've been through a dozen assistants these past few months, and the people I care most about in life are barely speaking to me.

Avery, thankfully, is, but that's it. Knox won't return any of my calls, and I know he's out there touring, and I haven't even seen him play live with his new band.

Ellie has moved across the country and settled in Charleston, and Avery told me she's doing really well. She's found a position at the same company, and it aligns with what she wanted. I'm proud of her for taking life by the reins, for not letting me apologize, and for not staying in Seattle when apparently that's not what she's wanted for a long time. She had been staying for me all along.

My Ellie was always putting me before her own needs, and that's just not right. My stomach churns every time I let myself wallow in self-pity for how I messed it all up.

After months of not understanding, it all clicked when I heard that. And that's when I realized that I knew what I needed to do. It's time to get my affairs and priorities in order and go back to the Carolinas to claim my girl.

Standing in front of these double doors, I understand that this decision is the first of many I need to make.

"Are you ready?" Avery asks next to me.

"Not really."

"I like this new, open version of you."

"I'm trying to do better."

She looks up at me and gives me a knowing smile.

"Think this is the right decision?" I ask.

Avery's still the majority shareholder of Rain Peak since she was the heir to his shares. With her backing, the rest of the board will have no option but to accept what I've come here to do.

"I think it's time you started living your life. Rain Peak is going to continue to soar, thanks to the foundation you built."

"Thank you," I whisper.

I straighten my suit jacket and stretch my neck.

"Let's get in there and set their world ablaze," she taunts.

"I will be," I groan out as I push open the door and let her in first.

Murmurs are going off around the room as to why I requested everyone be present for this board meeting.

"Good morning, ladies and gentlemen," I start.

I sit down in my seat at the head of the table as Avery takes the open chair next to me. She gives me a curt nod to continue.

"I have some news to share regarding a decision that I have not come to lightly."

All eyes are now fixated on me.

"Effective immediately, I will be stepping down as CEO and President of Rain Peak Corporation."

"What?" someone exclaims.

"Settle down, everyone. Let Fisher speak," Avery interjects.

"Thank you," I say to Avery.

Getting up from my chair, I start to pace along the front of the room before pausing and facing the board.

"Rain Peak has been one of my greatest achievements. I'm confident that I am leaving at a time when profits are in the black, company morale is above average, and client satisfaction is at an all-time high."

"You're really stepping down?" a board member shrieks.

"Yes. I'll be here over the next three months to assist with the recruitment of my replacement and to ensure it's a smooth transition. Then, of course, as a shareholder, I'll still be active in Rain Peak after that."

"Wow," someone else says as they settle back into their chair.

"Three months will be more than enough time. Until then, I will run Rain Peak as business as usual."

"And you support this, Avery?" a different board member asks.

"I do. It's time."

"Do you have a replacement in mind?" someone asks.

"In fact, I do."

"Well, who is it?"

"Doug Jones."

"Doug? Operations Doug?"

Avery laughs at the nickname.

"Doug, as in the Doug who knows Rain Peak just as well as Fisher does. The one who spends countless hours improving processes and teams, and that's just me getting started," she says.

"Let's start the interview process so we are able to review all potential candidates," someone chimes in.

"I'll have human resources get started," I answer.

Avery and I share a confident look with one another.

Step one, done.

We both head for the door to leave without taking more questions.

"That's it?" someone shouts.

"That's it."

I let Avery head out first, and I follow behind while hearing loud voices shouting behind me, still shocked.

"Heading to Los Angeles?" Avery asks as we walk out of Rain Peak.

"Have to handle step two."

We pause at the elevator bank.

"I'm really proud of you. It takes a lot to do what you are doing," she says.

"Thank you. I've been unhappy for a long time. It's about time I do something about it."

The elevator door opens, and we both step inside.

"Everyone deserves happiness. Sometimes, it just takes some of us a bit longer to figure out what that means."

"Hopefully, it won't be too late."

"Don't worry, it won't be."

The elevator door opens, and we both head into the parking garage. Avery pauses in front of her car service.

"Come on, let's share a ride to the airport. We're both going there anyway," she says warmly.

"I'll tell Darin. Give me a moment."

For the first time in months, I feel a small weight lifted off my shoulders. Now I hope this next step goes over better.

IN LA, I've made it to the venue. It's much larger than I was expecting it to be. I haven't paid attention to who they are opening up for during this tour. All I know is that his band has been topping the charts and are just getting started. He's accomplishing his dreams, and I'm so lucky to be his dad.

I don't fault him for reacting how he did when he found

Ellie and me together. He's needed time, but I need to talk to him. I have to let him know how much I care about him and always will.

"Mr. Underwood?" someone calls out as I enter the venue.

Spinning around, I see a petite younger woman with headgear on. She must work here.

"That's me."

"Oh good! I was afraid I would miss you, but Knox is right—you're hard to miss in a crowd!" she chirps.

"Knox?"

"Yes, he's asked me to bring you back to his dressing room. Right this way."

She turns and heads in the opposite direction I was heading. How did he know I would be at this show? I didn't attempt to reach out to him again, given how the past few months have gone.

Striding down the venue walkways, she slides a keycard through a digital lock, and we go backstage.

Three doors down on the left, a paper reads "Knox Underwood," and I'm taken aback. He decided to use my surname instead of his mother's.

I'm nervous to see him now. This is the talk that I've been wanting to have for ages. It's beyond the Ellie situation. Knox and I need to figure out a way to move forward.

"Go inside. He should be in there," the woman says and then walks away.

Opening the door, I see him fiddling with the strings on the guitar. He perks up when he hears me step through the threshold.

"Dad," he breathes out.

Thankfully, he looks relieved instead of angry, like the last time we were together.

"Knox, I'm glad you're ready to see me."

He places his guitar on the table in front of him and then walks over to me. I'm not really sure what his angle is.

"I'm sorry, Dad."

He pulls me into a tight hug.

This is nice, better than nice.

He pulls back, and it looks like tears are starting to form.

"Come sit down. I have a lot I want to say," he says.

"Me too."

We both take a seat around the coffee table.

"How did you know I was coming?"

"Avery."

This is starting to all make sense.

"What did Avery say?"

"What didn't Avery say to me?" He chuckles and runs a hand through his long hair.

"She told me what a fuck-up I had been. How long I've been holding a grudge for you not being there for my childhood when you didn't know I existed. Let's see, what else?"

"She didn't go easy," I say.

"Nah, but we wouldn't want her to."

"True," I say with a small laugh.

"She talked and listened about Ellie."

He swallows thickly.

"I'm sorry. I didn't realize. I didn't know. And fuck," he breathes out.

"Take your time."

"I didn't know because I never fucking ask about you. I don't know anything about you, really. And that's my fault. I was pissed as hell to know you were sleeping with my ex-girlfriend, but after talking to Avery, I realized how fucked-up our relationship has been for a long time because of me."

"Don't do this to yourself. I've never felt anything but

love for you. You're my son, and I'd like to have a better relationship. And before we go any further, I am truly sorry. Ellie and I were unexpected, and I was planning on talking to you about it."

"I know, Dad. I know."

"I love her... and I lost her."

Knox gives me a knowing look.

"You'll get her back. I know you will."

"I hope so."

"She called me."

I'm baffled.

"She did?"

"She told me how much she loves you. It was a punch to the gut knowing what I did to you both. I haven't called her back, but I'll talk to her soon."

"I don't want to lose you, Knox. I know how strange it might be, but I do love her too. I love you both."

"You aren't going to lose me."

He pauses.

"Will you stay after the show? I know there's a lot more for us both to say."

"Of course I will."

I stand, too, as the same assistant shares a five-minute warning.

"Ready to watch me play for five thousand fans?"

"I'm so proud of you."

Tears are welling in his eyes.

"I know you are. You always have been."

———

THREE MAJOR LIFE decisions happening all in the span of forty-eight hours. It's not reckless, considering I've been stagnant for months. With work being my priority for so many years, it's about time that I pack in everything I need to do to be happy.

Now, as I tour another home in Charleston, it's all hitting me how much I hope this helps. I can only wish it shows Ellie how serious I am about our future together.

All of these homes aren't Ellie and me. As nice as the beach and these residential areas I've been looking at are, we aren't destined for the suburbs.

"If this one isn't for you either, then I think it's time we go look at the available properties in downtown Charleston. I think there's one area in particular that might be a good fit for you," my realtor, Pam, says.

"Is that South of Broad?"

"It is. Are you familiar with it?"

"A friend of mine lived there before, but you may be right."

"I have several available," she continues as we leave this house.

I hop into her vehicle, and we drive the short distance to downtown. It's bustling with tourists and locals, but the vibrance of the city makes me already feel like this is where I should purchase property.

Pulling up to the first house, a rush of emotion runs through me. This is it. This feels like us. I didn't realize that it would be this easy to spot.

This home is two stories, with wraparound porches, a yard, and a swimming pool. It's blocks away from the action downtown yet easy enough to walk to. Ellie will love it here.

"I think this is it," I say to Pam.

"Wow, that is wonderful news. Shall we take a look around?"

"After you," I say.

Pam unlocks the door, and it confirms everything I need to know.

The pool is somewhere I can picture Ellie and me taking nightly dips. The patio area is expansive, and I can picture us hosting parties every season.

As we walk through the house, I see it's just the right size for us. Four bedrooms and three bathrooms, enough to have guests but not feel like we're living somewhere that doesn't fit.

It's coming so naturally to say what is and what isn't Ellie and me. Even though we were only in a relationship for a short time, I do know her better than I know anyone.

I'm transported back to that night when Ellie showed me how well I know who she is. She's been opening up to me all along. I just was too shortsighted to see it. To see her right in front of me, giving herself fully.

"Still think this is the one?" Pam asks as we linger in the entryway.

"This is it."

"The asking price is just over three million."

"I'll pay full asking. I'd like to get this settled as soon as possible."

"Understood. Let's head back to my office, and we'll get the paperwork started."

"Perfect."

We leave, and right as I'm about to get into Pam's car, I look back up at the house I'm about to make into our home.

TWENTY-SIX

Ellie

Four months later, December

"I CAN'T BELIEVE I'm about to do this." I groan and lean back into the couch cushions.

Harper and Avery both settle onto the sofa next to me. Harper looks over to Avery and back to me.

I'm at Avery's house for a girls' night, but it's really just me nervously asking about my impending trip to North Carolina—back to the cabin where Fisher and I admitted we have feelings for one another. And more importantly, where I told him to meet me if he could prove that I am a priority in his life.

"Am I missing something?"

I perk back up.

"No, you need to do this. You've been miserable without the man," Harper starts.

"Not miserable," I lie.

It's true. I'm happy I did this. The move to Charleston

has been better for my mental health and way of life. I've tried to enjoy the day-to-day as much as possible. Work has been incredible, and I'm already up for a promotion at my new company.

I work long hours and love every second of it. Then, I go to my nightly workout classes, have dinners with friends, and explore this historic city.

The only problem with how much I'm making this life my own is that I only want one person to enjoy it all with. Looking back, I wish I had called Fisher instead of waiting until December to see if he shows up at the cabin and still wants me. If he doesn't, I plan on drowning my sorrows with a nice bottle of champagne.

"You are. We love having you here, but this is what you want. And it's what he wants," Avery adds.

"Are you sure?"

"Yes. He wants you, and I can't wait for you to find out what he's been doing since you last spoke," she says.

"Avery, it kills me that you won't just tell me," I complain.

"It's not my story to tell."

"Fine." I groan.

"But we do have someone who is here to see you before you take off," Harper says.

She and Avery both stand and look nervously at one another.

I sit fully upright.

"What's going on? Is he here?"

"He's not, but I am," a male's voice sounds from down the hallway.

Heavy footsteps pad through the house, and I look up to find my ex-boyfriend in front of me.

"What are you doing here?" I ask, confused.

"Fair question. Avery invited me."

"Why?" I ask, still perplexed.

"We're just going to step out," Avery says.

Harper and Avery both leave without another word, and I'm left sitting here stunned. Knox is here and wants to talk to me. It's been so long. If he's here to tell me not to date his dad, I just can't do that.

Truthfully, I'm a little pissed off he never returned my call.

"To apologize."

I cross my arms against my chest.

"For what?"

"Come on, Ellie, I'm here to talk. Can we?"

I sigh and then pat the sofa cushion, inviting him to sit down too.

He comes over and sits down next to me, and we sit in silence for a few minutes.

"I was so angry," he starts.

I stay silent to let him continue.

"I was pissed at my dad and at you. He's my dad, Ellie. Can't you see how fucked that was for me?"

"I can. I truly do see that. But the way you handled it wasn't how it all should have happened. You're a grown man who dated me years ago. And need I remind you that you broke up with me?"

"I know. And I'm sorry for how I acted that day. It wasn't just about you two; it was something else that I wanted to be pissed at my dad for."

I nod to encourage him to continue.

"My dad and I have always had a complicated relationship, but I don't want that anymore. I told him that too when he visited me."

That catches my attention.

"You saw him?"

"Yeah, he came to my LA show a few months ago. He told me he wasn't going to stop dating you but that he wanted a relationship with me too."

"Wow."

My heart rate is picking up, and I can feel goosebumps pricking along my arms.

"Yeah, there's a bit more to it, but wow indeed."

"Well, I'm happy for you."

I shift my weight a bit on the couch to get more comfortable. I'm feeling restless as Knox speaks.

"Thank you. And I hope you and I can start new. I'm not going to lie; it's going to be weird as hell to see you two together, but I'll try."

I sink into the couch.

"If we get back together."

Knox smirks.

"I have a feeling the more you learn, the more you'll see that old man is obsessed with you."

That brings a smile to my face.

"Really?"

"Yeah."

"Can I give you a hug?" I ask.

"Come here."

Knox scoops me into his arms.

"I am so happy you two are friendly again," Avery says as she and Harper come around the corner.

I can feel Knox laughing and his chest vibrating. We let go of one another, and I see Avery and Harper are crying.

"Pull it together, you two," I say with a laugh.

"Now you know one step Fisher took," Avery says as she sits down next to me.

"A pretty important one."

"Maybe the most," Harper adds.

"Maybe."

BEING in front of the pond has a mixture of emotions roaring through me. I know I needed this time; I just hope that Fisher has really learned what he wants out of life.

Truthfully, I hope that it's still me. That we can be together and move forward in life as partners.

Even though it's December, it's not as snowy as it was this time last year. I suppose the lack of snowstorms is probably the reason why.

The snow is thinly lining the ground around me, but I can see grass and twigs popping through. The snow will come harder eventually, but this mountain can handle it.

I take deep breaths as I look out and wait for Fisher to arrive. Technically, I don't know for sure if he'll be coming. I've had to really trust my friends that they know what he's been up to and will be showing up today.

We have the cabin that started it all for the weekend if this goes according to plan.

I hear twigs and branches cracking behind me. My heart beats rapidly.

Deep breaths, Ellie.

Looking around, I see it's just a family of deer. More babies must have been born over the year. The family has expanded, and it looks like the same ones from before. Maybe it's a new family, but this still holds the same magic as it once did.

I face back out to the pond to watch small snowflakes start to fall.

It's getting chillier outside, and I contemplate going inside the cabin instead of waiting out here.

There is something peaceful about being near this pond. Even in the cold, it just feels like something out of a storybook.

More branches crack behind me, and I keep looking out at the water.

"Just as beautiful as I remember," a voice rasps.

I bury my face into my gloves as tears immediately prick through.

It's Fisher.

He came.

He still wants me.

Using the back of one of my gloves, I wipe the tears that are starting to fall. I turn around to face the man whom I've missed more than anything on the planet.

"You're here," I croak.

Fisher looks exactly as I remember. Thick black-rimmed glasses that I love, tattoos peeking out from the open dress shirt, and eyes that say everything I need. This man loves me. He always has and always will.

"I'm here."

I try to keep my tears at bay.

"Fisher, I..." I stammer.

"Let me, princess."

Fisher pulls out a tissue from his pocket and wipes away my fallen tears, then he scoops my hands into his.

"I love you. You brought me to life. I've missed you every second that we've been apart."

"I'm so sorry," I interrupt.

"Wait, please."

I nod for him to continue.

"You were right. What happened with Knox would have been easy for us to fix, but I needed to face my own truth. I had been going through the motions of life instead of living it. That is until we fell in love here in... what do you call it? Wonderland. I didn't stand a chance when it came to you."

"Fisher..."

He squeezes my hands.

"I didn't realize how many concessions you were making for me. I get it. I do now. So, I've made a few changes myself... for us."

"I never wanted you to change yourself."

"No, I had to come to terms with the fact that in order for me to get the girl, to get the son, to be happy, I had to make some decisions that weren't out of guilt for an old friend."

I nod.

"I quit Rain Peak."

"You what?" My eyes widen.

"My last day was in November."

"Fisher, you love working! Oh my god, I am so sorry. Please go back."

He grins.

"No, I loved working when I had nothing else. And I made another big change too."

"What's that?" I croak.

"I bought us a house."

"Wait, what? But we don't live in the same city right now," I ask, confused.

A wind chill makes me bury my head into Fisher's chest. He wraps me up in his arms and chuckles.

"Princess, I moved to Charleston. You're it for me. Can you say the same?"

I cry happy tears into his chest.

"Of course I can," I squeak.

I pull back and look up at him. Bringing his face into my hands, all I see is love.

"I love you. I love you so much," I confess.

"You better," he teases.

I grin and can feel warmth spreading across my cheeks.

"I love you too," he says back.

I press a kiss to his lips.

"Forever."

"Forever and always."

EPILOGUE

Ellie

Two years later

"I CAN'T BELIEVE how many people are here," I yell.

Fisher wraps his arm around my waist as we sway to the music.

"This is truly amazing. Knox did it," Fisher says in awe.

Thousands of fans are cheering around us for Wagon Chain to come out and play the show. Their opening act has been doing an amazing job, but we've flown back out to Seattle to see Knox's show and then head to Alaska.

This show coincided with the anniversary of my mom's passing. Fisher so graciously flew my sister and dad out to spend a long weekend in Alaska, where we can go on a whale-watching tour in her memory. We're meeting them there tomorrow.

They understood the significance behind the idea.

My dad also loves any chance he can spend time with Fisher.

Fisher and I got married in a small ceremony shortly after I moved into our home in Charleston. It was perfectly us. We still have no plans for babies, but I love being Auntie Ellie to Harper and Grayson's daughter. She's a precious spitfire, just like her mama.

"Are we going out with Knox afterward still?"

"That's the plan. Want to head backstage and see if we can catch him before they go on?" Fisher asks.

"That sounds great. I know he loves when you do that."

Fisher and Knox's relationship has changed drastically over the last two years. Slowly but surely, they were able to find their way to one another. Now, they regularly chat, and we try to see Knox as often as we can.

Fisher takes my hand in his and guides us out of the VIP section and toward backstage, where Knox and the rest of the band are waiting to go on stage.

As we walk past security guards, we flash our badges that grant us access. It's so surreal. Knox being a famous guitarist has been hard to get used to. It's crazy how many fans they have and how we see his picture on the internet now.

I couldn't be happier for Knox and Fisher. This is all Fisher ever wanted for his son—to find the happiness he had been chasing for so long.

Fisher and I walk down a long hallway and scan the dressing rooms for Knox's name.

Finally spotting it, Fisher does a few loud knocks. The sound from the opening act playing sounds loudly, even with how far we've walked away from the stage.

"Come in!" Knox shouts.

Fisher opens the door, and we see Knox strumming his guitar thoughtfully. He pops his head up and sees it's us, and a wide smile takes over.

"Dad, Ellie, I'm so glad you guys were able to make it tonight," he says.

"We are too. This is wild. First show of the new tour, and the crowd is electric. Have you seen it out there?" Fisher asks.

Knox laughs as his long hair swings back. He sets down his guitar and gets up from his seat.

"It's wild, right? What a year it's been."

Knox pulls Fisher into an embrace. After they pull apart, Knox wraps me into a tight squeeze.

"So happy for you guys," I murmur.

Suddenly, the dressing room door opens and bangs against the wall behind it. Knox and I break apart, and the three of us turn around to see who it is.

"Jessica?" Knox asks, confused.

"Hi, yes. Sorry to interrupt you," she huffs out, clearly out of breath from running down here.

"It's Wyatt," Jessica finishes.

Knox looks confused.

"What's wrong with Wyatt? I just saw him like twenty minutes ago."

"He's gone."

"Gone?" Knox asks, stupefied.

"Yes!" she shrieks.

"What do you mean?"

"Gone. As in, he's disappeared. He left a note for you. Sorry, but I read it."

"What did it say?"

"He can't do it. He needs a break."

Knox finally realizes what's happening.

I step next to Fisher to give Jessica and Knox some space.

"Fuck. Gather the band and find Pete. This is an emergency."

"Got it," Jessica says as she bounces in place.

"Now, Jessica. We're about to cancel the first show of the tour."

"Sorry! Right!" she shouts and hurriedly leaves through the door.

Knox faces us and looks sick.

"Knox, what does this mean? Where's Wyatt?" Fisher asks.

"Fuck, I should have listened to what he was saying earlier," Knox answers as he hangs his head back.

Knox comes back to us, and I see agony everywhere.

"Sorry, guys, but I have to go. I'll call you when I can, but this is bad."

"Of course. We understand," Fisher answers.

"We're here if you need us," I say.

"Thanks. I need to find Wyatt."

Knox heads out the door, leaving Fisher and me confused in his dressing room.

"What is he going to do?" I ask.

"I have no idea."

ACKNOWLEDGMENTS

Thank you so much for reading Fisher and Ellie's story. I appreciate you taking the time to pick Meet Me In Wonderland to read!

This book was a labor of love. I couldn't have done it without my support system: Brian, Allie, Courtney, Kymmie, Brittany, Kim, Angie, and Peggy. Thank you all for being there for my author journey.

Thank you to the team at Kat's Literary Services. Steph and Vanessa, you guys are rock stars, and I appreciate you both so much.

Sandra with Maldo Designs—thank you for once again designing an amazing cover and promotional graphics. It truly amazes me that you can bring my vision to life.

Jen, with Grey's Promotions, where do I start? You're such a good friend, and I'm so lucky to have you on my side as I promote these books.

To all of the influencers and creators on social media, every time you post about one of my books, it brings me such joy. Thank you endlessly.

Stay tuned because there is so much more to come!

ABOUT THE AUTHOR

Angel Anders is a romance author who loves the range of characters and complexities of stories that can naturally unfold when a story comes to life.

When she's not writing, Angel enjoys spending her days along the South Carolina coast with her husband, son, and dog. She enjoys strong coffee, white wine, and curling up with a good book by the fireplace.

www.angelandersbooks.com

9 798218 550462